Slightly Stalky

He's the one. He just doesn't know it yet...

Amy Vansant

ISBN-13: 978-0983719151

Vansant Creations, LLC / Amy Vansant
Annapolis, MD
http://www.AmyVansant.com
http://www.SlightlyStalky.com

Copyediting by Carolyn Steele.
Proofreading by Effrosyni Moschoudi & Connie Leap

DEDICATION

To the Chicken Club Crew.

CHAPTER ONE

One Week From Now...

Emily had barely shaped the crab cakes for dinner before Marc reentered the kitchen, freshly showered, wearing nothing but a pair of jeans.

That body.

He smelled of man scents she knew he hadn't found in her bathroom.

"You smell much better. Is that like deodorant or like cologne or like one of those body spr—"

Marc shut her up by kissing her again.

Nervous about the seduction in progress, she still appreciated his ability to quiet her babbling. If only Marc could kiss her quiet *whenever* she was about to say something stupid...

He pulled her close to him.

"I—" Emily tried to talk between kisses, but the way his hand glided beneath her shirt and across her spine made it difficult to catch her breath.

It had been so long.

His body steamed against her own as her palms moved across the rippling muscles in his back. His arms were so strong—she knew he could sweep her up and carry her to...*anywhere.*

She kissed him, hard.

That's when she saw the picture; a flashbulb bursting in her brain long enough to illuminate a man's face.

Sebastian.

Heaviness enveloped her heart. It was strange to be aroused and yet so sad at the same time.

She pulled away.

"You should know I'm sort of in love with someone else," she said as he nuzzled her neck.

Without releasing her, Marc leaned back until they could

6

look into each other's eyes.

"You have a boyfriend?" he asked.

"No, I'm just *waiting* for someone. I think."

"Waiting?"

"I wanted you to know, emotionally, my heart might be somewhere else."

He barked a laugh.

"You're so weird," he said, resuming kissing her. He worked his way down her neck, biting her lightly with each nod.

Fair enough.

She'd done her duty. She'd warned him she liked someone else. They were on the same page about what this was. She wasn't callously using him to break his heart. That, apparently, was laughable, so...

Marc's mouth again found hers, and she felt her hips tingle.

She silenced the voices in her head and gave into the moment. She kissed him, swept away by his sheer manliness. His hands slipped beneath her buttocks and pulled her hips against his. An aching need rose inside of her; a need she felt confident Marc could satisfy.

He lifted her, and she wrapped her legs around his waist. He continued to kiss her neck as he turned toward the bedroom.

Oh my God...

Emily paused to smile at Kady, who sat enraptured as she told her story.

"Then what? You can't stop *now*," said her friend.

Emily shrugged.

"That's when I ended up in the wall."

CHAPTER TWO

Current Day

"In college, you're constantly thrown into rooms with the opposite sex. College is a Petri dish of *lust*."

Emily sipped her Chardonnay, feeling stuck in a deep, buttery, oaky *rut*. She preferred a warm, chocolaty, cabernet-y rut, but summer meant mixing up her ruts.

Kady chuckled. "That sounds like the worst romance novel ever. *Petri Dish of Lust*."

Emily sighed and pushed a flake of peeled white paint back and forth with her toe.

"Seriously, where are you supposed to meet people after college?"

Kady shrugged. She and her boyfriend, Joe, were Emily's "hippie" friends. Kady and Joe lived in a fixer-upper they never fixer-upped, went to concerts featuring one endless song and ate unidentifiable plant pods on purpose. Emily had no interest in jam bands or kale salad, but she and Kady had other things in common, like wine, food, and books. Kady was also one of the warmest people Emily had ever met.

While the girls sipped wine on Kady's peeling porch, Joe attempted to roll a cigarette, tongue hanging from his mouth like an overheated Labrador's. Without looking up, he muttered, "Why don't you go to dart night at the Irish Rover?"

Emily scowled. "Irish Rover the *bar*?"

"Yes, the bar. They have a round-robin where you play darts for money. The place is full of men. It's a Petri dish of lust."

Kady groaned. "You have no idea how close that is to the

truth. That place is filthy."

Emily recalled the dartboard that once hung in her father's garage. As a pre-teen, she'd punctured more holes in the Philadelphia Flyers hockey team photo pinned *next* to the 8

dartboard than the dartboard itself.

"My dad had a dartboard, but I wasn't good." She gasped. "I threw javelin in high school—"

Joe barked a laugh, his floppy brown hair spilling to the left.

"That's like saying you'd be an excellent bowler because you played marbles," he said.

"Why? It's the same idea, right?"

"No. For one, you don't *aim* a javelin."

"Mmm. Excellent point."

Kady jumped in her seat. "Ha! Get it? Excellent *point.*"

"Bad dum dum," said Joe, providing a lackluster rimshot.

Emily ruminated on Joe's suggestion. She *did* love the idea of throwing sharp pointy things. She had a competitive streak. However, meeting men in a bar sounded so...*meeting men in a bar.*

On the other hand, she was tired of drinking café lattes alone at Grounded coffee shop under the guise of reading a book while not-so-secretly trolling for sensitive, literary types with insanely hot bodies. Avoiding eye contact with other singles was becoming pathological. None of the ladies at the coffee shop liked seeing their desperation reflected.

Emily knew which girls were on Coffeeshop Man Safari by the way their gazes laser-locked on women with boyfriends. Women with boyfriends always entered the Grounded arm-in-arm with their man, moving in slow motion, heads tossed back in the throes of an exaggerated laugh—those flashing white teeth activated jealousy processes in the brains of the hunters.

Judgment was passed.

The girlfriend was found wanting. Too tall, too short, too fat, too skinny, fashion-impaired, crooked-nosed, obnoxious, obvious, loud, mousey...

Wait, isn't one of her breasts smaller than the other?

Doesn't matter. She's not me.

After judging the girlfriend, the hunters' attention shifts to the boyfriend. He seems nice. Or douchey. While they're trying to decide, the *girlfriend* notices the lonesome latte drinkers. She smirks.

The jig is up!

Eyes dart away. Heads drop, and noses tuck into books. The hunters squash the urge to form an over-caffeinated, snarling wolf pack.

Emily didn't think she would meet the love of her life in a coffee shop, but she worked from home as a freelance writer and didn't get the daily human interaction other people took for granted. Her friends had lives and families of their own. She loved her dog, Duppy, but he wasn't much of a conversationalist. The chairs in Grounded weren't chatty either, but the constant flow of people walking in and out with their mochas and muffins made her *feel* social. It was like being at a party during that uncomfortable in-between-conversations moment. Awkward but, hey, anything could happen.

Emily realized Joe was looking at her.

She decided to play darts.

"When is it?" she asked.

Joe held up his freshly rolled cigarette, beaming.

"What do you think of this?"

"Nice," Emily said, having no real opinion on the quality of his workmanship. Her gaze lingered on Joe's ragged beard. It never grew in. He wore a flannel shirt, but it was Ralph Lauren. He wanted to be a hippie, but no matter how hard he tried, he always looked like he'd grown up in the affluent area of Short Hills, New Jersey.

Which he had.

Emily scowled at the cigarette. "Wait. Why do you need to roll cigarettes? You don't smoke."

He slipped the cigarette into the pocket of his flannel. "I thought it was something I should know."

Emily barked a laugh. "Why? In case you're teleported to the old West? Cigarette rolling is not something you *need* to know. Nobody ever screams, *This man is having a heart attack! Quick! Someone roll a cigarette!*"

"The plane is going down! Can anyone roll a cigarette?" Kady cackled, the dark curls framing her face bouncing.

Stone-faced, Joe ignored them.

Kady's giggles faded. "He said he saw someone roll one last week and thought it was cool. He *had* to know how to do it."

"Thank god he didn't see someone shooting heroin," muttered Emily.

The part of her not fond of Joe sneaked out for a visit, and she took a sip of wine to quiet herself. She didn't want to be

10

mean-spirited and offend Kady, and she knew better than to pick on a girlfriend's mate, even if the girlfriend initiated the attack. A week later, the same girl would reunite with the man she'd bashed, and then Emily would be *the jerk* for agreeing the guy was, "King Needle Dick of Loserville."

Unlike Joe, Kady was a genuine person and a true earth-mama-hippie. Kady liked jazz and cobbled together signature outfits from vintage clothes purchased on eBay. Kady thought the Eleventh Commandment should be *Thou shalt not shop at Big Name Stores*, because every time she found a classic piece of furniture, she'd discover some big store was already mass-producing carbon copies. It broke her heart.

She loved plants and insects and worked in the garden department of Home Depot to finance her tuition to landscaping college.

That was another fail for Joe. How many bohemians make six figures a year in corporate finance? He wore a tie to work and looked more comfortable in suits than hemp t-shirts—which was fine if he wasn't trying so hard to pretend he was a hipster. Emily knew it shouldn't bother her, but something about Joe felt disingenuous—he was a bored rich kid trying on new personalities, dating Kady to complete his hippie ensemble. Emily would never share this theory with Kady, but she *was* tempted especially because Joe wasn't always *nice*.

He didn't seem to appreciate Kady for *Kady*.

Emily sighed. The Joe-puzzle was unsolvable today; time to let it go.

"When is dart night?"

"Tonight," said Joe.

"That seems sudden. Should I go tonight? Do I have to buy darts? Should I practice throwing soft things first?"

"You could throw Q-tips," suggested Kady.

"You can borrow my spares," said Joe.

"Great," said Emily. She glanced at Kady, still unsure.

"We'll all go," Kady said. "It'll be fun."

Joe shook his head. "I don't want to go."

Kady pouted. "Why not? You were saying you wanted to go out, like, an hour ago."

Joe wrinkled his nose and then nodded his head from side to side, relenting.

"Fine."

"Fine," echoed Emily. "Good."

Emily supposed it wouldn't kill her to give darts night a try.

Unless someone had terrible aim, in which case, maybe it could.

12

CHAPTER THREE

The Irish Rover was a smoky saloon smothered in dark wood, Celtic knots, and Irish drinking songs stuck on endless replay. To the right of the entrance was an area the size of a large walk-in closet called "the snug" featuring a bar that began there, made a hard right, and continued to the back of the restaurant. The snug boasted two dartboards and four twenty-to-thirty-something-aged men practicing for Dart Night.

As soon as they entered, Joe peeled from the girls to offer his homemade cigarette to one of his smoking friends. Kady and Emily moved to the back of the pub to find the person in charge of the dart competition. She passed another pack of men practicing at additional dartboards.

"I feel like I'm man-shopping with you," said Kady.

Emily nodded. "Like we're shopping organic at *Whole Dudes*."

A short older man with an impish grin, shining eyes, and slightly pointy ears stood at the back of the bar, taking money and scrawling names on torn pieces of paper.

"Slow down and look casual," Emily stage-whispered into Kady's ear.

"What? Why?"

"Otherwise, he'll know we're after his pot of gold."

Kady cackled with laughter.

"The Leprechaun is Sean."

Sean the Leprechaun asked Emily and Kady for the ten-dollar Dart Night entry fee. Depending on the number of contestants, they could win much more, but they probably wouldn't.

Kady paid her fee and Joe's as well.

"You can get me back in drinks," she said.

"Can do."

At the bar, Emily ordered a Pinot Grigio for Kady and a vodka soda for herself. They sat at a tall, circular bar table to wait for the availability of a dartboard for practice. While Emily scanned the room, Kady busied herself reading the names carved into the tabletop.

The bar was packed. A whole ecosystem of dart players thrived a few miles from her home.

Who knew?

"I can't believe I'm doing this," she said.

A single shaft of late afternoon sunlight pierced the gloom of the dimly lit bar. Dust particles sparkled. Emily followed the light path from a small rectangular window to where it landed on the face of a brown-haired man sitting at a table near the back of the bar. A tiny brunette sat across from him. The girl had impossibly large breasts. She looked as if she was smuggling cantaloupes beneath her light summer sweater.

The light illuminated the man like an angel in a Renaissance painting; his blue eyes seemingly lit from within. Seeking relief from the glare, he turned his gaze in Emily's direction to find her staring at him.

Hello, there.

Their eyes locked until his busty tablemate slapped him on the arm, encouraging him to refocus on their conversation. When his attention returned to the agitated anatomical anomaly, Emily realized she'd been staring and looked away as her cheeks grew warm.

She took a moment to compose herself. It wasn't like her to stare at someone, but she couldn't shake the feeling that she knew the man.

"You have to see this guy," said Emily, tapping Kady's arm.

"Who?"

"Turn around. I can't look again. It's the table against the back wall. The guy who is...*glowing*."

She peeked as Kady twisted in her chair for a better view. As she did, the leprechaun released the back blinds, and the beam of sunlight disappeared.

"Who?" asked Kady. "I don't see any glowing men."

Emily watched as shadows fell across her glowing man and frowned.

"He's not glowing anymore."

"What?"

14

"He—never mind. He'll think we're nuts if he sees you gawking at him."

"Who?"

Emily rolled her eyes. "*Never mind.*"

Though darkness had fallen on the best-looking guy in the room, Emily wasn't entirely unimpressed with the bar. The male-to-female ratio at the Irish Rover crushed the coffeeshop, and the handsome-to-ho-hum numbers weren't bad.

She noticed a pair of boys abandoning the last dartboard in the back.

"I think a board opened up," she mouthed to Kady over the Irish music.

Kady removed two small black cases from her oversized purse and jumped from her stool to hand her bag to a giant woman pouring a drink behind the bar. The woman accepted the purse with her free hand and tucked it out of sight. Emily took a moment to eye the bartender; the Amazon was easily over six feet tall, with long, dark hair flowing over her shoulders. She wore a Renaissance-style green felt dress with a poufy, white cotton front. Her breasts spilled over her bodice like toothpaste bursting from a tube.

Emily scanned the bar to confirm none of the other bartenders wore costumes.

"What's with Henry the Eighth's girlfriend?" Emily asked Kady as they made their way to the dart area.

"Wendy? It's her thing. *Tips.*" Kady cupped her hands over her chest to manifest large, imaginary breasts.

Ah. That made sense.

Kady and Emily claimed the abandoned board. A movie-star-handsome man playing darts on the board beside theirs nodded his acknowledgment of Emily's arrival and then turned his attention to his game.

"Who's that?" Emily asked Kady.

"Ryan. Good-looking guy, huh?"

Emily nodded. *Yes, indeedy*, she thought, and then made a

mental note never to say "yes, indeedy" aloud.

Kady erased the scoreboard and prepared it for their practice game as Emily hovered, looking for an opportunity to introduce herself to Ryan. She couldn't get close without being obvious; an entourage of enraptured beta-men surrounded the ruling king of his court.

Kady creaked open one of her hinged black dart cases like a tiny coffin. She pulled her darts out and fiddled with the points.

Emily never dreamed throwing darts required so much preparation.

She caught enough nearby chatter to realize Ryan was sharing his latest sexual conquest with the crowd. His most recent night of passion ended with the girl needing an escort home, which he refused to provide.

"What did she say?" asked one of the other boys, barely able to contain his laughter.

"But it's dangerous out there!" said Ryan in falsetto, his hands in the air to mimic a damsel in distress.

The group erupted with laughter.

"You made her walk home alone?" asked someone.

Ryan offered a wicked grin.

"I walked her to the kitchen and pulled a knife out of the drawer."

The group fell silent as Ryan aimed his next dart, allowing the suspense to grow. He threw, hit his Marc, and turned back to his enthralled audience.

"*'You'll be fine,'* I told her," he said, pantomiming handing the girl the knife. "*Take this with you.*"

Laughter drowned the Irish music—no small feat. Ryan beamed.

"Then I went back to bed," he added.

His gaze caught Emily's, and she looked away.

Ugh.

Ryan was a *dick*.

With storytime over, the group surrounding Ryan scattered.

Kady looked up from her dart sharpening.

"You want me to introduce you to Ryan?"

Alarm bells still ringing in her mind, Emily shook her head. Ryan was knuckle-bitingly handsome, but she was too old to fall for bad boys.

At least *that* bad boy; he'd lost the element of surprise.

Someone lowered the lights in the restaurant and used directional can lights to illuminate the dartboards. One recessed light didn't get the memo and continued to shine brightly upon the man sitting directly beneath it.

The brown-haired cutie—spotlighted again.

A sign?

Emily tapped Kady on the shoulder.

"What's that guy's name?" she asked.

Kady turned. "Who?"

Emily pointed with her eyes.

"The guy in the *spotlight*."

Emily's pupils jerked to the right until Kady looked in that direction.

"I don't know what you're talking about," said Kady.

"*At three o'clock*," Emily said through gritted teeth.

Kady frowned. "I don't get that clock thing. Am I facing twelve, or are you?"

Emily huffed and turned. The bright light had dimmed, and the brown-haired man had fallen into shadow again.

What the hell.

Screw the lights—she pointed him out to Kady anyway.

"See the guy with the brunette at the two-top in the back?" She'd been a server for a summer in high school. All she'd taken from the experience was a habit of calling tables by their number of seats and a strong desire *never to waitress again.*

Kady perked. "Oh, that's Sebastian. He plays darts."

"Sebastian?" She'd been expecting something a little more like *John* or *Bob*. "Is he British or something?"

"I don't think so."

"Is that his girlfriend?"

Kady shrugged. "I don't know. I don't think I've ever seen her. She's tiny, isn't she? But—" Kady peered down at her chest. "That's not fair."

"Nope. I don't know whether to be jealous or worry she'll topple over and hurt herself."

"I'll ask Joe who she is. He used to come here a lot."

"Uh…" Emily panicked. She didn't want to draw attention to her obsession with the man at the back table, but she *did* want to know more about him.

She waited a moment too long.

When she reached to stop Kady, her friend was halfway to the front of the bar.

Kady disappeared in the direction of the front snug. A moment later, Joe and Kady's faces peered around the corner.

Emily groaned.

Joe and Kady disappeared. Emily took a deep breath and pretended to concentrate on her dart points though she had no idea what to do with them.

A minute later, Kady was back.

"Joe doesn't know anything about Sebastian, but he doesn't think that's his girlfriend," said Kady. "And he *left*."

"Who? Sebastian?" Emily turned to find Sebastian still in his seat.

"No, *Joe*. He said he didn't feel good. I wish he'd told me that before I paid the fee."

Kady flopped into a seat and demonstrated how to sharpen the point of a dart by swirling it in the top divot of a small cylindrical sharpening stone. Emily mimicked her. The motion felt like angrily stirring a tiny cup of coffee.

With their dart points gleaming, Emily threw a few, the muscles in her arm twitching with each aim. It took everything not to *spazz* and fling a dart into someone's face. She'd never been so *aware* of her arm before. The thought of throwing in a competition had her running for another drink.

After a few more practice rounds, the leprechaun called for everyone's attention as he slipped papers with the dart players' names scrawled on them into a coffee can.

Everything was super high-tech. Emily didn't know they even made coffee cans anymore.

Her stomach tightened into Celtic knots as she realized her fate sat in a can of Folger's Dark Roast. Kady should be her teammate, not some randomly selected victim. No one wants to get a new girl on her first night. She was the kiss of death, the Crusher of Dreams.

On the upside, Dolly Parton Jr. left, and Sebastian joined the dart group. He was *tall*. Emily loved tall. Maybe, as Joe thought, Hooters O'Houlahan *wasn't* his girlfriend. Maybe she was a friend, distant cousin, or friendly dental hygienist.

Anything was possible.

Emily considered bribing Sean to team her with the tall man

but decided losing the hottie's money would leave a poor first impression, especially if she spazzed a dart into his head. Better he stays safe on the other side of the room.

Sean pulled the names from the coffee can.

"Sebastian and..."

Emily's eye twitched at the sound of Sebastian's name. She'd *really* have to stop doing that.

"...Peter."

"Me and *who*? Was I second? Who was one?" asked a voice behind Emily.

Sean pointed at Sebastian. "Sebastian's the one."

Emily glanced at Sean. The leprechaun stared back at her.

"Sebastian's the one," he repeated.

Emily pointed to her chest. "Are you talking to me?"

Someone pushed past her. She stumbled forward, catching her balance against the back of the man in front of her. She righted in time to see the oaf who'd knocked into her was now shaking hands with Sebastian.

Ah, he was talking to Peter. Number two.

Sean next pulled Emily's name from the coffee can, followed by "Jack." Emily saw an older man she'd seen practicing earlier raise his hand. She waved back like an over-excited stage mom spotting her daughter at a dance recital.

Calm down, dork.

She felt lucky to be paired with a mature partner, one more likely to be a gentleman about the albatross around his neck. She hoped he had a strong back; he'd carry her all night.

Kady proved a better dart player than Emily, but both girls fell out of the running for the cash during early rounds. When Jack and Emily lost, she headed to the bar to buy her long-suffering partner a drink in return for his good humor and patience.

"Martini," said a voice to her right.

Emily turned to find Sebastian five stools away. She'd lost track of him during the rounds. Tall, neat, and thin; this man was her type. An adorable hybrid dimple/laugh line capped the right side of his mouth. If she'd built him online like a car, choosing her favorite mix-and-match bits, he'd look the same.

Now that he stood so near, Emily could see he was more than cute.

He was *gorgeous*.

Sebastian's head swiveled, and he caught her staring a second time.

"Hi," said Emily.

"Hey," said Sebastian.

She looked away.

Wendy the bartender delivered Sebastian's martini and turned her focus to Emily. Emily ordered herself vodka and a beer for Jack.

"Hey."

It was Sebastian again. He was mouthing something she couldn't decipher. She squinted, trying to read his lips.

It looked as if he said, "I love you."

Emily's face grew warm.

This can't be happening. Did someone put something in my drink?

"What?" she asked.

Sebastian held up his martini. He mouthed the words again.

"I love you."

She froze.

Seriously?

She leaned forward, pulled toward Sebastian's silent love call. Going to him seemed the polite thing to do. After all, he just confessed his love—

The thud of a cocktail and a beer hitting the bar made Emily jump and nearly slip butt cheek-first to the floor. She caught her balance and righted herself on the stool.

Smooth.

Wendy had returned. Emily worried the giantess would scare Sebastian away. *Couldn't she see they were having a moment?*

"Oh, he wants it dirty," said Wendy.

Emily swallowed. "What? Who?"

"Sebastian."

Emily whirled back to face Sebastian.

Whaa…?

Sebastian nodded at his drink again and mouthed those magic words.

"I love you," read Emily, whispering the words under her breath.

20

"Olive juice," said Wendy holding her thumbs up. "Gotcha!"

Olive juice?

Emily lipped the words "olive juice" followed by "I love you." They felt the same. She closed her eyes and wished herself somewhere far away.

I am a total idiot.

Sebastian looked at Emily, and she became aware of her one butt cheek clinging to the stool, locked in half-dismount. She flashed a quick smile, tucked her other cheek on the seat, and faced the bar.

She pretended to be fascinated by the bottles on the speed rack as Wendy grabbed a jar of olives. She walked over and poured a splash of olive juice into Sebastian's martini.

"Dirty enough?"

"Good, I guess. It's not for me; I owe Peter a drink."

Sebastian glared at the glass, his upper lip curling.

"Gross," he added before walking back to his partner, over-filled martini glass sloshing.

Wendy caught Emily's eye. "You okay?"

Emily took a quick sip from her straw.

"Awesome. Thanks."

She stayed at the Irish Rover for another hour, meeting more regulars. Everyone seemed friendly, and she had fun, even if she wasn't good. Players gathered in the snug as they fell from the competition.

Emily watched Sebastian talk, laugh and throw darts from afar, but his personality remained an enigma. He and his partner remained in the running to the end, finishing second. She was happy for him, but his success in the competition made it impossible to introduce herself. He never made it to the snug.

Maybe that was for the best. It was unsettling she'd nearly run to him in slow motion, arms outstretched, all because he asked for olive juice.

There was something about Sebastian. Emily couldn't shake it. Or stir it, for that matter.

By the night's end, all she knew about him was that he hated dirty martinis and hung out in a dart bar.

A penchant for dart bars wasn't something she looked for in a potential boyfriend, but she couldn't hold it against him, lest she be skewered by the shards falling from her own glass house.

After all, she was a dart player now.

22

CHAPTER FOUR

Sebastian moved the top cardboard box from his stack and opened the one beneath it.

"What are you looking for?" asked Greta.

Sebastian watched her rise from the sofa and walk into the kitchen. He hoped that meant she was making dinner. He was *starving.* She'd left the bar before the dart tournament with a promise to go food shopping. He didn't mind shopping or cooking, but when someone else said they would do it, it made it hard to *plan.*

"I thought I had another pair of brown shoes," Sebastian mumbled, rummaging through a box.

He'd been wondering about *shoes* during his final dart game, which is why he and Pete had finished second. Instead of concentrating, he'd been thinking about boxes, his work schedule, and the blonde at the bar he'd met when he went to get Pete a martini. She was maybe a little odd, but cute. He thought she was about to talk to him for a moment, but then she'd turned away. Just as well—at the time, he couldn't think of anything to say to her. He wasn't sure he remembered how to small-talk a girl. He wasn't sure he ever had known how. Somehow, they always ended up talking to him. He just answered.

Sebastian heard a low growl and glanced down to see Greta's Shih Tzu, Binker, staring up at him. The dog's googly eyes were milky with age. His lower teeth protruded from his flat face like a broken fence. Binker was blind, but somehow always managed to find him.

Greta reentered the room, looking very much like she wasn't

planning on cooking.

"You really should have gotten this dog braces. A retainer or something," he said, moving to another box.

Greta ignored him. "When are you going to move those boxes out of the living room? I gave you room in my closet. You've been here for months and still have most of your stuff in *boxes*."

Sebastian sighed. His old roommate had accepted a job out of state and sold his townhouse, leaving Sebastian homeless. He'd been seeing Greta for a few months, and she offered to let him move in with her. His gut told him it was a bad idea, but she'd begged him to stay, and her small apartment *was* near his work. It all happened too fast.

That was two months ago. His boxes had been sitting against the wall at the back of her living room ever since. He hadn't felt the urge to unpack. Something about having his life neatly stacked near the door gave him comfort.

"I'll move them. Sorry," he muttered.

He doubted there was room in Greta's closet for his boxes. She'd given him four inches of space to hang his shirts and suits for work, and they squished a little further to the right every day.

Sebastian abandoned his shoe search and stood, stretching his back. Bending was unkind to his six-foot-two frame. He heard Greta rustling in the kitchen.

Promising.

At the sound of the refrigerator opening, Binker waddled away, plowing headlong into a table leg. He shook his moppy head, shifted three inches to the left, and continued.

"Hey, did you stop and get food like you said you would?" Sebastian called.

"No, babe." Greta re-entered the living room with a bowl and sat on the short, plaid sofa in front of the television. She wore sweat shorts and a tee.

He knew comfortable clothes meant no chance she'd go out for food.

"I stopped at my sister's, and then had to rush back for my show."

Sebastian scowled.

Her *show*.

He'd rather chew off his arm than watch that vampire soap

opera.

His stomach growled.

"What are you eating?" he asked.

"Ice cream."

"For dinner?"

She shrugged.

Sebastian heard another growl, lower and angrier than his stomach's. Binker had returned. The gremlin-faced dog stared up at him.

He put his hands on his hips, a move that elicited another growl from Binker.

"I thought this dog was blind."

"*Totally* blind," said Greta.

"Then he uses his hate for me as an echolocation system. I guess I'll order pizza?"

Greta shrugged.

"Maybe I'll just go out."

"No!" Greta sat upright. "Stay and keep me company. This is *our* night."

Sebastian glowered at the television.

"How is it *our night* if you're watching vampires? Can't you record it, and we'll get some food? Or at least watch something we *both* like?"

"I *can't*," Greta said, making a pouty face, her voice high and whiney. "I *would*, but the girls at work will be talking about it tomorrow, and I have to be able to share."

Sebastian rubbed his eyes. He couldn't stand the baby-voice Greta adopted whenever she wanted her way.

"Look, I'll go out— "

"Topless," said Greta, cutting him short.

Sebastian dropped his hands from his face. "Who? The vampires?"

"What if I watched it topless? Would you stay then?"

Sebastian winced.

"Are you serious? That's so—*no*. I'd rather you grabbed food like you promised. If I'd known you weren't going, I would have."

Greta pouted again. "Come on, baby. Come sit next to me. My boobies want to watch TV with you."

He covered his face with his hand. "Oh god. You're going to make me throw up."

Greta put her bowl on the table and pulled off her t-shirt. She twirled it around her head and released it so that it landed at Sebastian's feet.

He sighed. When she did this sort of thing, he tended to relent, but not for the reason she thought.

She made him feel bad for her somehow. Like he needed to stay and protect her.

It wasn't lust.

What am I doing here? What am I—

Greta peered over her naked shoulder, patting the sofa beside her.

"Come sit next to Maxy," she purred.

Greta's middle name was Maxine. She hated her first name and waged a never-ending campaign, encouraging people to call her Max. It never stuck.

Sebastian walked around the sofa. Greta stretched her arms behind her head and shimmied.

She did have amazing boobs. He knew it, almost as well as she did.

Sebastian sat on the sofa. Greta smiled and glued her gaze to the television.

Sebastian knew his presence didn't inspire her happiness. That honor went to the pretty man with the fangs on the screen—the man who used a tremendous amount of hair gel for a night creature.

The Shih Tzu jumped on the sofa, wedging himself between them.

"Look little guy—"

Greta shushed him. She leaned forward and grabbed her bowl before sitting back, eyes locked on the television. She rested the ice cream in the center of her chest, her arms blocking his view of either breast.

"It's *on*," muttered Sebastian to the dog.

Binker grunted.

As an experiment, he moved his hand toward Greta.

The Shih Tzu growled, his alabaster eyes swiveling towards Sebastian. The dog flopped his moppy head between his paws when he pulled back his hand.

Sebastian waited a minute and then again reached toward

Greta.

Growl.

"This dog is *not* blind. And if he is, he's like, *Daredevil* blind."

"*Ssshhh*," hissed Greta.

26

On the television, a naked girl writhed on a bed of silken sheets. The fanged pretty-boy stood nearby, shrouded in darkness.

Sebastian sighed.

"I'm going to watch television in the bedroom."

Greta remained silent.

The moment Sebastian stood, Binker stretched to his full length and occupied the area where he'd been sitting. The dog expelled a rattily sigh.

Sebastian headed towards the bedroom, unbuttoning his shirt as he went.

"Take a box with you," called Greta without turning.

Sebastian paused. He turned, looked at the top cardboard box of his pile, and walked into the bedroom empty-handed.

CHAPTER FIVE

Emily awoke the following morning, consumed with how that blue-eyed devil Sebastian had stolen her heart without saying a word. Well, other than *hey* and *olive juice* and probably, *I just met the weirdest girl at the bar* once out of earshot.

She had to know more about him. She had to return to the scene of the crime.

But first—

What's that smell? Am I on the floor of a bus terminal?

Emily sniffed her pillow.

It smelled like a bar.

Before she did anything, she'd have to get a shower. Man-hunting at Grounded smelled like dark roast and desperation, but she didn't have to wash it out of her pillowcases.

Emily reached to pet her fuzzy mutt, Duppy, who'd taken up all the available space on her bed. She yelped as pain shot through her right arm.

Duppy lifted his head, looked at her, and flopped back to the mattress.

Touching the tender area on the inside of her elbow, she didn't recall falling, arm wrestling an MMA fighter, or betting someone she could do a hundred pull-ups. She flexed, touching her shoulder and stretching forward to test the ache.

The motion resembled throwing a dart.

Aaaah...

That made sense.

Pulling a muscle *throwing darts* had to be a new low for being out of shape.

What next? Tearing a ligament while filing her nails?

She offered Duppy a pat to apologize for waking him. *Poor Duppy.* His hair was thinning. He'd always looked like the offspring of some gorgeous Samoyed and a sewer rat, and age hadn't enhanced the more suspect aspects of his lineage.

She imagined fourteen years ago, Duppy's purebred mother had confessed to her girlfriend:

"Duchess, you wouldn't believe what I did last night. You

28

know that homeless cur who's been hanging around the block? The one with the mange? Well, I was in heat, and—*I slept with him.*"

Duppy was the result of that regrettable night of passion.

In college, she'd found him hiding under a car. He'd been barely bigger than a beer can. After a half-hearted attempt to find his owner, she'd kept him. Around that time, she'd read the biography of reggae great Bob Marley, in which the author described ghosts from Jamaican folklore called *duppies*. Her new puppy was white and came to her mysteriously, so naming him Duppy seemed a no-brainer.

Dup had been her companion through countless adventures, but at fourteen, he was an old man and did little more than sleep. She didn't like to think about her furry son's advanced age.

He would always be her baby.

After showering and throwing the previous night's clothes in the washer, Emily made a cup of coffee and went outside to read. Duppy padded along beside her to do his morning business. She lived in a ranch-style house with a brick patio in the back, so neither had to deal with stairs.

After her morning sabbatical, she worked for a while and then drove to a dart store called Bullseye's. When she'd asked, Kady said she could buy darts at *the dart store*. She thought she'd been kidding, but sure enough, a quick search proved there was such a thing as a dart store.

Who knew?

Pulling into the parking lot, she realized she'd passed the dingy strip mall store a million times without noticing it had a dart store.

She'd awakened to a new world—one of elbow pain and weird hole-in-the-wall stores once invisible to the human eye.

It was all very exciting.

She had to look the part; she was a dart player now. Now she was no better than Kady's boyfriend Joe—a test driver of personas. She'd buy darts to become *Emily the Dart Girl* just as Joe'd bought vintage cowboy boots and grown a scruffy beard to become *Joe the Hipster.*

Maybe she'd been too hard on Joe. She'd have to be nicer to him, or buy stock in Windex, what with all her glass houses.

She entered Bullseye's to discover the store sold pool tables and other bar game accessories. Bullseye's was Candy Land for bored drinkers. On the recommendation of the strangely greasy gentleman behind the counter, she bought a set of Black Widow darts and some extra flights. Flights, she now knew, were the plastic wings on the back of the dart. She'd seen Kady change her flights the night before and assumed that meant it was wise to carry a spare set. Apparently, if a dart bounced off the board and hit the floor, the flights often bent, making the dart less accurate. She also found it comforting to know that if she threw poorly, she could blame her performance on the flights and change them.

How often would she change her flights before becoming a better dart player? Five thousand? Fifty thousand?

Maybe I'll buy a hundred packs of those...

She searched for a *lucky* pack of flights, settling on a set featuring four-leaf clovers. While not unique, they suited the Irish Rover, and she was twenty percent Irish, so she wasn't a *total* fake.

She added another set with skulls—in case she felt particularly badass—and a dart board for practicing at home.

Stalking dart players was *expensive.*

Thank God Joe hadn't suggested she go to polo night—she'd be walking around with a pony and a backbreaking monthly hay mortgage.

Emily stopped in her tracks.

Oh no.

Am I stalking Sebastian?

She had a long and glorious history of crushes. She'd stalked a boy in high school until she broke him, and they'd dated for years. Maybe *stalked* was the wrong word. She hadn't stood in

the bushes with binoculars—she'd positioned herself like an innocent street sign in places she knew he would pass. Tailed him a *little*. It was a *Hey! Fancy meeting you here on the street where I have no logical reason to be! What a coincidence! This must*
30

be fate! type of stalking.

Was her new passion for darts all about Sebastian?

No.

No, dammit, I like playing darts. It's fun. It's my new hobby.

Hobbies are healthy.

Emily threw the dartboard in her trunk and swore to stop thinking about Sebastian.

Mostly.

Couldn't stalking Sebastian *be* a hobby?

Two new hobbies.

I am so *healthy.*

Anyway, she wasn't stalking anyone. She was giving love a chance. If romance was left to men, the human race would die out while they logged their fantasy football points and punched each other in the balls.

Everyone knew that.

She sighed. Maybe she should talk to Tessa.

Tessa would set her straight.

CHAPTER SIX

Sebastian stared into the bushes. He pulled at the chest of his t-shirt where it stuck to his skin, the fabric still damp with Greta's tears.

It's over.

He didn't love Greta. He'd read her all wrong. Every sweet note in Greta's voice sang from her ability to play him like a fiddle. With each soft touch, she caressed strings, manipulating him.

Greta's affections rang hollow, yet every time he tried to leave, she worked *feverishly* to make him stay. Why? So he could cover half her rent? So he could serve as a security blanket until she found a new man?

A week before, she'd gone to a meeting two hours away in New York. An hour after she was due to return, she'd called from New York to say she'd decided to stay the night at a college friend's apartment. She said it had been a long day, that she hadn't seen her friend in years, and it made more sense to stay. No biggie. He hadn't asked for excuses, but they rained on him like rice at a wedding. She'd thrown a whole handful, hoping one would stick.

That part made him a *little* suspicious, but he shrugged off his doubts and told her to have a good time.

He didn't give her sudden change of plans another thought, even when she called the next day to announce she'd be staying a second night.

Hm.

He didn't become officially suspicious until she returned and dumped her dirty clothes in the laundry basket. The lacy, black underwear topping that pile inspired a blip on his radar.

It had been a long time since he saw that particular pair of underwear. They'd been retired like an aging racehorse a few weeks after he and Greta started dating.

He didn't mind the *retiring of the sexy underwear* routine. He didn't even like frilly underwear. He preferred the comfort that
32

came with familiarity. He liked having *girlfriends*, not sex kittens. But why *did* that sexy underwear appear in the laundry? Why had Greta dragged them out of retirement like a broke boxer?

Sebastian knew he wouldn't ask. There was no point. Greta would never admit to cheating on him. He didn't want to hear lies or expend energy proving his suspicions. Maybe she happened to grab that particular pair of underwear. Who was he to say?

He inhaled through his nose and let it burst from his lips with an exaggerated *puhhh* that made his cheeks ripple. The whole incident reminded him of his stepfather. As a kid, he'd overheard that ass demanding to know why his mother had a spare pair of nylons in her briefcase.

"In case my stockings run," his mother had answered.

Sebastian remembered his mother's voice sounding strange—high and pleading. He couldn't see his mother's face but heard her shock and pain. Even as a teen, he knew his stepfather believed the nylons were evidence of an affair.

It was crazy to think his mother would have an affair. Sebastian knew girls at school who'd kept spare things in their lockers. Spare stuff was Girl 101.

He didn't want to be *that* guy. He wouldn't accuse Greta of having an affair because an unfamiliar, believed-retired pair of sexy underwear reappeared.

A month before the underwear incident, Sebastian raised the courage to tell Greta he wanted out of their relationship. He'd left work early and waited at the apartment, steeling himself for his well-rehearsed break-up speech.

Then Greta walked through the door crying—newly fired from her job. He couldn't leave her an hour after she lost her job. She needed a shoulder to cry on and his half of the rent more than ever.

He waited a few more weeks. Greta found a new job working with a big stadium's hospitality group and seemed happy. He again rehearsed his easy letdown speech.

Three words into it, her sister, Kimi, appeared at the door, sobbing that she was pregnant.

Houdini couldn't extract himself from a life with Greta.

Sebastian tried a new tack. He tried to *inspire* Greta to break up with him.

Nope.

The more he suggested they break up, the more she dug in.

Unfortunately, his relationship with her wasn't horrific enough to *demand* a resolution. It wasn't painful living with her. Thanks to their job schedules, they barely saw each other. They didn't have anything in common, but it wasn't like she was slowly poisoning his coffee.

As far as he knew.

Moving *on* meant the hassle of moving *out* and finding a new apartment.

Days came and went.

It was easier to stay.

Tonight, he'd tried to discuss moving out. His stay was supposed to be temporary. Maybe the phrase "move out" instead of "break up" would allow him to sneak the separation past her drama radar.

The second he said *my own apartment*, she burst into tears.

"Why baby?" she whined. She ran to where he sat on the sofa and jumped into his lap. Straddling him, she sobbed into his neck, shifting her hips just enough to make it clear the grinding effect was no accident.

"You can't leave me *now*. Why would you want to leave?"

His chin rested against her tear-soaked cleavage, her chest heaving with staccato sobs.

At that point, things got a little fuzzy. Ten minutes earlier, he'd had an excellent argument for all Greta's questions.

Now...

Well, now he was on the porch.

Sebastian heard the sliding door open behind him.

"Baby, I'm going out."

Sebastian turned. Greta wore full makeup. They'd barely been out of bed fifteen minutes, and she was dressed for a night on the town.

He didn't remember an invitation to join.

"Where? It's almost ten."

"It's my sister. She wanted me to meet her, and I totally forgot. You know how dizzy I can be." She rolled her eyes and stuck out her tongue to illustrate her point.

Flicking the hair from her face, the top of her breasts bounced behind her low-cut tee before settling back into the comfort of her *lift and shove together* bra.

"Why don't you ask your sister to come here?" he suggested.

"Sydney is coming, too. We're going to the Stone Horse Tavern for a quickie."

Sebastian grimaced. Greta's friend Sydney was always in the middle of everything.

If only I knew what Sydney knew…

"Whatever."

"Thanks, baby." She stepped out to kiss the top of his head. "Don't wait up. You know how Sydney gets."

Greta spun on her toe and bounced back into the house.

Sebastian called over his shoulder. "Wait, isn't your sister pregnant? Should she *be* at a bar?"

The slider door thudded shut.

"Don't lock the—"

He heard the flick of the lock.

Dammit.

Habit. She didn't mean to lock him out.

Ah well.

It didn't matter. She never remembered to lock the front door when she left. He'd walk around and use the front entrance.

He looked sideways at the lighter they used for the grill beside him.

He picked it up and flicked it on.

A dog barked, and Sebastian jumped. Greta's Shih Tzu stared at him through the slider glass. He ignored him and flicked the lighter a second time.

Binker woofed again.

"Shut *up*."

As Sebastian flicked the lighter on and off, a symphony of yapping burst from inside the house. The barking became louder and more frantic. Binker scratched at the glass.

Sebastian let the lighter die and hung his head.
The barking stopped.
He lit the lighter.
The barking resumed.
"Blind, my *ass*."
He twisted to glare at the dog. The barking stopped.
"Fine. I'll come inside."
Sebastian dropped the lighter.
Binker's tail wagged.

36

CHAPTER SEVEN

Emily called Tessa to an emergency meeting at Nice Legs! wine bar. Usually, she had to plan Tessa meetings months in advance, but she'd begged and gotten lucky. Her friend had kids now, and Emily scheduled time with her like one of Tessa's law clients. Kids were like little client meetings that never ended.

"I think the first step is to admit I've always been a tad stalky," Emily said, spinning her wine glass on the table the way she always did right before she spilled wine everywhere.

Tessa put her hand on Emily's to stop her from twirling. Her jaw clenched, her eyes went gunslinger-squinty.

Emily released the stem of her wine glass and slowly pulled her hand away like a camper who'd reached for a soda, only to find a snarling wolf on the other side of the cooler.

Tessa was small but terrifying.

Emily knew she could spin her ferocious Chihuahua of a friend like a wine glass if she had to, but it didn't matter. For every teaspoon of Emily's slapdash nature, Tessa was one full cup of *precise*. Not only did she not do dumb things, she prevented *others* from doing dumb things—like stopping Emily from playing with stemware.

Tessa was like a bitchy superhero.

"So you're officially admitting you're a little stalky?" Tessa asked.

"Little Stalky," echoed Emily. "Sounds like The Green Giant's son, doesn't it? *Lil' Stalky*?"

"The Green Giant has a son?"

"Well, there's Sprout, of course. The little Brussels-sprout-looking kid, and Lil' Stalky is his tall, gangly son."

"Ah, I remember. Sprout was stout."

Emily nodded. "Right. And I'm thinking Lil' Stalky looks enough *not* like Sprout for Green Giant to wonder if Mrs. Giant was maybe messing around with the milkman."

Tessa scowled. "Do vegetables drink milk? Who has a milkman? Is it always 1860 in Green Giant Land? And why are milkmen always so horny?"

"These are all good questions."

Tessa leaned forward and whispered, "What does Mrs. Giant do when the Green G's away at the canning convention? Hmm? I ask you that."

Emily snickered. Tessa was both fierce and fun. Her personality was like using a knife to tickle someone.

"I think Jack climbed more than the beanstalk if you know what I mean," Emily suggested. "Luckily for Mrs. Giant, DNA testing hasn't been invented in magical canned-vegetable land."

"Indeed. Lucky Ho Ho Ho."

Emily's gaze fell to their shared cheese plate. She'd already eaten her portion of the bleu cheese, but Tessa had let her half rot. It made Emily *crazy*. Tessa had otherworldly willpower *and* couldn't gain weight if she beer-bonged lard milkshakes. Occasionally, Tessa pointed to the tiny roll of skin hanging over her size-negative jeans and moaned, "Look at this, what do I do about this?" and Emily had to fight not to choke her.

She considered herself a normal-sized person, but standing next to Tessa, she looked like a Sasquatch.

Emily glanced at her watch. How long since Tessa's last bite of cheese? Ten minutes? Twenty?

Polite-time had expired.

Now it was cheese-for-all.

"Just eat it," said Tessa.

"What?"

"If you stare any harder at the bleu cheese it's going to burst into bleu flames. Just eat it."

"Was I staring?" Emily scooped the moldy goodness onto a cracker before her friend could change her mind.

Bleu cheese gone; only the sharp cheddar remained between them.

Patience.

Emily tried to distract herself from the cheese. "Anyway, back to you talking me off the wall. Stop me from doing unladylike things."

Tessa chuckled. "You? Unladylike? When I look up *demure* in the dictionary, your photo stares back at me."

Emily scowled as Tessa continued.

38

"Weren't you the one who made a doll out of that freak Daniel's hair in high school?"

An approaching server overheard Tessa's comment and glanced at Emily like she was wearing a straight jacket.

Emily smiled back at the server, whose gaze fell on the nearly empty cheese plate. Emily instinctively covered the edge of the cheeseboard with her fingers, ready to wrestle it from the server's grasp should he lunge for it.

"Did you just growl?" asked Tessa.

"I'm sorry, what?"

The server left.

Emily leaned forward to hiss at Tessa. "*I did not make a hair doll.* You always say that, and it makes me sound like a lunatic. What I did was romantic. I took some of his hair and sort of *bunched it together*."

"Like a doll."

"*Not* like a doll. It was a loop of hair. Sometimes a loop can look like a head, that's all. It wasn't like I built a shrine with burning candles and chicken bones."

"As far as I know. How long did you end up dating that guy anyway?"

Emily sighed. "Eight years, which is like twenty-five in emotional rollercoaster years. I had to buy him a ticket to California to get him away from me long enough to find the strength to break up with him."

"I still haven't decided if you're an idiot or a genius with that move."

"It's a fine line."

"Who did you stalk after that?"

"No one, remember? Brad stalked *me*. And I was so flattered I nearly married him even though he bored the hell out of me."

"That killed three years?"

"Close to four. It broke my heart to break his heart."

"You're terrible at this. Maybe you should take a vow of chastity. Stalking people gets you in trouble; *being* stalked gets you in trouble... It's a classic 'damned if you do' situation."

"You're married and retired from romance. You forget the hair-doll days were the good old days. I miss infatuation. I haven't been inspired to stalk someone in a very long time. I miss the game. The intrigue—"

Tessa's head cocked. "Is it that you haven't been inspired? Or have you been court-ordered to stay thirty yards from all men?"

"Very funny. I'm serious I—"

Tessa's phone rang, and she held up a finger to put Emily on pause. Tessa leaned sideways to rummage the purse at her feet, and Emily took that opportunity to pop the remaining chunk of sharp cheddar into her mouth.

She had a problem with cheese. Cheese and wine. And chocolate. And bacon. And vodka.

My God, I am riddled with problems.

Tessa sat up, glanced at her phone, and then set it down on the table. She noticed the empty cheese board, arched her right brow, and took another sip of wine.

"You work out of your home. It isn't a mystery why you can't meet anyone. Who are you going to stalk? The UPS guy?" she asked.

Emily grinned. "Piece of cake. I'd keep ordering things."

"You need to get out more. I guess if following this Sebastian dude will get you out of the house..."

Emily's eyes popped.

"I have your permission to stalk him?"

"That's not what I said. But I guess you could stalk him *a little*, for the greater good."

"Yay." Emily rapidly clapped only the tips of her fingers in silent celebration.

"But no hair dolls," added Tessa, pointing. "And I don't want to be called to your restraining order hearing."

"Deal."

Emily smiled. Everything felt better with Tessa's blessing. She'd intended to stalk Sebastian regardless, but now, if it didn't work out, she could tell Tessa it was all *her* fault.

"My problems are solved. What's new with you?"

Tessa straightened. "Ooh, I forgot to tell you. I joined a running group. I'm going to do a marathon."

Emily's expression fell.

The thinnest girl in the world *enjoyed* running.

She sighed.
"Ok, now you're just being a jerk."

CHAPTER EIGHT

Two days after dart night, Emily returned to the Irish Rover at the crack of happy hour to find the bar area empty, but for two people: a giant, bespectacled man, and Sebastian.

Emily nearly fainted with happiness. Finally, she'd *meet* Sebastian. Was it luck? Fate? Stalker intuition? Something brought them together. The God of Vodka, perhaps.

Sebastian and Four-eyes sat at the front snug bar. It seemed cheeky to plant herself on the stool between them, so she roosted at the tall bar table flush against the snug's front window directly across from the boys. Nervous to throw darts in a small space next to other victims—er, *people*—she unzipped her case. Instead, she'd sharpen her new points on her new sharpening stone. They might be dull from languishing in Bullseye's display case.

Emily slid the darts from her nylon case, feeling very *legit*. Real dart players had cases, and hers was sleek yet large enough to carry darts, her license, credit card, compact, and lipstick. It was *perfect*. Emily took a deep, cleansing breath.

Be cool.

She pulled her lipstick from its special pocket and faced toward the window to reapply. She'd bought a new color for the case. She'd searched for a lipstick called *Bullseye Red*, but settled on *Coral Reef*. The color was bold for daytime, but as Emily sat at her kitchen table, glancing back and forth between the case, her watch, and the late afternoon sun streaming through her window, she realized *dark* happened too late at night.

She couldn't wait that long to go to the Rover.

She slid the lipstick back into its pocket and noticed a price tag on the table beside her case. She tried to pick it up, only to find it attached to her pack.

Oh no.

How had she not noticed the tag on her dart pack as she lovingly filled it with accessories? She couldn't look more like an amateur if she'd strutted in wearing a t-shirt emblazoned with *Dart Players Do It With a Point.* She was officially the biggest 42

dork ever to enter the Irish Rover.

They would sing songs about her:

> *She played darts once then bought the whole kit,*
> *The stuff was brand new but she still played like shit*
> *And a hydie diedy deedle doodle…*

Emily shot a glance towards the snug bar. The boys had their backs to her. No one had seen her shame.

Hope sprang eternal.

Emily yanked the tag, but the transparent cord holding the ticket in place resisted breakage like military-grade fiber; possibly alien in origin. She looped in her finger and pulled as hard as possible, grunting with the strain. She cleared her throat to cover the grunt.

The loop refused to snap. Her finger, lashed by an angry red indentation, throbbed.

Emily raised the case to her mouth, tapping it against her chin as if deep in thought. Her eyes made a second sweep of the room.

No one was looking.

She turned to the window and shoved the plastic into her mouth, positioning the cord between her eyetooth and lower canine. She gnawed, lips pulled tight across her teeth, nibbling at the loop like a rabid squirrel.

"What can I get you?" said a voice.

Startled, Emily jumped, the dart case shooting from her grasp like a freshly caught fish determined to return to the sea. She bobbled the pack hand to hand, finally slapping it to the ground with a loud thud. Spiking the case to the floor seemed the only logical way to end her horror. She almost immediately regretted the decision.

She stared at the case at the foot of her stool.

"You never told me you could juggle."

Emily recognized Sebastian's voice. She lifted her head; her dry upper lip still stuck to her gums, her teeth bared in a frozen snarl.

"*Gaaah*," spat the bespectacled man at the bar.

Emily met gazes with the three people gawking at her: the big guy in glasses, who'd already spit his drink in horror; Sebastian, sporting a barely perceptible smirk of amusement and Giant Wendy the Bartender, hands on her hips, awaiting an answer to her question.

Emily licked her upper lip back into submission.

"Whoops."

Emily hopped from her stool and retrieved her case, maneuvering the tag, so it remained unnoticeable to the group. As she watched the big man wipe his cocktail from his chin, she questioned whether the price tag remained her number one concern. Spiking her case to the ground was climbing the Dork Hot 100 Chart. Impersonating a beaver was number one with a bullet.

"Dropped my case." She held it in the air like a small nylon trophy. "Got it."

She placed the case back on the table and smiled at Wendy.

"What can I get you?" repeated the giantess.

"To drink?" Emily asked as her hair fell over her eye. She tucked it behind her ear and then tossed her head, a move she thought would appear sexy and casual. The hair she'd secured fell back across her face, so she pushed it behind her ear and tried a second sexy head toss, dislodging the lock afresh.

This happened several more times.

Wendy scowled. "Yes. What can I get you to *drink*."

Emily fixed the hair one last time and resisted the urge to head-toss. Composed, she opened her mouth to answer and then fell dumb, unable to think of a drink.

Any drink.

Did drinks have names?

She searched Wendy's face for assistance, but the woman's expression telegraphed only a strange cocktail of annoyance and pity.

Emily swallowed. "I, uh..."

"Get her a Chicken Club," said a voice.

"Chicken?" echoed Emily.

"Chicken *Club*."

The voice wasn't Sebastian's, so it had to belong to his bar buddy.

Emily focused on the man. She guessed his height at six-four, his body built like a linebacker's, several years out of training. Though physically imposing, his thinning hair and

44

round, wire-rimmed spectacles softened his appearance.

"I'm not hungry," she said.

"It's not a sandwich. It's a drink. Vodka and soda with a splash of cranberry."

"Oh. That'll work." Emily nodded her head like a paint mixer.

Wendy disappeared behind the partition separating the snug from the rest of the bar.

"You, uh..." The big guy pointed to his mouth and made a circling motion around his lips. "You got a thing going on there."

Emily covered her mouth with her hand. She turned to her table, zipped open her case, and retrieved her compact. Flipping it open, she peered into the mirror to find her freshly applied lipstick smeared far beyond the boundaries of her lips. The area on her pack where the plastic tag loop pierced her nylon case also sported a fresh coat of lipstick.

She noted she should always shove her dart case in their mouths *before* touching up their lipstick.

Wiping her mouth to look a little less like a four-year-old playing with mommy's makeup, she cleaned her case as best she could and ripped off the paper price tag. She left the plastic ring attached until she could find metal shears or a blowtorch.

Maintenance completed, Emily turned to find the two men at the bar had politely returned to their drinks rather than watching her piece her face back together. She noticed both had pale pink drinks in pint glasses.

She cleared her throat, but the men seemed unfamiliar with the international gesture for catching someone's attention and refused to turn.

"Is that what you're drinking? Those manly pink drinks you have there are Chicken Clubs?" she asked the backs of their heads, chuckling.

The men's heads swiveled to face her. They stared, their faces blank as wax figures. During their deep silence, Emily reconsidered her last comment.

"Just kidding. About the manly part. I mean, about inferring that you aren't manly—"

Ohmygod, why can't I shut up? Why don't I just point at their penises, laugh, and call it a day?

Emily thrust her hand toward the cuddly linebacker.

"I'm Emily, by the way." She noticed a smear of lipstick on her thumb and quickly wiped it away with her other hand.

"Benny," said the adorable goon, shaking her hand once she had replaced her original offering with a cleaner version. "This is Sebastian."

Sebastian nodded and extended his hand. Emily shook it, her gaze darting from his eyes to the floor.

She mentally groaned as she released his long-fingered paw. Unless Sebastian was from a land with no women, he had to know she found him attractive after playing touch tag with his eyeballs.

"So, why do you call them Chicken Clubs?" she asked, turning back to Benny.

She felt every molecule in her being screaming, "*Help me, Benny. Please make the awkward go away.*"

"On a business trip, I bumped into some guys who called them that. The bar had it so 'Chicken Club' printed out on their receipts, so the guys who drank there could write their drinks off as a business expense."

"Ah. Very clever."

'Very clever?' Who am I, Sherlock Holmes?

Sebastian sniffed. "Unless their boss wondered why they ate six chicken club sandwiches for lunch."

Emily turned to him. "I saw you playing darts the other night."

She meant, *I stared holes through you while you were playing darts the other night*, but avoided wording it that way, demonstrating a surprising show of restraint.

Baby steps.

"Me?" asked Sebastian.

Emily nodded.

He squinted at her. "Oh, right. You were at the bar."

"Right. You were getting a martini, and you forgot to ask for olive juice."

Emily trailed off, choking back a flood of unnecessary details to avoid sounding like a stalker. *Oh, and a lock of your hair had fallen across your forehead, and I remember your shirt had a small cranberry-colored stain on the sleeve and...*

Benny took a sip of his drink. "Sebastian's really good. I mean, not as good as me, but..."

Sebastian rolled his eyes.

"You were there at the end, weren't you?" Emily said, gently prodding Sebastian to speak. He had a nice voice; no discernible accent of any kind; masculine, but not gruff. "I mean, you almost won, didn't you? I think I saw you in the finals—was that you? If that's what you call them, *finals*? Are they called something else in darts? I mean, did you win?"

Wow. Is there a Pulitzer Prize for speaking? I am the Siren of Subtle today. Hey, as long as we're sharing, Sebastian, here are some photos I took of you. And here's a Ken doll; you can see I cut off his face and pasted a picture of your face in its place. Hope that's cool—could I have a few of your fingernail clippings? What blood type are you?

"We came in second," said Sebastian.

Emily took a deep breath and exhaled for what seemed like an hour.

Oh Sebastian. You poor, insanely attractive thing. You have no idea what is going on in my head, or you would have leaped from the bar stool and sprinted down the street on your long, sexy legs ten minutes ago.

Sebastian swiveled his knees toward Emily and rested his back on the partition splitting the snug from the rest of the bar. Emily moved behind Benny and took a spot at the end of the snug bar. Wendy brought her Chicken Club, and just like that, Emily joined the boys at the bar. She was like a bumbling explorer stumbling onto the tribe she'd hoped to study.

"So what do you guys do?" she asked, remembering what normal people said in situations like these.

"Lawyer," said Benny.

"I thought you looked shifty."

Benny's smile morphed into a grimace. She wasn't the first to throw a "lawyers suck" joke his way.

Emily focused on Sebastian and chanted in her head like she was playing craps.

Come on, say novelist-slash-Internet mogul! Millionaire-

entrepreneur-who-single-handedly-saved-all-the-stray-puppies-in-Thailand! Seven come eleven!

No. No, he couldn't say those things, she decided; too braggy. He would say he tinkers with stuff, but by that, he'd mean he invented the iPhone. Or, he'd say he's a philanthropist, or he'd say—

"I'm a manager," said Sebastian.

Manager?

"Oh, like an office?" she asked.

"No, like a store. Retail. At the Cove Center."

"Oh. Cool."

Okay. Maybe not Internet mogul cool, but that was fine. She'd never dated anyone for money or fame before; no reason to start now. And who knew? Maybe he still saved puppies on weekends.

Should I ask him about puppies?

"What do you do?" asked Sebastian.

"I'm a writer and have a little web development company."

Website development company always sounded better than *I sit at home in my pajamas, moving things around on my monitor.*

"You live in town?" asked Benny.

"Yeah."

Emily grimaced. She hated saying "yeah." She practiced saying "yes" instead of "yeah," but the habit remained. It was like trying to kick heroin. She imagined. She didn't know.

"Well, I live on the outskirts of town," she added, wanting to be completely honest with her new friends about everything except the fact she was stalking one of them. "I have a house in Thicke Woods."

"Cool, wanna date?" said Sebastian.

Sipping from her Chicken Club, Emily gagged and coughed it back into her glass. She covered her mouth and looked up at Sebastian, who appeared alarmed.

"You okay?" he asked.

Benny laughed. Emily's eyes watered. She used a napkin to wipe her mouth and fought to ignore the vodka in her nasal passage.

"I'm fine," she wheezed, taking another sip to clear her throat.

"Sebastian wants your house," said Benny.

Emily swallowed, pleased to find standard breathing

patterns had commenced.

"What?"

"*Do you want to date,*" repeated Sebastian. "I have a weird housing situation right now, so *if you've got a roof, I'm yours,* is 48

what I was saying. I was kidding."

Emily nodded. "Ah. Got it."

She liked how *I'm yours* rolled off Sebastian's tongue. The *if you've got a roof* part barely registered. Apparently, if someone was attractive enough, her body released a hormone that ensured she only heard what she wanted to hear when he spoke.

That explained a lot.

Emily was preparing to ask Sebastian what he meant by a "weird housing situation" when more people entered the snug and diverted Sebastian's attention from the sputtering girl with the literal drinking problem.

After one or two failed attempts to reignite a more intimate conversation, Emily did her best to remove her laser focus from Sebastian and blend with the others. After all, she wanted him to like her, not file a restraining order. Tessa had warned her about that.

Emily recognized people from Dart Night. It seemed on non-tournament nights, the dart crowd gathered to freeform gamble. It cost five dollars to play, and luckily, Emily had brought cash to lose in the interest of practice. She played single for these games; she didn't need to embarrass a partner. A few less competitive players took it upon themselves to school her on board number two, while the big league players like Sebastian shot on board one.

Emily discovered the board in her dad's garage had been an American dartboard. At the Irish Rover, all the boards were of the English variety, and Cricket was the game of choice. The object of Cricket was to close your numbers by hitting three darts in the pie slice for that number. The numbers you had to hit were fifteen through twenty and bull's-eye. Most players started by closing twenty and worked their way down to keep people from "pointing" them. If someone "closed" twenties, for example, by hitting three of them, they could then hit more twenties to score twenty points per dart against a player who still had that number "open." In the end, if the player with the most points closed the board, it was over because there was no way for the other player to continue pointing the winner while they attempted to close their board.

Emily discovered she loved playing darts. She quickly adopted dart slang, calling "fifteens" "fives," for example, and learned how to write scores on the chalkboard. She even managed to keep her mouth shut when she wasn't sure about something, so she didn't do the equivalent of screaming "touchdown!" at a baseball game.

Thanks to one or two lucky games and Benny's amateur status, Emily only ended five dollars down after two hours of play. That rate wasn't bad at all in the grand scheme of paying for entertainment.

Maybe having a job was overrated. Maybe she needed to join the dart tour.

Enraptured by competition, Emily didn't notice when Sebastian disappeared. At some point, she looked for him, and he was gone. She was disappointed her interactions with him were over for the day but happy she hadn't noticed him leave. It proved her new hobby wasn't all about Sebastian.

Or the sexy little scar on his left cheekbone.

CHAPTER NINE

Emily was working on a hair salon's website when she heard knocking on her front door. She hated when people knocked on her door. Not because she minded the intrusion, she just had ridiculous nipples.

Movie girls were helpful when deciding if your body parts conformed to societal norms or if you were a freak of nature destined to flee from pitchfork-wielding villagers. Her circle parts, the areolas, were normal if naked girls in movies were any indication.

On the other hand, her nipply parts were like pencil erasers and needed to be contained in public, strapped down like King Kong on his way to New York City.

She felt confident they weren't *freakish*, but they weren't little nubby things either. And she *hated* wearing a bra. Why would she wear a bra in her own home when she didn't need its gravity-fighting abilities? But though her breasts weren't pendulous, if she didn't wear a bra, visitors had to stare down the barrels of her nipples like she was a gunslinger. She knew if that happened, she'd say something like, *"They aren't loaded!"* which would make everything *so much worse*. If she said, *"Do you feel lucky? Well, do ya, punk?"* to the FedEx guy, she'd never get another delivery.

"Just a second, hold on, I'm coming! Hold on!" she screamed as she tore off her t-shirt, applied a padded bra, and reapplied the t-shirt. In the meantime, Duppy took his usual spot behind the front door, barking his head off. At forty-five pounds, he sounded like a five-hundred-pound hellhound. Handy for a woman living alone.

She answered the door to find a man in a black suit holding a pamphlet.

"If you want him in your heart, just ask," he said.

Emily sighed. Her neighborhood posted signs to warn away sales door-knockers—magazine subscriptions, meat in a truck, religion, politics—but nothing stopped the onslaught of peddlers.

"Thanks, I'll do that." She took the pamphlet and closed the door.

She tossed the paper in the trash as her coffeemaker caught her eye. She needed caffeine but didn't feel like home-brewed coffee. She craved human interaction and not the kind that arrived, unannounced, on her doorstep with pamphlets. She worried if she stayed at home, her mind would drift to Sebastian, and she'd end up at the Irish Rover even earlier than usual.

She threw on shorts and a polo and drove to Grounded. It wasn't prime man-watching time. At this hour, people rushed in, grabbed a coffee, and sprinted to work. No one lingered to read, crunch spreadsheets, or do whatever people with real jobs did. It was the perfect time for head-clearing, surrounded by the hustle and bustle, yet completely alone.

A woman burst out of the coffee shop as she arrived, and although Emily was the perfect distance from the door, the woman didn't hold it open for her. She did everything but push the door closed and nail it shut.

"So polite," Emily muttered under her breath. She didn't think she'd said it loud enough for the woman to hear, but as the woman hustled away, she yelled, "Shoulda asked—shoulda moved faster!"

Emily opened her mouth to respond, but the perfect retort didn't jump to mind. She entered the coffee shop and stood behind two people, a man and a woman dressed in suits. Not ordering at the speed of light topped Grounded's sin chart, falling just behind *asking for "a coffee."* The line moved faster than she expected, and she panicked as the barista's attention turned to her.

"I want something different," she blurted.

The teen stared at her blankly, the subtle shift of his weight

52

from one foot to the other the only sign that he'd heard her. Someone behind her groaned.

She panicked.

"Can I get a double espresso, but with whipped cream on top? Is that weird?"

The kid shrugged.

"Ask, and ye shall receive," he said, writing her name on a cup.

A few people were waiting, so Emily found a seat. She'd brought a book, figuring she'd finish her coffee and then head home and get to work.

"Sebastian!" called a barista.

Emily sat up like a meerkat and scanned the shop. She didn't see Sebastian, but no one moved to claim the coffee. *There couldn't be two people named Sebastian in town, could there?*

"Sebastian!"

No one moved.

Could he be here? Her initial excitement gave way to trepidation. "Coincidental" meetings were her modus operandi, and they'd worked for her in the past, but if she bumped into Sebastian again so soon, he might get suspicious.

Or frightened.

A suited woman stepped to the counter.

"Do you mean Samantha?" she asked.

The barista studied the scribble on the side of the cup.

"Probably. Half caff latté?"

The woman nodded and took the coffee.

Emily's expectant heart fell.

Fate dropped Sebastian in her lap at the snug bar. It was too much to expect it to happen again.

"Amy?" called the coffee guy.

Emily's phone rang. She looked at the caller ID. It was her mother.

"Hi, Mom."

"Amy?" called the barista again.

"Do you want Sebastian?" asked her mom.

Emily blinked. Her mother's ability to sense what she was doing at any given moment was legendary, but this took her superpowers to a new level.

"What did you say?"

"Do you want sea bass, hon?" repeated her mother. "Your father has some, and we're coming down, so we can bring you some if you want it."

Emily closed her eyes and chuckled. Her parents lived a few states away, but they also owned a small house near Emily, and they periodically came to stay. Her father fished and often caught enough to share.

"Sea bass, hon," echoed Emily. "Sure. Thanks."

"Oh good, I'm glad I called. I figured it couldn't hurt to ask."

They said their goodbyes.

"Amy?" called the barista again.

Emily looked around the store. Only she remained.

"*Emily*?" she asked.

The teen shrugged. "Probably."

She retrieved her coffee. Before she could take her first sip of joe, a brilliant idea flashed across her brain.

I'll ask Sebastian out.

Forget the stalking, forget the unrequited crush lingering for weeks or months, forget waiting for someone to notice her, or for the perfect moment to strike.

She would ask *him* out.

Why didn't I think of that before?

She'd been waiting for inspiration—a *sign*—but clearly, she was a love *genius*.

CHAPTER TEN

Asking Sebastian out at the Irish Rover was a bad idea; too many people, too much noise, and if he said no, she couldn't bolt out of the bar and run home without suffering massive humiliation. No matter how discreetly she asked, she'd be forever known as *the chick Sebastian dissed.* The Rover would name a drink after her, called *The Desperatio*—made with vodka, cranberry, and loser tears. Spurning someone would be forever known as *pulling an Emily,* as in, "Man, Bob really gave that girl the Emily!"

No.

Asking Sebastian out at the Rover was a no-go.

And no matter how private the location might be, Emily couldn't go to Sebastian's home. First, she had no idea where he lived. Second, there was no logical reason she *should* know where he lived, so appearing on his doorstep would make her Creepy McCreeperson.

Emily knew Sebastian worked at a home decor store at the Cove Center shopping plaza, which only had one such store; Über Home. There was nothing strange about shopping; she could stop at Über Home and be "surprised" to see Sebastian.

"Oh hey! Sebastian, right? Fancy meeting you here..."

Wait, no. She couldn't say "fancy meeting you here," without sounding like a dame from a 1940s rom-com.

"Oh hey, Sebastian, right? Ha—we've got to stop meeting like this..."

No. Even worse.

I should punch myself in the head for even thinking that cliché.

"Oh, hey, Sebastian, right? You work here?"

Duh, *no*. He doesn't work there—he likes to sneak into stores and see how long he can stand behind the counter waiting on people before the owner throws him out.

"Hey—how are you?"

Better. Not clever or memorable, but better than embarrassing herself.

She didn't worry too much about what to say next because if it took her an hour to decide how to say *hi*, she and Sebastian would both be dead from old age before she found the nerve to *proposition* him.

She took a deep breath and mentally embraced the notion if she felt this strongly, it must be *fate*. Yep. *Fate*. As sure as bite marks in Christmas cookies meant Santa had visited. Never mind that Mom's breath smelled like chocolate chips. Or that when you suggested leaving out sugar cookies, Mom, the chocoholic, insisted on Toll House. Look away from the crumbs on her pajamas...

Emily didn't know why she carried a torch for this man, but she had to end her puppy love. Nip stalking in the bud. Either he was interested in going for a drink with her, or he wasn't—either way, once she asked, she could move forward.

No more planning. She'd go to Sebastian's work and ask him for drinks or coffee—something non-threatening—and leave. Emily scrutinized her house for a spot she could fit new furniture, just in case. Über Home was nice. Maybe she'd buy a new sofa. It would depend on how much she panicked.

The last time she saw Sebastian, he'd arrived at the Irish Rover at 4:20 p.m., wearing khakis, a button-down white shirt, and a loosened tie—clearly a work outfit. No one would dress up for the grungy Rover. If Sebastian left work and traveled directly to the bar without changing, she could reasonably induce he clocked out at four.

Why didn't I ever consider becoming a detective?

Emily checked her stove clock. It was 2:10 p.m. She still had time to catch Sebastian at work, assuming his schedule was consistent, he worked Fridays, and he hadn't installed snipers on the rooftops to take her out should she come within fifty feet of him.

So many ifs.

Emily went to her bedroom to choose the perfect outfit. Broad daylight seduction attire required sexy yet subtle;

waltzing around a shopping center at three in the afternoon in a plunging neckline and four-inch heels was conspicuous. The second-to-last thing a stalker wanted to appear was *conspicuous*.

The first, was full-blown crazy.

56

After trying four outfits, she found a coral summer tank with a touch of glitz along the neckline. The tank enabled her to display flesh yet appear casual.

Perfect.

She paired the tank with a linen skirt and inspected the outfit in her full-length mirror.

Nipples. All she saw were nipples.

She couldn't wear a proper bra with a tank. She knew people walked around with bra straps peeking from beneath their tanks all the time, but she also knew her mother would appear on a flying carpet woven from a shredded copy of *Miss Manners* if she wore bra straps in plain view.

Her mother was five inches shorter than she was but very much like Tessa in that small-but-terrifying way.

From a sex appeal perspective, the tank was perfect, but if she walked into Über Home without proper nipple padding, all Sebastian would see was the perfect place to hang his jacket.

Emily walked to her office to fetch a roll of tape. She removed the tank and attempted to tape down her offending nubs. They refused to be contained. Cellophane tape was no match for nipples determined to stand at attention.

Emily moved to the hall closet. After digging, she found a roll of medical tape in a first aid kit so old the bloodletting leeches were dead.

She cut a chunk of white tape and slapped it over her springy nugget.

Close.

She cut a second piece and crisscrossed the first to double down.

Success!

Slipping back into her shelf bra tank, Emily reviewed her progress in the mirror. No nipple in sight. She looked like a normal girl.

After makeup and hair, the time was three-fifteen. Time to go.

Emily put one foot into her car and stopped, struck by a memory from her college public speaking class. She made an about-face and headed back to the house.

She beelined for her liquor cabinet, poured a vodka shot, and tossed it back. Vodka helped when speaking in front of strangers in college; hopefully, propositioning men at strip malls fell under the same category.

Sebastian's shopping center was five minutes from Emily's house. She found a parking spot and sat in her car for five minutes, wishing she'd brought the *bottle* of vodka. And a Valium. And a better body with bigger boobs and smaller nipples. Thicker hair. Blue eyes. A fuller mouth—

"Screw it."

She burst from the car as if escaping a carjacking. The vodka had kicked in. She felt calmer. She strode towards Sebastian's store, bubbling with confidence.

She made it three feet from the Über Home door before her stomach dropped to the pavement and her mouth went dry.

Deep breaths. He's just a guy.

Emily stared at the door. Her face felt cold. The sun's reflection upon the all-glass storefront prevented her from seeing inside.

Maybe Sebastian isn't even there. Maybe I should go—

A woman exited the store and politely held the door open for Emily. She glared at the woman. *Where did she get off being so helpful? Where's the rude woman from the coffee shop when I need her?*

She wasn't ready. She stood, frozen, the air conditioning from the store wafting over her. The woman cocked her head, making it clear she wouldn't hold the door all day.

Fine.

Emily offered the woman the best smile she could muster, with all the muscles in her face petrified by fear.

She stepped inside.

The store was freezing.

Terrified the cold would cause her nipples to rip free from

their chains, she covered her chest with her elbows under the guise of scratching both temples. Aware the awkward maneuver made her look like a comic book telepath attempting to read someone's mind, she crossed her arms against her chest.
58

There he is.

Sebastian stood behind the payment counter, looking down at something. His tall, square frame made Emily swallow, but she had no saliva to aid the gesture. What little saliva she possessed shot down the wrong pipe, and she began to cough.

Gag, really.

This wasn't a polite, Jane Eyre, sort of cough—more the hacking, desperate-for-breath bark of a tuberculosis victim in the last throes of a long battle to survive.

Sebastian looked up from his desk. Emily saw his face twitch with recognition. At least, she thought it was recognition; it might have been disgust. He may have needed to sneeze. It could have been anything. It was hard for her to tell because she was hacking up a lung. She stifled her gagging, which turned her barks into sputtery lip explosions. She sounded like a racehorse with croup.

Emily steadied herself on a sofa back and turned away from Sebastian, hoping she could stay conscious long enough to crawl out of the store and back to the safety of her car. She had a brief image of herself lying on the store floor, surrounded by paramedics...

She reaches out a dainty hand to touch Sebastian's cheek—

"I'll always love you," she whispers.

"We never had our time," sobs Sebastian, kneeling at her side and shaking his fists at the heavens. "Why? Whyyyyyyyyy?"

She turns her head to the side so as not to see his pain and lets the darkness take her.

"I'm so cold. I'm so—"

"Are you okay?"

Emily refused to look at Sebastian and sat on the sofa she'd used to steady herself. She cleared her throat. If she concentrated, she could keep from coughing. She could be silent—now, she just had to figure out how to be invisible.

Don't notice me. I'm not here.

His face hovered near hears. "Emily? Is that right? Are you okay?"

She nodded.

"Oh, I know. Hold on."

Sebastian jogged to his desk and returned to offer a handful of tissues. She nodded to acknowledge his kindness and then waved him away. He stood straight and took a step back. Emily cleared her throat again, blew her nose, and then inhaled like a canary testing mineshaft air. The tickle in her throat disappeared.

She looked up at Sebastian and offered him her most winning post-near-death-experience smile.

"Hey, thank you so much."

"Got it now?" he asked.

"I am *so* sorry," she croaked, pointing to her throat. "Wrong pipe."

"Oh, I hate that. Don't worry about it. Was I right with the name? Emily? Irish Rover girl with the house?"

"That's me." She offered a hand to shake and then thought better of it. Her hands were full of used tissues.

"I came from my house, in fact," she added.

He scoffed. "Show off."

She laughed. It felt like her head was vibrating. She had to hurry and complete her mission before her skull spun, *Exorcist*-style.

"What's up? Can I interest you in a lovely divan?" he made an exaggerated sweeping gesture with his hand.

Emily glanced around the store.

Should I buy a sofa?

No. She needed this to be over.

"I, uh, I was wondering if, I dunno, maybe sometime you'd be interested in going to lunch?" she asked, trying to hold Sebastian's gaze as long as her quivering head would allow. Her cheek twitched.

He is definitely going to ask if I need an ambulance.

She stood there for what felt like three or four days, waiting for Sebastian to answer. He blinked and pulled his head back in surprise, or shock, or horror. She wasn't getting any better at deciphering his expressions now that she wasn't suffocating to death.

He frowned. "Oh, I—I can't."

"—or coffee, or a drink. It doesn't have to be a whole lunch or anything," she heard herself say.

He bit at his lip. "No, it's not that. I—"

"That's cool, okay, just a thought," she said, cutting him short and shrugging to imply she hadn't even meant to ask him out.

Did I ask you out? This damn Tourette's. I'm so sorry.

"I have a girlfriend," he said.

He said *girlfriend* in the same tone a person might mention herpes, like, "I'm sorry, but I'm afraid you have *girlfriend*."

Emily realized she'd ceased breathing and took a sharp, shaky breath. Smiling, hands flailing, she said: *Nobiggie sorryseeyouatdartsokwellIguessI'llletyougetbacktoworkbye!*

Sebastian stared at her, speechless.

Emily darted around him to scurry out of the store, her face as red as the throw pillows on the $999 pullout couch behind her.

As she reached the door, she heard a voice.

"Don't forget me!"

She froze, her fingers resting on the handle of the exit.

She turned.

Sebastian seemed as surprised as she did, his hand raised, half covering his mouth as if she'd caught him in mid-sneeze.

"Okay," she said and bolted from the store.

She sat in her car until the sweat beaded on her forehead. She started the ignition and turned up the air.

Don't forget me?

Emily shifted her car into reverse.

What the hell am I supposed to do with that?

CHAPTER ELEVEN

Sebastian opened the door to his apartment and walked inside. Binker raised his head from the sofa and growled.

"Don't start with me," said Sebastian, throwing his keys on the kitchen table.

The dog's head flopped back to the cushion.

Sebastian changed from work clothes to sweat shorts and a tee. He felt tired and vaguely sad. His mind kept wandering to the girl in his store.

Emily.

He couldn't believe she'd come to his work to ask him out. Part of him wondered if she was a little nuts. How did she know where he worked? Had he mentioned it at the bar? He couldn't remember.

She was cute, really cute, and something about her had put him at ease, like he'd known her for years. As strange as the experience had been, a smile crept to his lips as he recalled how shaky she'd made her pitch. To think he could make someone that nervous surprised him.

It was flattering.

Sebastian's gaze drifted to Greta's side of the bed, and the collection of frames arranged there—photo after photo of Greta and her friends, smiling, posing, frozen in time at one party or the next. He'd never really noticed them before. He stared at Greta's grinning face. She was stunning, but he felt dread when he looked at her now.

Dread of their inevitable breakup.

Dread they would never break up.

He wanted their relationship to be a distant memory, but he couldn't stand living through the drama of a breakup.

As one thing or the other delayed his plans to leave, he'd

never considered he was missing a chance to date other people. He was so unhappy in his current relationship that starting another seemed like a hassle, a lesson in futility ending with him in the same position he was in now. Maybe that was

62

another reason he never found the courage to leave.

Sebastian didn't know anything about Emily. He might never see her again. But he'd *hated* telling her he couldn't go out for a drink when, in his heart, he'd left Greta months earlier. He was, at best, romantically lazy; possibly depressed. Something about that girl in his store made him smile; gave him a tiny hope for happiness.

Someone appeared to kick his miserable butt into gear, and he'd turned her away.

Sebastian heard a thud that shook him from his thoughts. He wandered back into the living room to search for the source.

Another dull thump. Sebastian walked to the front door and opened it.

"Oh, you're home," said Greta, nearly falling into the apartment. She'd been trying to balance a box of wine against the door while she fished for her keys.

"Here." She handed him the box.

Sebastian took the box and moved it to the kitchen counter.

"You're home early. What's this?"

"Free wine. I have a bottle from each supplier vying for the beverage contract at the stadium. My homework is to taste-test them all."

Sebastian opened the box and peered inside. "They're all open."

"I might have started already," said Greta, smirking.

"If you drank them at work, why did you bring them home?"

"I tried them with a girl *from* work. Not *at* work." Greta threw her arms around Sebastian's neck. "Now I get to try them again with you."

She offered him a kiss, but he pulled away. Whenever Greta threw herself at him, she was up to no good, and he wasn't feeling playful.

"I thought you seemed in an unusually good mood," he mumbled.

"I am," she said, heading back into the living room.

"You still like your new job?"

"Oh, I love it."

"Good. And your sister? How is she handling the pregnancy?"

"The preg—?" Greta turned, her face twisted with confusion. As she met eyes with Sebastian, her features melted into a perfectly unreadable mask.

"Oh, I forgot to tell you. She isn't pregnant anymore. Lucky, I guess. I mean, a shame in one way, but lucky in her case. False alarm."

"Oh. Work is good, sis is good...how are your parents?"

"Good," said Greta, flopping beside Binker on the sofa. "What's with all the questions, Sebby? Go pour us our first taste test."

"So, you're in a good mood, and nothing is wrong with the world today?" Sebastian asked, moving to the cabinet where they kept their wine glasses.

"Yep. All is great with the world."

Sebastian grabbed two glasses and pulled the first bottle from the case. He poured an inch of wine into each glass and carried them to Greta.

Greta took the glass and held it up. "What should we toast to?"

Sebastian held his glass near hers.

"To the end of our relationship." Sebastian stifled a laugh, suddenly feeling giddy. He didn't mean to be cruel, but he'd surprised himself by saying his thoughts aloud.

Greta rolled her eyes. "Very funny."

Sebastian stared at her, questioning his courage to forge ahead.

No sense stopping now.

"I'm not kidding. Let's toast to our future—our *independent* futures."

Greta's goofy wine smile collapsed.

"What?"

He shook his head. "Don't pretend you're shocked. You know it. We've been done. You've moved on, and I've tried to end this three times."

Sebastian considered voicing his suspicion that she was seeing someone else but decided against it. Greta fighting a break-up was one thing; Greta insisting she wasn't cheating was a whole other mess. He'd be on the defensive with no proof. That diversion alone would shove the breakup itself to the back burner.

If she was cheating, it didn't matter. He wasn't jealous—he

64

didn't care enough to be jealous. That, if nothing else, was a massive clue the relationship was doomed.

"What are you talking about, *three times?*" asked Greta.

"Every time you hear it coming, you throw out some new tragedy to stop me. This time, no tragedy. I double-checked."

Greta's eyes welled with tears. "But Sebby, I *love* you. You can't."

"Stop it. *Please.* You only *love me* when I'm trying to leave, or you're not getting your way."

Her eyes screwed shut—lips pursed so hard they turned white. She looked like a two-year-old throwing a tantrum.

"You're still here. You could have moved out by now. You *want* to stay with me."

He shook his head. "I just hate change. But you're right. It's my fault. I should have left a long time ago. Come on. We've only been dating like four months—"

"Six."

"—and it's not like it was ever a wild love affair. We just fell together."

She scowled. "Then why did you move in?"

Sebastian looked away.

That's a good question.

He sighed. "You offered, and it seemed like a good solution, and I liked you—"

"*Liked?* Past tense?"

"You know what I mean. Look, I feel like we're getting off the point. *The point* is we're done—"

"No! We're *not* broken up. You're just in a bad mood."

She pounded her fist into his thigh, and he jerked his leg away. "Ow! Cut it out. I'm not in a bad mood."

"You pulled away from me when I tried to kiss you. You're in a bad mood."

"*No*, I didn't feel like kissing you. I know you can't imagine a world where someone doesn't want to kiss you, but it happens."

She rolled her eyes. "Pfft. We just had sex, like, yesterday."

"That was a mistake," mumbled Sebastian, embarrassed he hadn't been stronger.

"What's that supposed to mean?"

He huffed. "What do you get out of trying to make me stay? You don't want me here. Not really. You just don't want to be alone."

Greta scowled, but he pushed on.

"Look, I'm going to start looking for a place tomorrow."

"You don't have one already?"

"No. I'll go to my brother's for now."

"All the way there? You don't have to go—you can stay here tonight." Greta's glare softened. Her arm moved. Sebastian winced, but she placed her hand gently on his knee this time.

He froze like a hunted rabbit.

Her fingers ran along his inner thigh.

"Greta…"

"Stay until you find a place," said Greta, her voice low, her eyes brimming with tears. "We'll just be friends. I promise."

Sebastian swallowed. He thought about the long drive back and forth from work to his brother's house. He was happy he'd found the perfect time to break up with Greta but wished he'd found an apartment to escape to post-breakup.

"*Please*," she pleaded.

He sighed. "Fine. I'll stay until I find a new place. But we're *roommates* now."

Greta squealed and hugged him, sloshing his wine on the sofa. He held his hands over his head, protecting his drink and waiting for the celebration to end. She pulled away and stared into his eyes, a sweet smile on her lips. Sebastian stared back at her.

They remained that way for too long.

"You're freaking me out," he said.

Greta laughed. She stood and headed for the bedroom.

"I'm going to change. I'm so glad you're staying, no matter what we are."

As the sound of the closing bedroom door faded, Greta's last words registered with Sebastian.

"We're *friends!*" he called after her. "*Roommates!*"

His eyes closed, and he shifted and allowed his head to flop against the sofa's backrest. He felt Binker waddle across the cushions and collapse onto his legs.

"Not you, too." He lifted a hand and petted the dog, who snuggled deeper into his lap.

A few minutes later, Sebastian heard the bedroom door open.

"What do you want for dinner? Do you still want to try the
66

white wine? Should we have chicken?"

Sebastian followed Greta's voice as it moved behind him and turned to see her walk into the kitchen. She wore an oversized t-shirt that barely covered her rear end.

"Seriously, Greta?" he asked.

"What?"

"Just a tee shirt?"

She huffed. "Oh, now we're broken up *and* I'm supposed to be uncomfortable in my own home?"

Sebastian rubbed his face with his hand.

He *really* had to find an apartment.

CHAPTER TWELVE

Emily lay in bed, staring at the ceiling.

She'd asked out Sebastian hoping to jumpstart a romance or nip one in the bud.

Instead, Sebastian managed to turn her down *and* give her hope.

Don't forget me.

Who says that?

Sebastian had a girlfriend. He was unavailable. End of story, no matter what nonsense he called to her as she left Über Home. He wasn't available.

Done.

Right?

Now she could get out of bed.

She remained in bed for another hour.

Maybe there were other possibilities. She ran through the facts, each time arriving at the same conclusion: Sebastian wasn't available.

She released a long, exaggerated sigh, dramatically pantomiming her frustrations for an invisible audience.

Screw it. Moving on.

She threw herself out of bed and padded to the shower to prepare for a rare morning client meeting.

I am a strong, single woman! I don't need Sebastian and his confusing messages.

She passed her full-length mirror.

I will embrace the day!

She caught a flash of white in the mirror.

I will—Wait, what the hell is that?

Emily stopped and took a step back. She stared at her naked

body in the mirror.

There were white Xs in the center of each breast.

Her boobs looked like the eyes of a dead cartoon character.

Nipple tape.

She'd undressed in the dark and slipped into bed. She'd forgotten about the tape. Thank god there hadn't been a fire, and she'd gone running naked into the yard; her elderly neighbors would think she had a bondage dungeon in her basement.

Emily stepped closer to the mirror and picked at the tape's ends. She never imagined it would be so sticky. She could have hung a television on her wall with it.

She peeled the tape a millimeter at a time, removing several layers of flesh regardless of how fast or slow she progressed.

"Ow ow ow ow—" she chanted through gritted teeth.

An eternity later, tape removed, she gaped at the strips of raw, red flesh remaining, perfectly X-shaped, across her nipples.

How lucky Sebastian hadn't swept her into his arms and carried her off to the mattress section. How could she have explained the tape?

It would have been the shortest relationship on record.

Trying to find joy in a bullet dodged, she tossed the tape into the trash and stepped into the shower. She usually worked at home, but a local truck parts company had begged her to help design their website and insisted she work from their office. Summers were slow, so she accepted, even though getting dressed in the morning felt like a nightmare.

There was no reason for Emily to work at a client's office, but the customer waxed poetic about the good old days "when people met eye to eye" until she'd raised the white flag and agreed.

She should have never gone to his office. That had been the first warning sign. Client meetings were best by phone. There was no reason to get fancied up and drive half an hour to have a ten-minute conversation. A phone call—or even better, an email—saved the client time, too. They didn't need to act out their ideas with hand puppets.

Unfortunately, she needed the cash, so soon she was looking for parking dressed in a sensible skirt.

The lobby area of Emily's new temporary workspace came straight from the Office Lobby Handbook. Chairs for visitors, business magazines no one ever read scattered on a table, a vaguely motivational poster of a wave crashing against the shore meant to imply the company's determination; and a cheap tabletop fountain filled with rounded pebbles, tinkling a steady rhythm.

The fountain kept visitors calm in the event they realized they were wasting their lives at meetings.

The fountain didn't work for Emily. She'd worked from home for too long. The low sputter-hum of the water-pumping motor made her want to pelt the receptionist with the rounded pebbles.

She considered bolting for her car, but before she could move, a young man around her age entered the reception area. Her eyes swept his body from head to toe and back again. She settled back into her seat and decided to stay.

Hello there, sailor.

The man boasted a perfectly tussled crop of black hair, enough five o'clock shadow to highlight a razor-sharp jawline, and green eyes. Emily looked for a hidden camera. The magnificent creature standing before her had to be a joke. They'd hired a model to make a fool of her.

Finding no camera, she refocused on the guy, now stretching a hand in her direction to shake.

Momma likey.

Emily preferred taller and slighter builds on her beau hunks; this guy was muscular and under six feet tall. Her friend Kady loved "football bodies." Emily preferred "soccer bodies." Still, there was no denying the raw, masculine sex appeal of this fellow.

"Hi, are you Annie?" he asked as she stood to shake. He throttled her hand as if trying to choke the life out of an attacking boa constrictor.

"Emily," she corrected, stifling a whimper.

"Oh, sorry, *Emily*, got it," he said, blushing.

He actually blushed. In two seconds, he'd shown her both strength and tenderness. He might as well have been a shirtless firefighter carrying a litter of kittens from a burning building.

70

"I'm Marc. I'll be overseeing the computer stuff that you do."

The computer stuff that I do? Okay. She smiled and nodded. *Close enough, hot stuff.*

"I'll take you to see Dad," he said, turning and motioning her to follow. He pounded down the hallway as if he'd much rather be running through a jungle, knocking over small trees.

Wait. Did he say Dad?

Emily winced.

Marc was the boss's son.

Well, if she was going to sabotage this gig, she'd identified the most enjoyable way to do it.

Marc led Emily into his father's office. With his perfect salt and pepper hair, emerald eyes, and equally sharp jawline, there was no mistaking the person behind the desk as anyone but Marc's pop. He looked like a man who hadn't heard the word *no* since birth.

"I'm Emily," she said, reaching across the desk to shake his hand.

"Roger." The man gave her hand a quick jerk. He didn't stand. "You're the little lady taking us into the twenty-second century, huh?"

Roger chuckled and looked at his son. Marc grinned, but his eyes darted to Emily's. He seemed embarrassed.

Score one for Marc for noticing that calling people *little lady* wasn't cool.

Emily offered a tight-lipped smile. "I guess I am," she said, sitting in the barely padded chair in front of Roger's desk.

Roger motioned to his son. "Marc here will be in charge. You have that list of what we want on the website?"

"Hm? Oh, yeah," said Marc. He reached into his pocket and pulled out a folded piece of yellow legal paper. He opened it and sat beside Emily.

"So..." he said, scanning the page. "We want a home page..."

Emily tried not to groan.

Oh boy. This is going to take a while.

"Well, sure," she said, launching into her timesaving speech. "Of course, we'll have all the usual things like home, contact page, about you—"

"We don't need anything about me," said Marc, cutting her short.

"No," agreed Roger. "We don't need anything about Marc. He's just overseeing the web project."

Emily shook her head. "No—by *about you* I meant about the *company*. Sorry. I meant a page where people can read how long you've been in business, awards—things like that. A company bio."

"Oh. That's a good idea," said Marc.

Roger nodded. "Good idea."

Emily pretended to write something down. Marc and his father hadn't touched on anything unusual yet, but it made people feel appreciated when she wrote things down.

Often she wrote, *Things like that.*

"We want all the social media," said Roger, falling back on the only buzzwords he knew. "And Photoshop."

"Um, Photoshop is more of a *program* to make graphics—"

"I have a blog," said Marc.

Emily looked at him. "For the business?"

"No, for me. I post my photography on there and shots of my band."

"Your band?"

Roger nodded. "He's good with a camera. We'll want a link to his Instramamagram."

Emily grimaced to keep from laughing aloud.

"You don't want links to personal sites on your business website. Every outgoing link you have that takes clients away from your site—"

"I have a Tiktok account," said Marc, in the same rapid cadence a child says, "*we went to the zoo today and I saw a bear!*"

She eyed him. Was Marc having a conversation with an invisible person? Was this person asking him to name social media sites and rewarding him with a lollipop for each one?

It was official. She'd lost control of the meeting.

"I, uh, pictures are great. In-house photographers are a bonus."

She glanced in Marc's direction but he offered no help against his father's old-fashioned requests. She couldn't have been more on her own if the two had pushed her from a plane over the Amazon with a week's rations and a Boy Scout survival kit.

"Tell you what," snapped Roger a little too loudly. "Why

72

don't you two go to Marc's office and work out what we need? I don't need to be involved."

Marc nodded and stood. He smiled at Emily, oblivious to the tension in the room. He was like an adorable puppy. Though, she was sure even Duppy knew you didn't put a link to your personal "Instramamagram" account on your business page.

She took a deep breath.

"Sounds good," she said, standing. "Nice to meet you, Roger," she added. She lifted her hand for a parting handshake and then snatched it away when Roger offered a curt nod and lifted his phone to make a call.

He did not intend to shake her hand a second time.

Busy guy. He probably had to check his AOL stock.

Emily followed Marc to his office, where she outlined what she'd do to ensure they had the best truck parts site possible.

"Cool," said Marc when she was done.

She held his gaze and nodded slowly, waiting for the other shoe to drop.

Marc proved shoeless.

He had no comments and no thoughts to add. He bounced in his chair, bobbing his head.

She huffed a sigh. "Okay then. I guess I should get to work?"

"Sure. I'll show you your office."

Marc took her to a small office next door to his. The room was empty, but for a desk, computer, and a calendar featuring a girl in short shorts rubbing her tush against a semi-truck.

Nice.

She smiled. "What else could I need?"

He stared at her and she realized he thought she'd been quizzing him.

"No, I mean, I've got everything I need. Thanks."

"Oh, cool." Marc spun and disappeared down the hallway. A moment later, he returned to thrust a pile of white papers at her.

"Here are all the parts we need to put on the site."

"Great," Emily said, wondering if her tiny office window was high enough off the ground to throw herself out of it.

Marc turned to leave and then paused.

"You know, I don't want to make you feel scared, so don't take this the wrong way..."

Scared? Emily braced herself. *What, is he a werewolf or something?*

"Do you want to get a drink after work?"

Her mind went blank; her jaw hanging slack. She closed her mouth and heard the click of her teeth echo in the awkward silence of the room.

"I mean with me," added Marc.

"No, no, I got that."

"You can *totally* say no. This isn't, like, office *assault* or something."

"Harassment."

"No, I'm saying it *isn't* harassment." Marc waved his open palms at Emily as if warding her off.

"No, you should call it *harassment*, not office *assault*," she explained. She laughed. She couldn't help herself. She'd entered the *Twilight Zone.*

Marc laughed with her, his white teeth flashing, his perfect pecs bouncing in his tight t-shirt.

"Sure, I'll get a drink," Emily blurted.

She didn't mean to say it, but she had a new soft spot for people with the courage to proposition strangers—especially when they looked like the cover of a steamy romance novel.

"I'm still not linking the business site to your Instagram account," she added, accompanied by a corny wink she immediately regretted.

"No, that's cool." He flexed one pectoral muscle and then the other. Emily watched them dance in his shirt.

Did he even know he just did that?

Grinning, he left her office.

Emily slapped the giant list of truck parts to her desk and flopped into her chair. She thought of Sebastian and suffered a wave of guilt. He'd told her not to forget him, and the very next day she'd accepted a date with a gorgeous truck part prince.

She scowled.

"Don't be an ass," she said aloud to herself.

I can't let myself pine after an unattainable man, even if it seemed like fate that we—

"Oh, hey," said a voice, breaking Emily's train of thought.

Emily spotted Marc's head peeking from the side of her doorway.

74

"Yes?"

"I meant to apologize for my dad and that 'little lady who's taking us to the twenty-second century bit."

Emily laughed. "Thanks. I noticed that you noticed."

Marc nodded. "I know, right?" he said, rolling his eyes. "The twenty-second century is like a thousand years away, Dad, *duh*."

Emily's smile lingered a second longer before vanishing.

"Wait, *what?*" she asked, but Marc was gone.

CHAPTER THIRTEEN

A few days after Emily's first day as a trucking company employee, Kady stopped by Emily's after work to sit on her back patio drinking wine. Emily stared at her glass and considered the possibility she'd become predictable. Maybe she'd pour a bourbon next round.

Kady took a sip from her glass. "Let me get this straight. You went to Sebastian's work and asked him out?"

Emily nodded.

"And he said no because he has a girlfriend, but then told you 'don't forget me?'"

She nodded again.

"And then the next day, a gorgeous trucking hunk asked you out for a drink?"

Emily grinned. "When you put it that way, it sounds pretty cool."

"When I put it that way, you sound *badass*! How'd the drink with the hunk go?"

"Good," she said, shrugging. "He isn't anyone I'd want to date in the long term, but it was nice. He's super sweet. He's like a puppy. A sexy, sexy puppy."

"Why no long-term?" asked Kady.

Emily sighed. "He told me that thanks to lifting heavy truck parts at his father's warehouse all day, he is *totally fatigued*."

Kady tilted her head to the right. "You don't want to date him because he's tired?"

"No. He thinks *fatigued* is another way to say he has a good physique, like, 'Dude, I've been lifting all day. I am *totally fatigued*.'"

Kady snorted a laugh. "Oh no. That's not good. So, he's not

the brightest bulb on the tree?"

"No."

They pondered in silence for a minute.

Emily shrugged. "Like I said, he's super sweet, and I'd like to

76

eat Cheetos off his abs, but I don't see us in a long-term relationship."

Kady sat up. "You saw his abs? Tell me more."

"The whole bar saw his abs. It's how he describes *fatigued*." Emily laughed and put down her glass so she could pantomime the part. "I said, 'You're fatigued?' and he said, 'Yep! Check it out!' BOOM! *Shirt lift.*"

Katy covered her mouth to keep from spitting out her wine. "That. Is. *Awesome.*"

Emily giggled. "It kinda was."

"So did you...?" Kady asked, raising her eyebrows until they almost flipped to the back of her head.

"No. It was our first drink together, and I work for his dad. I dunno if sleeping with the boss's son is smart."

"Since when have you done anything smart?"

"Good point."

"It's been a while, though, hasn't it?"

Emily sighed. "Let's just say I hope it's like riding a bike."

"It pretty much is. Except the bike wears out before you get where you're going most of the time."

Emily chuckled. "But you're like, 'Oh no bike, I'm finished, that's okay, no worries...'"

"And the bike is like, 'I thought so. I *rock.*'"

The two women collapsed into giggles.

"What are you going to do about Sebastian?" asked Kady when she regained her composure.

"Nothing, I guess. He's got a girlfriend, and until he doesn't, what can I do?"

"You could kill her."

"I know, but that's so messy."

"True."

"What about you? Anything new and exciting?"

Kady looked away and twisted a piece of her long curly hair around her finger.

"No..."

"What? Something's up."

Kady took a deep breath.

"I don't know. It's Joe. He's being really weird."

"How can you tell? He's a non-smoker who taught himself how to roll cigarettes."

"That's just it. Suddenly he's learning all sorts of things he didn't care about five minutes ago. Just like—"

"Just like when he met you and wanted to know about everything *you* were interested in," Emily said, finishing her sentence.

"Exactly."

"Like what?"

Katy frowned. "All of a sudden, he's really into baseball. He *hated* baseball. Now he's going to games once a week with this guy, Max, from his office. And he's bringing home different bottles of wine every night, mostly white. And they aren't for me. *He* drinks them."

"Well, it's summer. That's the only time I drink white."

"But he hasn't had wine in years. Suddenly he's trying to learn what *oaky* tastes like. Yesterday he asked me to taste his glass and tell him if I thought it had a peppery finish. When I said *yes*, he did a fist pump like he'd won the lottery."

"Did you ask him what's up with all the wine?"

"Yes, sort of. He said he'd been stuck on beer too long, and it was time to expand his palate."

Emily shrugged. "That's why I started eating humans. You know, you can only eat chicken and fish and beef for so long."

Kady nodded. "True. Maybe you could eat Sebastian's girlfriend."

"New boyfriend *and* lunch, two birds with one stone," she said, grabbing the empty wine bottle and heading inside to grab a new one. "Brilliant!"

The next day at work, Emily was adding truck parts to the website's database when Marc bopped into her office.

"Whatcha doin'?" he asked.

Emily stopped typing and swiveled her chair to face him. He

leaned against her doorway, sweaty, mopping his face with his shirt, which he had removed and balled into a makeshift handkerchief. She watched his muscles rippling across his ribs, beautiful as a pianist's elegant fingers caressing the keys of a 78

perfectly tuned instrument.

Kady was right. It had been too long since she'd had sex. Comparing men to finely crafted musical instruments had to be an early sign of withdrawal.

"What am I doing?" Emily echoed, trying to focus on anything other than Marc's torso. "Same thing I'll be doing until my fingers fall off. I never dreamed trucks had so many parts."

"Got any big plans tonight?"

Emily shrugged. "I have to mow my lawn."

Outside, it was ninety-four degrees with eighty-five percent humidity. She was not eager to mow, but if she didn't soon, her neighbors would revolt.

"Ooh, I'll do it," whooped Marc, raising his hand over his head.

Emily jumped in her chair, startled by his sudden outburst.

"Mow my lawn? It's like a thousand degrees outside."

"You got beer?"

Emily thought for a moment. She wasn't much of a beer drinker, but she usually kept some on hand for her dad and brother should they stop by.

"Some, I think. Maybe like six?"

Marc grimaced. "Mm. Well, I can pick some up."

"You can have it all. I'm not a beer drinker."

"No, I know."

Oh. Got it. Six isn't enough.

"Write down your address, and I'll meet you there in an hour."

Emily jotted down her address.

"You're seriously going to mow my lawn?" She held out the slip of paper, and he bounded over to retrieve it.

"Yeah, I was going to work out, but I'll do this instead. You have a universal machine?"

"A what?"

"Free weights? You have free weights, maybe?"

"I have ankle weights and little pink barbells that came with an aerobics video I bought ten years ago."

Marc stared into middle distance, deep in thought.

"Ankle weights," he mumbled. He spun and sprinted out of her office, screaming, *"See ya soon!"*

Emily turned back to her monitor and rubbed her eyes.

If men expected sex after buying a girl a drink, what the hell did they expect after mowing a lawn?

Emily's imagination drifted back to the vision of Marc's glistening torso in the doorway. She was going to end up in a special hell where girls who abandoned their principles for a side of beefcake spent their days roasting in hellfire, just out of reach of a cool vodka and lemonade.

Mmm.

Vodka and lemonade.

An hour and a half later, Emily sat on her front porch, drinking an ice-cold vodka and lemonade, wearing her oversized shades, and lazily watching as Marc strolled back and forth behind her lawn mower. He'd wave like an excited schoolboy every few minutes, and she'd wave back. By the end, she'd started to wave in different styles, once slowly, with her fingers closed, like a pageant girl, next in the strange air-cupping motion of the Queen of England. Marc didn't seem to notice. He grinned and pushed—sweat beading on his tanned forehead and gliding across his angular jaw.

Ugh. Why do the dumb ones have to be so damn handsome sometimes?

She felt like Mrs. Robinson, except Marc was her age. Physically, anyway. He *had* to know they had nothing in common. Of course, he was probably only after one thing, which she was starting to think might work fine for her as well.

"Looks good?" said Marc, mowing up to her lounge chair and cutting the engine almost in time. She brushed away the bits of grass settling across her bare feet.

"Looks great. Ready for that beer?"

"Hell, yeah. That'd be awesome."

He pushed the mower back toward the shed as she left.

"Bring like four," he called over his muscular back.

She nodded. Inside, she grabbed four of the beers Marc had brought with him. Having no cooler, she put some ice into a

80

bowl and artfully arranged the beers on top of it.

Eat your heart out, Martha Stewart.

She found Lawnboy on the back porch, sitting in a patio chair, shirtless and glistening. She put the ice bowl on the short glass table between them and took her seat.

"Cool," said Marc, cracking open a can and finishing it in one long gulp. He crushed it in his hands and glanced at her for approval.

Should I clap?

She offered him an appreciative smile, and he grinned back, mission accomplished. She suspected he had some Neanderthal checklist built into his brain:

Show woman me perform manly duties.

Check!

Show woman how strong me is.

Check!

"Well, I appreciate the lawn," she said to jumpstart the conversation.

He shrugged. "No biggie. I like working outside. I was thinking of starting a landscaping business, but you know, Dad was all like, 'You're going to come work for me, Son' so..."

"I guess most would consider you lucky to inherit a business, but people don't realize what a burden it can be, too."

Marc popped and finished his second beer. This can he sat beside the bowl, having already proven he could crush it should it attack.

"People expect a lot from me," he said.

Marc rarely spent time in the office. From what Emily could gather, his father relegated him to monkey work around the warehouse. She wasn't sure how much his father *expected* from him, but she'd only been at the company for a week. She didn't know their family history or his full resumé.

He opened a third beer and drank half. As he tilted back his head to finish, Emily studied the sinews of his neck and the sweat pooling in the "V" notch of his throat. His collarbones gracefully stretched from either side of that limpid sweat lake, traveling to the tips of his broad shoulders like a mountain pass.

"Could I make you dinner?" she asked before the thought gelled in her brain. She wasn't sure why.

He looked hungry? A maternal instinct to feed him?

He chose to crush the third can. The suggestion of food stirred something primal in him.

He held her gaze with his green eyes and realized what was happening.

Oh shit. I am totally going to sleep with this guy.

Emily swallowed. "I, uh...I have some crab. I could make crab cakes? Or, we could do steaks on the grill—?"

"Would you mind if I got a shower?"

"No, of course not. I can get you a towel."

Emily stood, and he mirrored her. She considered a joke about not having dry clothes that would fit him, but he cut her short by leaning forward, putting his knuckle under her chin, and guiding her lips to his. Emily felt sure she'd seen John Wayne use that same move in some old Western.

Emily felt lightheaded and took a deep breath.

He smelled like a wildebeest.

She had never been so attracted to a wildebeest.

"I have some clothes in my truck," he said.

He walked around the house to get his clothes. Still in shock, Emily stumbled toward the house to find a towel for his shower.

When he entered the house with his spare jeans, Emily met him in the kitchen. She introduced him to Duppy, and then led him to the guest shower. He paused at the threshold of the bathroom. Emily sensed he was about to ask her to join him, so she spat, "I'll get the crab cakes made," and jogged back down the hall. Her voice crackled with nerves; she sounded like a teenage boy hitting puberty.

Twenty minutes later, she was wrapped around him like a baby koala.

Oh my God...

She wrapped her legs around his waist. He continued to kiss her neck as he carried her toward the bedroom.

She felt almost dizzy.

Is this happening? Is this—

Nope.

Suddenly, a blood-curdling yelp echoed against the walls. Emily heard the scrabbling of claws on the rug.

She knew that sound. She heard it at least once a week.

82

Duppy.

Her dog had been snoozing in the hallway when Marc came wheeling around the corner with a woman clinging to his chest. There was no way he could see Duppy below him.

After releasing a panicked cry, Dup scampered to safety, but the forward momentum of Marc and Emily's entanglement no longer held in Marc's favor. They moved much faster. Marc fell forward, desperately trying to catch his balance and keep his feet without dumping Emily to the floor.

Before Emily could unwrap her legs, they reached the end of the hallway. Emily's head and back plowed into the drywall. There was a crunching sound and then nothing but panting— her own and Marc's. His body pressed hers to the wall like she was a mounted butterfly. She couldn't move, pinned as she was by his bulk.

He huffed. "Holy shit. That was close."

Emily released a little grunt. It was hard to breathe with his Marc's chest pressed against hers.

"*Close?*" she croaked.

"Are you okay?" He asked, his mouth muffled against her neck.

She unlocked her ankles, and Marc steadied her butt as she lowered her feet to the floor. Once standing, he released her, stepped back, and stretched his back.

She eyed the hole in her drywall.

"Did you just plow me into the wall?"

He scratched his head and offered a sheepish grin. "It was the dog. I couldn't see him—"

"Oh, I know. I almost step on him all the time. He's a menace."

She rubbed the back of her head and stepped back to inspect the wall. Part of it had buckled against one of the studs.

"That's no problem. I'm really good with drywall. I did my buddy's whole apartment."

Emily cracked her neck. "Great."

"And my ex-girlfriend's bedroom wall," he added.

Emily squinted at him.

"Seriously? You've done this before? Should I ask?"

He shrugged. "It's a pretty cool story."

"That's okay."

She sighed. The mood was broken, and she was glad. She glanced at Marc's jeans and found the bulge she'd felt a moment before had disappeared. Good to know plowing women into walls didn't excite him.

"Guess what part of us broke her wall," asked Marc, grinning.

Well, sometimes, it excited him.

"Guess," repeated Marc. "You'll never guess."

Emily walked down the hall toward the kitchen.

"How about those crab cakes?" she asked.

84

CHAPTER FOURTEEN

"You want to get some dinner?"

Emily swiveled her chair, intending to turn down Marc's invitation. The thought of touching that body excited her, but she wasn't sure she had it in her to *use* him, even if he approved. After their mishap in her hallway, she'd found the strength to end romantic entanglements for the day—surely, she could find that strength again. Plus, he was the boss's son; things couldn't end well.

A moment before, she'd been daydreaming about Sebastian. The curve of his smirk, the brilliant cobalt of his eyes, his lips, as they mouthed the words, *"I can't; I have a girlfriend..."* in slow motion.

Formulating a gentle letdown for Marc, she turned to find him standing in her doorway, shirtless, as usual. Shirtless was his uniform when working in the un-air-conditioned warehouse, a fact that delighted *him* to no end. Other than a defiant two-year-old she once saw speed-strip in a store to protest his mother's reluctance to buy him a video game, she'd never met anyone so eager to rip off their shirt.

Emily allowed herself a quick ogle of Marc's physique. A fine sheen of sweat covered his taut body...and he held the most adorable Jack Russell puppy she'd ever seen in his arms.

What the...

"You've got to be kidding me," she muttered.

"Did you see the puppy?" he asked, walking the squirming ball of adorable to her. "George brought him in."

Emily involuntarily squealed with delight as Marc placed the puppy in her lap. Marc sat on his heel beside her and scratched the dog wherever he could sneak past her puppy-snuggle attack.

The mingling scents of puppy and raw man made Emily delirious. Someone needed to create a cologne—*Men with Puppies.* If they spritzed it at female shoppers in the mall they'd make a fortune.

"So, see you after work?" asked Marc.

"Yep," she said before she realized he wouldn't be bringing the puppy.

Dammit. How does he get me to agree to things before I know what I'm saying?

Marc pried the dog from her hands and toddled off.

Emily sighed. She hoped to find the strength to turn him down next time, but he'd probably show up with a basket of kittens or a baby hedgehog wearing a monocle and top hat. Then, all bets were off.

Emily and Marc left work to grab dinner. He was fun to hang out with. There was no chance he'd launch into a dissertation on the rise of the anti-hero in modern television or run through a list of U.S. Presidents by year of election, he was always in a great mood and listened when people talked. He was sweet and insanely hot.

Emily *wanted* to fall in love with him. She really did. There was just something missing.

In the middle of dinner, Marc's buddy called to invite him to a pay-per-view wrestling match. Marc asked her to come with him, but she declined and suggested he go without her—effectively removing the wrestling match between herself and her raging hormones from the evening's fight card.

Whew. I guess.

Driving home, Emily found herself thinking about the man she *really* wanted to share a puppy with. She'd had daydreams in which she and Sebastian bought a dog together.

Is that weird?

She couldn't ask Tessa.

Tessa would have her committed.

She didn't know why she was so obsessed with Sebastian; she'd barely talked to him, and other than the time he'd actively

86

turned her down, they'd never been alone. Her obsession with the boy reminded her of corny novels where the lead characters' eyes met, and they fell in love like victims of a witch's spell. It made no sense, but was kind of wonderful...if a tad bittersweet.

Heavy on the bitter.

Marc was nice and fun to ogle, but sometimes conversations with him were like trying to pull-start a bad motor. Marc's dad didn't have an engine part to fix that. The night they'd broken her wall, they'd ended up watching a movie where the hero spent all his time sweating and carrying guns. Emily didn't mind; she liked movies she didn't have to think about, but this particular film lacked *any* sense of style or intrigue. Better plot lines came from her neighbor's six-year-old playing pretend in the front yard. Though, to be fair, the kid might be a genius. She'd seen him create dialog for two trashcans, three bushes, and a tree that made total sense.

Long story short, Hollywood couldn't make enough action films to fill a lifetime with Marc.

Emily didn't know if she and Sebastian would click any better. She just had a *feeling.* A debate raged in her head over whether her infatuation with Sebastian was a byproduct of loneliness or love at first sight.

She wasn't sure she believed in love at first sight.

It had never happened before.

On the other hand, she'd been single for nearly two years and, during that time, had *never* been so inexplicably attracted to someone.

Maybe if she discovered the origin of Sebastian's attractive, unknowable quality, she could approach her feelings for him more sensibly.

Stalking Sebastian wasn't crazy—it was *science.*

She promised herself she wouldn't go to the Irish Rover. She promised herself repeatedly as she made a U-turn and headed back downtown. She promised herself as she pulled into the parking lot of the Rover.

Inside the Irish Rover, she was both disappointed and relieved to find big Benny alone in the dart snug. She hadn't seen Sebastian since asking him out and dreaded their next, awkward encounter. For now, she could relax—safe as an anonymous rejectee for a little longer. Hopefully, Sebastian hadn't told everyone about the stupid girl who'd come to his work to ask him out. He didn't seem the gossipy sort. If he were, at least his blabbermouth behavior would turn her off him for good.

"Hey, Benny," she said, tossing her dart case on the snug bar.

"Hey. Back for more punishment?"

He unzipped his case and retrieved his darts, checking the flight on each as he placed them on the bar.

She slapped a five-dollar bill on the bar. "I robbed a liquor store on the way here and told them to give me all their fives."

"You're going to need them."

"Step to the line, sucker. I could use the practice before the real dart players show up."

Benny cocked an eyebrow. "You're implying I'm not one of the heavy hitters?"

She shrugged as he walked to the line of board one, the preferred location, a foot closer to the bar than board two. He threw and missed the board.

His dart clattered to the ground.

Emily snorted a laugh. Even she didn't miss *the whole board.*

"Not a *word*," he said, throwing his second dart.

They threw a few practice rounds and then "diddled for the middle," a phrase she'd discovered wasn't as pornographic as it sounded. Both aimed to hit the bull's eye—the owner of the closest dart went first.

Emily won the diddle. She'd hoped to hit three twenties and close that number with her opening salvo, but instead, she'd hit one twenty, missed to the left (the one), and slopped into an eighteen, which, luckily, was a number that counted. She marked the chalk scoreboard accordingly, and Benny stepped to the line for his turn.

"Nice slop," he said.

"I meant to do that," said Emily, taking a sip of her pink Chicken Club. The drink had magically appeared. Anyone who drank Chicken Clubs became part of the "bottomless vodka" club. She didn't need to order drinks anymore. She showed up,

and a Chicken Club manifested. The hard part was *stopping* the appearance of drinks when it came time to leave. Sometimes she stayed at the Rover an additional hour because she was slow to ask for her check and found herself bound to a new cocktail.
88

Who was she to complain about prompt service?

Emily gulped her drink in preparation for Sebastian's arrival. She needed liquid courage to see him again.

She and Benny threw two more games. Between smack talk and chit chat, Benny mentioned Sebastian.

"Does Sebastian have a girlfriend?" Emily asked, trying to sound as innocent as possible.

Benny paused and studied her. She found his silence unnerving.

"Dark hair with, uh..." Emily trailed off. Benny picked up her slack.

"Huge boobs? Gazongas? Melons?"

"Bingo."

"Yeah, that's Greta." He shook his head, a gesture she didn't miss.

"What was that?"

"What?"

"You shook your head."

He shrugged. "Greta's a pain in the ass."

"How so?" she prodded. She couldn't help herself. This news couldn't have made her happier if he'd just cured the common cold.

"She's just..." He rolled his eyes and snapped his four fingers against his thumb like he was working a hand puppet. "Bitch bitch bitch, moan moan moan, me, me, me."

"She complains a lot?"

"Yes. But it's more sinister than that. She *loves* drama. Feeds off it."

"Really? Sebastian doesn't seem like the drama-loving type."

"He isn't."

"So why is he with her?"

"Off the top of my head, I can give you two reasons," said Benny, throwing his darts. He hit one twenty and missed twice.

Emily waited for Benny to continue. He noticed her expectant gaze and cupped his hands a foot in front of his pectoral muscles.

"Duh," he said.

She frowned. "Oh. *Those* two reasons."

Benny continued. "I mean, I don't know if that's true. It's my guess. Sebastian doesn't talk about his love life, one way or the other, but I can tell you he doesn't seem happy. Whatever powers 'the girls' had on him wore off a long time ago, but he's terrible at breaking up with people. His last girlfriend celebrated her fiftieth wedding anniversary with some other guy before Sebastian broke up with her."

Emily heard the sound of angels singing.

Sebastian was unhappy. Hallelujah!

Her smirk caught Benny's attention.

"Look at you. You love my man, Sebastian."

She felt her cheeks flush. Was it too late to pretend she was asking about him for a friend?

Probably.

"Sooooo...you think they're about done?" she asked.

"Who?" said Sebastian, walking through the door behind Benny.

The blood drained from Emily's freshly flushed cheeks. She felt lightheaded. She'd probably missed brain damage by a hair's breadth.

"Some actor," said Benny, without missing a beat. He plucked the last of his three darts from the board.

Sebastian shrugged, uninterested in Hollywood gossip.

Emily smirked at Benny. She wanted to hug him.

She noticed Sebastian looking at her.

"Hey," she said, flicking her head back and forward in the standard, super-cool, I'm-acknowledging-your-presence maneuver.

"Hey," he responded. He held her gaze for a moment and twitched a half-wink. Whether he did it to let her know there was no reason for her to feel awkward or by accident, she didn't know; it made her feel better. For the first time, she thought she might survive the evening and not die of embarrassment.

Hall and Oates' *Rich Girl* came on the radio. Sebastian hummed along to the song. The Rover spared patrons the Irish jigs until later at night and tended to play old music for the older clientele who came for the early bird shepherd's pie.

"Little known fact," said Emily. "Hall wrote this song about a stuck-up boy who used to date his girlfriend but changed it to 'rich *girl*' because it worked better that way for the radio."

Sebastian nodded. "Huh. I absolutely do not know what to do with that information."

90

She looked at her toes. "I like trivia," she mumbled.

"Hit me with another," said Sebastian.

Emily looked up. "Another factoid?"

He nodded.

She chuckled. "Okay...um, did you know the dot on a lowercase i is called a 'tittle?'"

Sebastian and Benny laughed.

"You said *tittle*," said Benny, pointing at her.

"Okay, maybe that was a bad choice," admitted Emily.

Sean delivered Sebastian his obligatory Chicken Club. Taking a seat at the snug bar, he leaned against the dividing wall and surveyed the game's chalk scoreboard.

"Looks like you're getting your ass kicked, Ben," he said.

Emily was winning, but not by much.

"I'm up next," he added.

"Alrighty there, Superman," said Benny.

Emily stepped to the line to throw. Benny looked past her, and she paused, curious about what drew his attention.

"And here comes Lois Lane," he grumbled.

Someone knocked into Emily's shoulder as she prepared to throw. She ceased her forward motion and stepped from the line. Greta breezed past to stand next to Sebastian at the bar without acknowledging her.

Sebastian scowled. "Seriously? People are trying to play."

"Sorry," said Greta without looking at Emily.

Sebastian remained agitated. "Hurry up. What do you need? Or move over here while people are playing." He gestured to the seat beside him.

"I'm not staying. I'm meeting Sydney next door. Don't forget we have to help my sister move tomorrow. You promised."

Sebastian looked down and nodded. When he looked up, he seemed surprised to find Greta still standing there.

"Got it," he muttered.

Greta glanced at Benny, gave Emily a visual once-over, and left the bar. Emily could tell by Greta's expression that

Sebastian's girlfriend didn't consider her a threat.

Benny chuckled. "What time *is* your curfew, Sebastian? I always forget."

Sebastian frowned. "Funny. You're a funny guy."

Emily took her turn and returned to her cocktail, which happened to be sitting on the bar very close to Sebastian's.

She watched him chew on his lip, deep in thought. He looked up and, caught staring, Emily's face spasmed. Her first instinct had been to look away, but it was too late. Captured by Sebastian's gaze, she felt half her face bolt to the left while the other half played it cool. The result felt like fighting off a sneeze.

Aghast, she released a tiny moan, shorthand for the full-blown scream of horror playing in her head.

Seriously, how could Sebastian not succumb to sexy moves like the full-face-spasm-grunt?

"I don't understand Superman and Lois Lane," Sebastian said, his eyes never leaving Emily's. He didn't laugh at her, so she clung to hope her spasm wasn't as noticeable as it felt.

"Hm?"

"Superman and Lois. What's the attraction?"

She cocked her head. "Um, he's *Superman*?"

He shook his head. "Nope. Superman couldn't get Lois Lane. Not that she's anything special, but Superman doesn't even have a job."

Emily laughed. "What are you talking about? Superman has a job. He's a reporter."

Benny nodded. "For the Daily Planet. I think. Or is that Spider-Man? Doesn't he work at a paper, too?"

"He's a beat reporter," said Sebastian, pulling his darts from his pocket. "Plus, he's probably been laid off by now. What would Lois see in him?"

"He's *Su-per-man*. He can get Lois anything she wants," said Emily.

Sebastian scoffed. "Except a house and three squares a day."

Emily barked a laugh.

Benny finished his turn, and she moved to the line to throw her darts. She tried to ignore the conversation because laughing would kill her aim but to no avail.

"Superman could burrow into the ground and bring back diamonds. He doesn't need a job," said Benny.

"Now he's a mole-man?" Sebastian shook his head, put a five-dollar bill on top of Benny's, and stepped to the second board's line to throw practice darts. "Anyway, Superman would consider that *stealing*, or at the very least, stealing jobs from wherever the diamond mines were. Morally, he couldn't do it.

He'd be broke. If I could be a superhero, I'd be Batman."

Emily scowled at Sebastian. As an avid superhero fan and recovering comic book enthusiast, she didn't like this debate's direction.

She scoffed. "Batman doesn't even have superpowers. You'd have to work out and stay in shape."

Sebastian scratched his nose. "But I'd be super rich. I wouldn't have to worry about anything. I mean, I'd be a little moody—"

Benny laughed. "You'd be moody as hell. That guy is nuts."

Sebastian stared into space, lost in his Batman daydream.

"I'd dig a tunnel from my house to the neighbor's and use *that* as my bat cave."

"The neighbors might have something to say about you popping up in their living room," said Emily.

He shrugged. "I like Aquaman, too."

Emily scowled.

Okay. That's taking it too far.

"Aquaman? Talk about dudes without a job. He's next to useless unless some drama is going down on a *boat*."

Sebastian looked at her as if she was crazy.

"Um, he can talk to dolphins. *Hellooo*—"

"So? How often does talking to dolphins come in handy?"

He shrugged. "If you could talk to them, you'd know."

"Aquaman is kinda cool," mumbled Benny.

Emily couldn't agree.

"Aquaman is *stupid*. I'd be Jean Grey from the X-Men. She has telepathy and telekinesis which—"

Sebastian cut her off.

"*Whoa*. First off, you obviously know *way* too much about comic books and you're geeking out. Second, Jean whoever-she-is, is not a real person."

She gaped at him.

"None of them are real people."

"I mean she doesn't count," he clarified. "You have to choose from classic superheroes. Superman, Batman..."

"They're all DC comics."

"Then DC rules. Wait, what is Daredevil?"

"Who's Daredevil?" asked Benny.

"A blind guy, but all his other senses are heightened," said Emily. "Daredevil is Marvel. You read Daredevil? You can't call me a geek if you know who Daredevil is; he's not as well known."

"I live with Daredevil. Only he's a dog. If Daredevil is Marvel, then *definitely* DC rules."

"A dog? What are you talking about?"

He sighed. "Don't ask."

She let it drop.

"I'm more of a Marvel person. I used to read *X-Men*," she added.

Emily toyed with admitting she had a large collection of *X-Men* comics at home. In college, she'd found reading about the strong female leads therapeutic while suffering through a bad breakup. Sebastian *started* the superhero argument, but the nerdom of owning *two thousand comic books* might be too much this early in their relationship.

"When did the X-Men show up?" asked Sebastian. "Like the sixties? They don't count. They're freaks. They probably work as carnies when they aren't fighting crime."

She laughed. "They don't work as *carnies.*"

No one was going to call Gambit and Wolverine carnies.

Sebastian sucked his tooth with his tongue and smiled just enough to activate the laugh line-dimple hybrid to the right of his mouth.

His smirk switched a light bulb in Emily's brain as she realized he didn't *care* about superheroes.

He was messing with her. He was arguing for the sake of arguing.

How had he known she felt so passionately about superheroes? Was she such a dork he could sense it? Was it dumb luck?

Emily eyed him suspiciously.

The corners of Sebastian's blue eyes wrinkled as he tried, unsuccessfully, to swallow a grin.

Does he know I've caught him?

"I'd be Batman," he repeated.

"Whatever," she said, taking a sip from her drink.

Benny stared at the two of them.

"Are you two going to flirt all night, or are we going to play darts?"

Sebastian shot Benny a look and returned to his corner seat.

Benny threw his last dart. He lucked into a bull's eye and won. Emily grimaced and pushed the two fives on the bar towards him, acknowledging her defeat. The big guy retrieved his darts from the board and grabbed one of the fives, leaving the other as the down payment on his next game with Sebastian.

Sebastian stepped to the line to diddle. As he aimed his dart, Benny looked at Emily and winked. She glowered at him to show she disapproved.

Then she looked away to hide her giddiness.

CHAPTER FIFTEEN

Sebastian opened a cardboard box and peered at his belongings, wondering where they'd travel next.

Greta was late. After the breakup, he'd felt guilty enough to agree to help move her sister, Kimi, into her boyfriend, Brian's, house. They were supposed to be at Kimi's apartment at ten a.m., but Greta disappeared that morning and had yet to return.

It was nearly eleven.

Sebastian pulled two mugs from his cardboard suitcase and put them in Greta's kitchen cabinet. He didn't like those mugs. No reason to cart them to the next place. He didn't like having a lot of stuff. Every time he moved, he left a little of himself behind.

He needed his truck empty for Kimi's move, or he'd have already shifted his boxes out of the house. The next time he went to his brother's, he'd take them. Since the breakup, he'd become a nomad, spending some nights at his brother's house, crashing on Greta's sofa on the others. If he stayed more than four days in a row at Greta's, she demanded his reinstatement as her boyfriend. Sometimes she cried. Sometimes she walked around half-naked. Sometimes she screamed. Staying at his brother's was inconvenient— Garrett lived nearly an hour away from work—but, sometimes, it was worth it to avoid the drama.

He'd investigated several possible apartments, but each had problems. The ones he liked were too expensive. The ones he could afford were too depressing. One had crime tape loosely wrapped around the handrail like a forgotten Christmas garland. When he asked to see the bathroom in that apartment, the landlord glanced at a sealed door and said it was *under construction*. His lips said *construction*, but his *face* said they hadn't found a cleaner stringent enough to remove the bloodstains from the wall.

Sebastian felt like an ass. He had to get out of Greta's house, but most days, he worked until five o'clock, and driving to his
96

brother's at rush hour was *insane*. Instead, he'd go to the Rover and walk back to Greta's apartment. He wondered if her location, walking distance to his favorite pub, had weighed more heavily on his decision to move in than he'd realized.

Sebastian reached into his pocket, searching for his truck keys, and instead retrieved a slip of paper scrawled with a list of possible apartments. He wadded the paper into a ball and threw it toward the kitchen counter. It missed and fell to the floor.

As he closed the cardboard box, a flash of white caught the corner of his eye, and he turned to find Binker galloping toward him, the wadded piece of paper in his mouth.

"What the—"

Sebastian sat on his heels and took the paper from the dog. Binker panted, his milky gaze bouncing back and forth between the wadded paper and Sebastian.

He threw the paper six feet across the room. Binker wheeled and cantered after it. He ran directly to the wadded note, picked it up, and trotted it back, dropping it neatly at his feet.

"Blind as an eagle," Sebastian mumbled.

He threw the paper several more times before Greta walked into the apartment.

"Sebby?" she called.

Sebastian stood from his squatted position behind the sofa, paper in hand.

"Come here. Check this out."

"What are you doing behind the sofa?"

"Just come here."

Greta walked around the furniture.

"See this?" He held the crumpled note aloft.

"Yes."

"See your stupid dog?"

She glanced at Binker, standing before them, panting.

"I guess..."

"Watch *this*."

He threw the paper over Binker's head, just as he had five

times previously.

Binker didn't flinch. He remained staring at Sebastian's shins, happily panting.

Greta put her hands on her hips.

"Right, it's *Binker* who's stupid. You're the one playing fetch with a blind dog."

Sebastian sat back on his heels to glower at the dog.

"*Go get it,*" he hissed, pointing toward the paper.

Binker lay down and rolled on his side, his tongue rolling from the side of his mouth like a tiny red carpet.

Sebastian sighed. "You little scam artist."

Greta went to her bedroom.

"Are you ready to go?" she called.

He stood. "I've been ready. Where have you been?"

"My sister and I went and got our nails done."

Sebastian's eyes widened. "Before we spend the day moving?"

She popped into the doorway, topless, bra hanging from one arm.

"Oh, I didn't even think of that," she said, covering her mouth with her hand, long nails on full display. "Ha—I guess we won't be much help."

Gritting his teeth, Sebastian executed a quick about-face. "Can you put some clothes on?"

She huffed. "Oh, jeeze, I'm getting *changed.* Don't look if you don't want to see."

"I *wasn't looking.*"

Sebastian stared at his feet. Binker peered up at him, paper in his mouth.

He clenched his fists and released a muffled scream of frustration.

Moving was hell. Sebastian, Brian, and two of Brian's friends shuffled boxes, sofas, a huge entertainment center, and a Foosball table. Greta and Kimi packed in slow motion, careful to protect their manicures. Greta took after her small-framed Japanese mother, but her sister was big-boned like their German

father. Kimi could have been *helpful*. When Sebastian muttered
something about the girls' ill-timed manicures, Brian tittered
nervously and glanced at Kimi to see if she'd overheard. It

98

seemed best to avoid asking Kimi to do things she didn't want to
do.

The sisters had some things in common.

By the time they finished, Sebastian was starving.

"Let's stop and get dinner," suggested Greta as they headed
home in his truck.

Sebastian nodded. It was rush hour and a bad time to head to
his brother's house. He was tired and wanted to flop on a sofa
but knew there was little to eat at Greta's. The longer he lingered
alone with her, the better chance some drama would erupt, so
the idea of eating out appealed to him. At a restaurant, he could
eat and enjoy the safety of a public place.

They chose a pub with good, cheap food. Nothing fancy. As
they waited for their burgers, Greta relayed her nail salon gossip
to Sebastian. Apparently, one of the nail technicians had shaved
her head. Another had gained a few pounds. The quality of the
gel manicure had plummeted. One wealthy patron forgot to tip,
and the whole salon erupted in Vietnamese chatter. Greta could
only imagine what they were saying.

Riveting stuff.

Sebastian spotted an adorable dirty blonde enter the
restaurant. He froze, his hamburger resting on his bottom lip.

It was Emily—the girl who had asked him out. The girl he'd
had so much fun talking to at the Rover.

He put down his burger, grinning without meaning to, and
then noticed a muscular man shadowing his adorable dart
buddy. She and the man took a seat near the bar. They laughed
like old friends.

Or lovers.

Sebastian looked down at his plate. He felt emotion rising,
crashing like waves against his chest. Was it anger?

No...*jealousy.*

He was jealous.

Weird.

He glanced at the couple again, and the feeling intensified.

I know that guy.

Why did that make it worse? Sebastian rummaged through his memories. *High school.* He'd gone to high school with the guy. He hadn't seen him around in a few years...*what was his name?*

Marc.

That was it. *Marc.* His father owned the big trucking business on the outskirts of town.

Sebastian swallowed, forcing down a surging tide of disquiet. Marc was a good-looking guy. Rich. Outgoing. He'd been quite the panty-dropper in high school if he remembered right.

He was also an *idiot.*

He'd use Emily and toss her away.

What was she doing with him?

Emily asked him out, and already she was dating Marc? He'd broken up with Greta. Soon, he'd be out of her house, and he'd thought maybe—

He didn't realize he'd been staring.

Now he could see Emily was staring back.

On an urge, he stood and walked towards her. He didn't know why, but he couldn't stop himself.

What would he do when he reached her?

"Where are you going?" asked Greta.

Her voice sounded miles away.

CHAPTER SIXTEEN

Emily and Marc sat on her sofa, watching movie credits roll. Once again, Marc had stopped by her office and suggested they grab dinner. Again, she'd meant to say no but agreed.

Marc didn't know what *fatigue* meant, but he was a genius at getting girls to go out with him. It helped that he was nearly always shirtless and had the body of an underwear model. That was like fishing with dynamite.

This time, he asked if she had a particular streaming channel. She admitted she did; the next thing she knew, they were watching a pre-dinner movie. She'd only meant to stop home long enough to let out the dog.

"That was pretty good," Emily said, gesturing to the screen. "When he tore the fifth guy's head off, I thought that might be overkill, but no, totally made sense. I was a fool."

He licked his lips. "I kind of feel like I should kiss you now— But not really, you know?"

She chuckled. His comment sounded like an insult, but instead of miffed, she felt relieved.

"I know *exactly* what you mean."

Marc tilted his body toward her and laid his head in her lap. She stroked his hair as if she'd done it a million times before. It wasn't sexual; it just felt natural.

"We're not ever going to date, are we?" he asked.

"No," she said after a moment of thought. "I know I'm insane. You're so freaking hot. I just have this...*thing.* I can't shake it."

Marc sighed. "That's cool. I still like hanging out with you."

Emily smiled. "Me too. This is nice."

"I'm kind of lonely, though," he added.

Emily stopped petting and looked down at Marc's beautiful face.

"Oh jeez, Marc, you could get any girl—"

Marc barked a loud laugh that made Emily jump.

"Ha! Not *that*. Jeeze, Emily, I get laid all the time."

She chuckled. "Of course you do. What was I thinking?"

"I mean I'd like a *real* girlfriend. I thought you'd be a good *real* girlfriend, but it's cool. You're a little too thinky for me, anyway."

"Too *thinky*," echoed Emily as she resumed petting his head.

Marc nodded and closed his eyes.

"I suppose this means you're not going to mow my lawn anymore."

"Oh, hell no. Think of all the other girls whose lawns I have to mow now."

Emily smacked him lightly on the temple, and they laughed.

"You want to grab some dinner, buddy?" he asked.

Emily nodded. "That sounds like a plan, pal."

Marc bounced up. He tilted his head towards Emily and looked out from beneath his brow with those piercing green eyes. A lustful thought flew through Emily's mind, and she shut the door on it.

Marc looked at her as if he could read her mind.

"Just to be clear. I'm totally good with this friend thing, but if you ever want a quick—" He thrust his hips back and forth. "...just ask."

Charming.

She nodded. "Oh, don't worry. You'll be the first to know."

They hopped in his truck and drove to a downtown restaurant. Marc ordered a beer. Forgetting herself, she ordered a Chicken Club and then had to explain what it was to the server.

"We have next Friday off," said Marc scanning the menu.

"The office is closed?" She didn't think it was a holiday, but since she usually worked from home, she wasn't privy to the complicated world of corporate holidays.

"Supposably," he said.

"Suppo*sedly*," she corrected.

She'd promised herself she wouldn't correct Marc's English

anymore, but he didn't seem to mind. Once, after Marc mentioned "the pointy things on top of castles," she asked, "You mean turrets?" He'd started laughing hysterically and screaming, "Asshole! Penis!" Then she had to explain Tourette's
102

and turrets were two different things, all while he shouted, "Shitballs!" at her.

Emily scanned the restaurant until her gaze passed a pair of eyes staring back at her. The moment didn't register until her stomach twisted into a pretzel.

Sebastian.

"Oof," she said aloud. It sounded as if she'd been punched in the solar plexus by a small mammal. An otter, perhaps.

Across the restaurant, Sebastian stood and headed toward her. Emily froze like a store mannequin.

"Hey," said Sebastian, arriving tableside. He turned to Marc. "Hey, Marc."

Ice ran through Emily's veins. She knew she had to be whiter than a girl in yoga pants at a farmers' market.

Sebastian and Marc knew each other.

Stupid, stupid small town!

Marc grinned, his expression registering recognition. "Hey, Sebastian, man—I haven't seen you in *years!*"

"Nope." Sebastian shook Marc's hand, but his gaze remained locked on Emily. His expression was unreadable. Very kissable but unreadable.

Why are you looking at me? Stop that.

"You guys know each other?" she squeaked.

"Dude, we went to high school together," said Marc.

He called her *dude* a lot.

"I think the last time I saw you, Sebastian—jeez—Billy HipHop's summer party? Maybe four, five years ago?"

"Probably."

Marc laughed. "Oh dude, that's right. I remember because I did that thing where you do a tequila shot, but you snort the salt and squeeze the lemon in your eyes."

Sebastian rolled his attention back to Marc, appearing decidedly unimpressed.

"You *what?*"

Marc chuckled. "It wasn't my idea. It was a *thing.* Everyone was doing it."

"Right." Sebastian offered Emily a quick sidelong glance, and she suffered a strong urge to crawl beneath the table.

"By the second or third time, it wasn't too bad," mused Marc.

"You'd probably lost all feeling in your eyes at that point," suggested Sebastian.

Emily groaned.

Oh, Marc. For the love of...

Sebastian focused on Emily again. The expression on his face wasn't puzzling to her now. He was wondering what she was doing with Marc. The guy he knew from high school. The guy who squeezed lemon in his eyes for fun.

Ohmygod. He thinks I'm dating Marc.

Marc scratched his chin. "I think I messed up my truck pretty badly, too, by the end of that party. I still have a scar on my hand—No, that might have been from playing the knife game..."

Emily nervously twirled her drink, a tight-lipped smile plastered to her face. Her mind was whirling. Should she find a way to tell Sebastian that she and Marc were just friends? Would he believe her? Was it his business?

No.

She decided. Sebastian had a girlfriend. It wasn't like she was cheating on him, even if she *was* dating Marc.

She and Sebastian talked at least once a week at the Rover, but every night he went back home to Greta.

"So you know my girl, Emily?" Marc asked.

Emily looked at him with horror.

My girl? Why did he have to phrase it like that?

"We met at darts," said Sebastian.

"Oh right, you play darts on Wednesdays when I'm at softball," said Marc, pointing at her. "Cool. That's so crazy you guys know each other."

Emily stopped herself from slapping her hand to her face. Marc couldn't have implied they were a couple more if he'd grabbed her face and shoved his tongue down her throat.

Something snapped in her head. She felt trapped. Her chest tightened. She wanted to get away.

Now.

"I'll be back in a second," she said, standing.

Stepping on the foot of the bar table, she stumbled. Sebastian caught her arm and helped her right herself.

"Easy there, Grace," he said.

"Emily," corrected Marc. Emily and Sebastian both looked at him.

Marc smiled back.

104

"Thanks," Emily mumbled to Sebastian, pulling her arm from his grasp.

She speed-walked to the ladies' room. The small room was blessedly unoccupied. She entered and locked the door behind her.

The exchange between the two men in her life was unbearable. She pressed her back against the cool tile wall to steady herself.

Am I having a heart attack?

Why is it so hard to breathe?

She inhaled, but it didn't feel like any oxygen reached her lungs.

She cleared her throat and took slow, deep breaths as she slid down the wall to a squat, her butt hovering inches above the floor. She wrapped her arms around her knees, closed her eyes, and imagined calming thoughts.

Amidst fantasies of warm beaches and fuzzy bunnies, another idea screamed through her brain like a freight train, flattening the seagulls and crushing the rabbits.

She'd left Marc and Sebastian alone.

She should have stayed for damage control. Without her there to manage the conversation, Marc would find a way, without meaning to, to imply they were married with triplets on the way.

Crap.

Emily stood, took a quick look in the mirror to ensure she didn't look as crazy as she felt, and opened the bathroom door. She returned to the table, breaking into a trot every third step.

When she got there, Sebastian was nowhere in sight.

"Hey," said Marc as she sat back down.

Emily ignored him and scanned the bar.

"Crazy seeing Sebastian again. I haven't seen that dude in years."

Emily nodded and chewed on her lip.

Sebastian wasn't back in his seat.

"What's wrong with you?" asked Marc. "You look like that dude from the movie when he thought he was being followed by the alien assassin."

She took a long drink from her vodka. "Oh, Marc. Marky, Marky *Marc*."

"What? You're being weird. Not that *that* is all that weird, but—"

She put her hand on his.

"You know how I told you I liked some other guy?"

"Yeah. *That* cock-block." He guffawed at his joke.

"Sebastian," said Emily.

Marc blinked at her.

She repeated the name. "*Sebastian*."

"Yeah...?"

Emily prayed for Marc's rusty gears to turn. Finally, his eyes widened. She heard the creak of machinery coming to life.

"Wait..." He tucked back his chin and surveyed her face.

Here we go...you can do it...

"Your dude..." Marc removed his hand from beneath Emily's. He pointed at her with his index finger and then jerked his thumb toward the back of the bar. "*...is Sebastian*?"

She nodded.

"The guy you like is Sebastian Krzyzanowski?"

Emily nodded again and then knit her brow.

"Wait, what's his name?"

She couldn't believe it had never crossed her mind to ask his last name.

"Krzyzanowski. My man Krazy Krizzy. His mother's like, full-on Polish."

"Krzyzanowski," Emily repeated.

Jeez, what a mouthful.

Marc grinned and shook his head. "Old Sea Bass. Who knew? Now I'm *really* jealous!"

"People call him *Sea Bass*?" Emily recalled the confusion with her mother on the phone and chuckled. "That's a thing?"

Marc thought for a second. "No. Now that you mention it, I think he kicked some kid's ass for calling him that."

He tilted his head and stared at the ceiling, like a bird searching the treetops for predators.

"Come to think of it. It might have been *my* ass."

"Well, now Sea Bass thinks we're dating. You called me *your girl.*"

"Oh, *nah.* I'm sure he knew what I meant. He wouldn't think we were dating."

"I— *Wait.* What do you mean he wouldn't think we were 106

dating? I'm not hot enough for you?"

Marc laughed.

"You should *be* so lucky," muttered Emily.

"Bring it, baby. Any time."

She rolled her eyes.

"You are totally nuts," Marc added, taking a sip of his beer.

She tilted her head back and exhaled.

"I am *going* nuts." Emily spotted Sebastian and Greta walking toward her. She hadn't noticed Greta at his table. He nodded as he approached, and Emily offered him a nervous smile. The action made Marc turn, and he watched Sebastian and Greta approach.

"See ya, dude," said Marc, holding out his hand.

Sebastian slap-shook Marc's outstretched hand as he passed. Greta never glanced at Emily, but caught Marc's eye and smiled, eyelashes batting so hard she might have bruised her lower lids.

Once they'd safely passed, Emily turned and watched the couple leave. A soup of relief and depression boiled within her.

"That's Sebastian's girlfriend?" asked Marc, his eyes still on the door.

"Yes."

"Her tits are *insane.*"

Awestruck, Marc shook his head, like a tourist witnessing the grandeur of the Grand Canyon for the first time.

Maybe the Grand Tetons.

Emily scowled at him.

He giggled. "Yours are nice, too, but seriously... You are *screwed.*"

CHAPTER SEVENTEEN

Emily dressed for dart night, more nervous than usual about seeing Sebastian. For weeks, she'd had her crush to nurture, and now not only did she have to wait for Sebastian and Greta to break up and for Sebastian to realize she was his ideal mate, but she had to worry he thought she was dating Marc.

She'd read two books and drunk approximately forty-five thousand cups of tea over the weekend. When she felt low, she curled in her window seat with a cup of tea and a good book. The act was so melodramatically pure. She'd performed similar one-woman plays in college, sitting on her wide windowsill, staring forlornly through the glass. If it was raining, even better. Staring into the rain might win her an Oscar. In college, instead of tea, she'd systematically dip an entire package of shortbread cookies into a jar of Nutella, but the concept was the same.

Emily liked to think she'd grown. In college, she'd run to the mirror to watch tears slide down her cheeks and pretend she was in a heart-wrenching music video.

She hadn't done that for at least two or three years.

There were a handful of people at the Irish Rover when Emily arrived. She was agitated and not above taking out her frustrations on a rube. The second board was open, and she challenged a new guy, determined to kick his ass.

Emily won five dollars before Sebastian came through the

door. He perched on his usual corner stool and ordered a Chicken Club.

"Hey," he said when he caught Emily glancing his way.

"Hey," she echoed.

108

The rube asked for a second game, and Emily obliged. She tried to concentrate but felt Sebastian's presence, like he was standing beside her, stroking her arm. She wanted the game to end so she could stand at the bar and make idle chit-chat with him. Maybe this time, she would say the perfect thing to make him fall madly in love with her.

She rushed her throws and returned the new guy's five dollars. One of the regulars challenged the newbie to a game, and Emily agreed to sit out a round.

She stepped to the end of the snug bar to reclaim her Chicken Club.

"So, Marc, huh?" said Sebastian. His voice had the lilt of a child teasing another kid on the playground.

"I've been working on a website at his father's truck store," Emily said, playing it as cool as her spazz-inclinations would allow her. "I guess you knew him in high school?"

"We weren't really in the same crowd, but yeah. He dated a few girls I knew." He made air quotes as he said the word "dated."

Emily scowled and aped his air quotes. "What do you mean *dated*?"

He raised his brows and shrugged, looking away as he did.

She dropped the topic. She knew he was implying Marc had a way with the ladies, which wasn't breaking news. She felt protective of her friend and wished she could tell Sebastian that Marc had always been a gentleman to her. Other than the time he slammed her into the drywall.

On the other hand, Sebastian's curiosity about Marc meant that seeing her with her handsome friend made an impression on him. Warning her about Marc meant that either Sebastian was concerned for her, which was cute, or he was jealous, which was even better.

More people arrived for Dart Night, and the crowds made it easier for Emily to resist the urge to orbit Sebastian, waiting for something to click.

She and her randomly selected Dart Night partner played the strongest team in the first round and lost. There were fewer competitors than usual, and the night wrapped early. That made Emily happy because though she lost the big game, she preferred freelancing in the snug. The extra Wednesday night dart players made finding a partner for snug games easier. The key was to find a strong partner who didn't mind having a cinderblock tied to his ankle.

She was plotting a potentially profitable pairing when Sebastian called her name from his seat at a nearby table. It was 9:15 p.m., and the drinking patrons had overrun the Rover's dining area.

Sebastian sat with the pretty man, Ryan, whom she'd noticed her first night at the bar, and a striking redhead with hair flowing like lava across her shoulders. The girl sat on Ryan's side of the table. Emily had seen her in the bar before but didn't know her name.

"Emily!" called Sebastian again. "Come sit." He motioned her to join the table.

Emily felt pain in her right ankle.

"*Ow.*"

The only person close enough to kick her was Benny.

She scowled. "Why'd you do that? That *hurt.*"

Benny waggled his eyebrows and motioned to Sebastian's table. "You're getting the call to the big leagues."

She huffed and leaned down to rub her anklebone. "I regret talking to you about him."

Benny grinned.

Gathering her darts, Emily snaked through the crowd to Ryan and Sebastian's table. She took the empty booth space beside Sebastian. The basic math made her giddy.

1 couple + Sebastian + Me = 2 couples.

Everyone in the bar could see what Sebastian had not yet grasped.

They made a *lovely* pair.

"I'm Emily," she said, sliding into the booth beside and extending a hand to the redhead.

"Jessica," said the girl.

Since the night Emily first overheard Ryan brag about his love life, they'd interacted many times during various dart games. She'd gotten to know him as more of a bachelor wise-ass than her first impression of him—a psychotic misogynist. Not that he was a *good* guy. Dating him had to be a nightmare, but the story with the knife probably wasn't true.

Probably.

110

Anyway, Emily had no plans to date him, and he was perfectly pleasant at the Rover.

"So, Emily, I guess you're wondering why I called this meeting," said Sebastian.

"Because you missed me?" She grinned, pleased with her response. She embraced the bravado brought forth by cocktails.

Sebastion shook his head. "Yeah, *no*. I have a question for you: What does P.S. stand for at the end of a letter?"

Emily glanced at Ryan and Jessica and found them both staring at her.

"Don't know?" asked Ryan.

"No. I know." Emily paused, wondering if she was being set up.

She decided it didn't matter.

"It stands for *postscript*," she said.

Jessica pointed at Sebastian. "Ha! He told us it stood for *personal space*."

"Damn," muttered Sebastian. "Okay, you can go now, Google. I'll call you back when we need more information."

Emily's jaw fell slack.

"You asked me over to ask me *that*?"

Sebastian nodded.

"Shoo shoo," he said, accompanying the comment with the appropriate hand gesture, ushering her from the booth.

Emily glared at him. The awkward silence grew. Finally, she curled her lip and began to slide from the booth.

"I'm kidding!" said Sebastian, putting his hand on her leg to stop her from leaving. She wore shorts and felt the warmth of his touch on her bare thigh.

She looked down at his hand and then caught his eye. He looked away and returned his paw to his own lap.

He seemed flustered.

Was that a moment?

He gestured to the couple on the other side of the table. "Okay, but seriously—now tell them you were kidding, and P.S.

really stands for *personal space*."

She shook her head. "But it doesn't. It's *postscript*, like, a thought you add after the rest of the letter, post-letter."

Jessica sighed. "I thought it stood for *psss*. Like *Psss, I have another secret.*"

Ryan patted Jessica's hand. "And that was an excellent guess."

Jessica beamed as Ryan turned his focus to Sebastian, beckoning him with his index finger. "Pony up."

"Fine." Sebastian slapped a dollar on the table.

Emily couldn't let it go.

"Why would it stand for *personal space*? That doesn't make any sense at all."

Sebastian rolled his eyes. "If you're writing a letter to someone, *clearly*, you want personal space. You're far away from that person, and probably for a good reason."

"Probably as far away as the 1800s," muttered Ryan, taking the dollar.

Sebastian shrugged. "Hey, I call 'em like I see 'em. I don't make the rules."

Emily saw this argument resembled Sebastian's Batman rant. He purposely drew people into idiotic arguments for his own amusement.

Ryan yawned loudly, and all eyes turned to him.

"Let's hop around a bit," he said. "I've been here all night."

"Hop around," said Jessica, giggling, holding her hands beneath her chin to mimic rabbit paws.

Sebastian glanced at Emily, but they looked away, each fighting the urge to laugh.

"Sounds good," said Sebastian.

"Sure," said Emily.

The four settled their tabs and stepped outside into a fog of humidity. After the dry chill of the air conditioning, it felt like a warm embrace. They walked down the street in the aimless way people do, right before someone says, "Well, I guess I better get home."

Emily couldn't let that happen. She wanted to keep Sebastian near for long as possible.

"Want to go out on my boat?" said a high, desperate voice she didn't recognize.

Who said that?

Eyes trained on her.

Oh no.

I said that.

Emily's father kept a seventeen-foot center console Parker at
112

a nearby marina. She knew where the keys were and how to operate the boat, and her dad didn't mind if she used it. He didn't expect her to tool around the Chesapeake Bay in the middle of the night with a boat full of drunks, though, no matter how crucial the move might be to her love life.

"Boat sounds perfect," said Ryan.

"A boat?" squealed Jessica.

"I guess..." said Sebastian.

Emily swallowed with a smile frozen to her lips.

Shit.

The group's weaving path shifted in the direction of the marina. Emily practiced a speech explaining to her father why taking the boat out in the middle of the night seemed reasonable. The last time she'd taken it, the wind pushed her into another boat's propeller, rubbing away part of the "P" in Parker.

She'd demoted the "Parker" to "Farker."

She fought her rising dread.

The things we do for love.

At the marina, the group piled into the boat, and, old salt that Emily was, she lowered the engine. She ran through her mental checklist four or five times, worried she'd do something to blow them all into lust-filled chunks of meat.

She made a note that *Lust-filled Chunks of Meat* would make an excellent sequel to *Petri Dish of Lust*.

She pointed to the aft. "Ryan, release those lines in the back. Sebastian, you go to the bow and let loose that line. Then fend the poles as I pull out; I might need some help. Same goes to you on the fending bit, Ryan."

"Aye-aye, Captain," said Ryan, untying the back lines.

Sebastian looked at Emily, his face awash with confusion.

"What do you want me to do?"

Emily pointed to the front of the boat.

"Go up front, untie that line, throw it up on the dock, and then, as I pull out if I start to drift toward any of these poles or another boat, push against them, so I don't hit them."

"Ah. That makes more sense. Stop talking like a damn pirate."

Sebastian walked to the front of the small boat, untied the line, and threw it on the dock. Released, Emily shifted into reverse and pulled slowly from the slip. When she drifted too close to the back of another boat, Ryan leaned out and pushed off, saving the day.

So far so good.

Emily putt-putted from the marina into the middle of the wide Severn River, where even the worst captain couldn't scrape the name from her boat.

She cut the engine, and the four of them bobbed in the dark, the only sound the gentle lapping of the water against the boat. Conversations from the bar picked up where they'd left off beneath a bright summer moon, the crew whispering so as not to disturb the peaceful evening.

Ten minutes after positioning themselves in the center of the river, Jessica announced she was hot in a breathy, dramatic voice usually reserved for soap queens and porn stars. A mischievous grin crept across her face.

"I'm going to go *swimming*," she said.

Emily peered at the black water.

Oh, that seems like a terrible idea.

Jessica spun away from the group and whipped off her shirt. Her bra snapped open as if on the remote control and dropped to the deck. Skirt shimmied down.

Emily watched, speechless.

Redheads. What can you do?

Jessica gracefully dove into the water.

"I did not see that coming," said Emily.

"I did," mumbled Ryan.

The boys seemed oblivious to Jessica's antics. Ryan had seen Jessica in every possible state of undress; her naked swimming held no mystery. Sebastian's neck vertebrae appeared fused; he never swiveled in Jessica's direction, no matter how loudly she called or giggled. Emily guessed years of practice had taught him never to look at another guy's girl, particularly when she was naked.

"Come in!" Jessica called, motioning to Emily from the water.

Emily took a moment to consider her level of intoxication

and found it lacking. She wasn't drunk, making getting naked and diving into murky waters a tougher leap—*literally*. She'd never been a skinny-dipping-in-the-middle-of-the-house-lined-river-at-midnight type before, but she hadn't been in this 114

position, either.

If circling Sebastian like a moon hadn't convinced him of her adoration, would nudity?

She watched Jessica swim around.

It does look like fun...

Seeing the boys distracted by conversation, she made a split-second decision to split the difference. Slipping out of her summer dress, she left on her underwear and slid into the water.

"Yay!" yipped Jessica, ruining her attempt at stealth.

The girls paddled in the water by the side of the boat, clothed by darkness. The boys ignored them, other than declining Jessica's invitations for them to join.

"This feels so good, doesn't it?" asked Jessica.

Emily had to agree.

It really did.

The water was warm. Along the banks, the dock and porch lights of the waterfront homes danced with their rippling twins reflected on the river. Even the boys fell silent as if they didn't want to disrupt such a perfect evening.

As Emily put her foot on the lowest rung of the boat's ladder, preparing to climb back into the boat, the water around her burst with eerie purple iridescence. For the first time, she understood why people in alien movies froze when beautiful but ultimately deadly lights appeared.

They're *pretty*.

Jessica gasped. "Oh, Ryan, *look*."

The boy's heads appeared over the side of the boat. They noticed the ethereal glow, their eyes growing wide with wonder.

"What *is* that?" asked Sebastian.

"Maybe shrimp? Iridescent shrimp?" guessed Emily.

"Huh," said Sebastian. He looked at Ryan. "See? I told you she knows everything."

The movement of the girls' legs made the ghostly spectacle brighter, and they remained in the water, kicking to create bursts of light.

Emily was enthralled by the natural wonder—but annoyed it had taken glowing crustaceans to make the jackasses in the boat notice two naked girls.

When the novelty faded, the girls climbed into the boat and dressed. Emily moved to the helm, and Sebastian took the seat beside her. Ryan joined Jessica in the back. The moonlight on the water glistened around them, as beautiful as glowing shrimp. Emily looked at Sebastian and found him watching her. The moon lit the curve of his cheekbones and darkened his jawline, painting him with manly, romantic shadowing.

"That was sort of magical," she said.

Sebastian nodded. He looked away, but she could see he was smiling.

Emily turned the key and shifted into forward gear, fluffing her wet hair in the breeze as they roared back to the marina.

Ryan and Jessica canoodled in the back of the boat.

"Emily," said Sebastian, yelling over the engine. "Do you—"

She held up a finger to signal that she needed quiet.

"One second, I have to park this damn thing," she called back.

Emily slowed and made her way to the slip. Her approach was diagonal but passable. Jessica, falling asleep on Ryan's shoulder, jumped as the boat bumped into a piling.

"Impressive," said Sebastian as she cut the engine.

"Thank you." She closed her eyes and bowed her head to demonstrate she accepted his gracious compliment with great tongue-in-cheek humility. She nearly remarked that she was a girl of many talents but realized how cheesy-sexpot it would sound, especially after the skinnydipping.

"Were you going to say something a minute ago?" she asked.

Sebastian shook his head.

"No. Just good job."

Ryan stood and retied the back line. Sebastian moved forward to retie the front, and Emily watched him do it. She was sure he'd had more to say than *good job*. She regretted shushing him, but she'd been flustered planning her approach to the marina.

"Help up?"

Emily looked up to find Ryan off the boat, offering a hand to her. It was low tide, and the boat sat four feet below the pier.

Though there was a ladder, getting out would be more difficult than getting in had been.

"Thanks," said Emily, accepting his hand.

Ryan aided Sebastian next, and the four wandered back to
116

the Rover, where their vehicles awaited. They each offered one version or another of "see you later" and left. It was late, and everyone was tired.

Nothing romantic—just four tired boaters.

One question dogged her, though.

Was that a date?

CHAPTER EIGHTEEN

After their midnight boat ride, Emily sensed a growing intimacy between Sebastian and her, but reading him proved impossible. She saw him at the Rover two or three times a week. They talked, laughed, maybe even flirted, and then...*nothing*. She had to remind herself that he had a girlfriend. What did she expect?

While Emily's love life floundered, her dart game improved. Worst-case scenario, she might never win Sebastian's heart, but she could become a dart shark.

College and an unused teaching degree—all to join a dart tour.

Her parents would be so proud.

Playing a five-dollar game, standing at the dart line just inside the Rover's front door, Emily felt someone slap her ass, *hard*.

She spun.

"Hey girrrl," said the slapper.

Greta.

Emily gasped and then slapped her hand to her mouth, horrified she'd responded to the vision of her conquest's girlfriend that way.

Greta continued to the bar without acknowledging her shock.

The women had seen each other a few times but had never been introduced. That made the playful slap odd, to say the least.

Why would Greta suddenly give me some sorority girl high-five? Was it like a Mafioso's kiss of death?

Anxiety flooded her veins as she scrambled for a reason Greta might slap her. She came up with four:

A: Greta was in a super-friendly mood, and Emily had become such a fixture in the snug she felt the urge to acknowledge her presence. *Innocent.*

B: Sebastian's girlfriend knew about the boat ride and
118

Emily's crush and offered this passive-aggressive gesture to make it *clear* she knew. *Worrisome.*

B, Subsection 2: Greta slapped her with a poisonous dart to constrict her throat until she admitted her crush on Sebastian. Greta would then administer the antidote, but only after Emily promised to pack up and leave town. *Crazy.*

C: Greta had a crush on Emily. An interesting twist but doubtful. Greta looked at every man that passed like they were steaks and she was a starving wolf. She doubted she was Greta's type. *Porno plotline.*

D. Emily was really, *really* overthinking the whole thing. *Winner.*

"Uh., hey," said Emily, in a much-delayed attempt to re-establishing her composure.

Greta stood at the bar and held up a hand without turning to acknowledge Emily's hello. A second later, another girl burst into the bar, nearly falling into Emily, before collapsing on Greta's back. Greta and the girl screeched and erupted into giggles.

"It's about time, Sydney. You almost knocked over my new handbag."

Her friend eyed the bag. "Oh, it's *gorgeous.*"

Greta nodded. "He gave it to me."

Emily missed her next toss, and her dart clattered to the faux brick floor. She didn't catch the girls' entire exchange, but it was clear Greta's relationship with Sebastian was healthy enough for him to buy her an expensive handbag.

It was hard to concentrate on darts and eavesdrop at the same time.

She felt sick.

Greta and the girl left the Rover, chattering like finches. As they walked by the window, Emily noticed Greta slip and nearly snap an ankle as she struggled to walk in her high-heeled sandals.

Reason E for the butt-slap; Greta was drunk.

Emily took a deep, cleansing breath. The slap didn't mean Greta was plotting her death—buzzed Greta wanted to party with her friend. Emily had the most accessible tush for smacking at the moment Greta felt like smacking tush.

Right up until the day I wake in a trunk, wrists bound with an Hermès belt and a silk scarf stuffed in my mouth...

She re-focused on her game. She won and pushed herself into a second round against a short, dark-haired newcomer. She needed something to keep herself from staring at the vision burning in her mind's eye of Greta's stupid orange handbag.

Sebastian entered and took his usual spot in the snug. They exchanged the usual hellos.

"Hey," she said.

"Hey," he said.

She felt uneasy. She didn't know what she expected, but it was never enough. She didn't expect Sebastian to kiss her—not even a little Parisian *kiss! kiss!* on either cheek. Still, the Hey-Hey always felt like a letdown.

Heck, his girlfriend felt me up before he did.

After the midnight boat ride, she thought things would be different or at least *progress.* Instead, Sebastian apparently went home and bought Greta a handbag to assuage his guilt.

Emily made short work of her foe at the dartboard. The guy gave up and left the snug. Emily took the opportunity to sidle up to Sebastian.

"Greta was here a little bit ago," she said. She winced to hear the bitter edge of her tone.

Sebastian looked at her with no emotion.

She continued.

"She slapped my ass."

That caught his attention.

"She *what*?" he asked.

"She slapped my ass. I was at the line, and she walked in and slapped my ass and said, 'Hey girrrrl...'"

Sebastian rolled his eyes.

"She's like that. And I think she's hanging out with some of her girls today. She's probably already plastered."

Emily nodded. "She did seem buzzed. "You, uh..." Emily hesitated, afraid to continue.

"What?"

"You didn't tell her we went out in the boat or anything, did you?"

"*No*," said Sebastian, visibly annoyed. "We don't talk. We aren't—"

Sebastian ran his tongue over his front teeth, agitated.

120

"Just don't worry about it," he said.

Emily felt chastised. She shouldn't have brought it up. Maybe the conversation felt too much like *drama*.

"Sorry. I wanted to be sure she wasn't mad at me for nothing—"

He turned on her. "Why? Why do you care what *she* thinks?"

"I—don't. I just didn't want a boat ride to get you in trouble—"

"Get me in—" Sebastian grit his teeth. He seemed angry, but the emotion passed, and his face relaxed. His voice lost its edge.

"I'm sorry. I'm not mad at you, and I'm not in trouble. Just don't worry about it."

He looked away.

Emily took a sip of her drink to smooth the weird lump in her throat.

It's probably my foot.

She didn't know what to make of their exchange. She hardly had a moment to wonder before someone blinded her by placing a hand over each of her eyes.

"Guess who?" said a man's voice.

Oh no.

Emily turned on her stool to find Marc standing behind her, grinning as usual.

"What are you doing here?" she asked.

"I dunno. Softball is over." He reached into his back pocket and produced three darts. "*Viola*! Bet you didn't know I play darts, too."

He pronounced *viola*, vee-ola. It implied he'd *read* the word and sounded it out, so not too bad.

"I didn't know you played." Emily looked at Sebastian. "You guys know each other, of course."

Sebastian and Marc exchanged nods.

"You want a game?" asked Marc.

Sebastian shrugged. "Sure."

Excited, Marc gave some invisible foe a head butt. "*Yeah*. Get some. Let me get a beer and take a couple practice shots, and then we'll play. Cool?"

"Icy," drawled Sebastian.

Marc laughed and left the snug to find a bartender.

Emily watched Sebastian pull out his darts.

"I don't think he plays much. You're going to kill him," she said.

He remained silent, but she watched as the corner of his mouth curled into a smirk, making his hybrid dimple-laugh line more prominent. She wanted to kiss it, but that would be weird. If not sexual harassment.

Marc came back, beer in hand.

"Ten dollars?" asked Sebastian.

Emily shot him a glance.

The going rate is five...

"Whatever," said Marc. He set down his beer, pulled out a sloppy wad of cash, and put ten on the bar. Sebastian did the same.

"High rollers," mumbled Emily, taking a sip of her drink.

"Rich kid," Sebastian whispered in her ear before stepping to the line.

A shiver ran down her back as his breath caressed her ear.

Chuckling, she took a sip of her drink.

Calm yourself.

For the next hour, Marc and Sebastian hogged the near board. Other players came and went, striking up games on the second board, but Marc and Sebastian held their ground.

Marc erased the board in preparation for another game. Sebastian moved to the bar and picked up a pack of cigarettes someone had left there.

"Check it out," he said to Emily.

Sebastian put the cigarette in his right palm, which he held open and flat in front of him. He checked to be sure she was watching and then slapped his right wrist with his left hand. The cigarette jumped into the air, flipping as it arced toward his mouth. He caught it, positioned perfectly between his sexy lips.

"Oooh. You're *so* cool," said Emily.

"I know. I can't help it."

"You're up," snapped Marc, clearly unimpressed.

"Do not put that back in my pack," said Sean behind the bar, glaring at him.

Marc played darts shockingly well. The two men traded games as Emily watched and occasionally played beside them against other competitors on board two.

It grew dark outside. She started another Chicken Club and 122

settled on one of the stools to watch the boys' never-ending war.

"Is it best out of...*something*?" she asked.

Neither of them answered. Sebastian concentrated, preparing to throw. Marc stood at the end of the bar, glaring at him. Emily had never seen Marc so serious.

Sebastian missed the sixteen on his last dart, and Marc stepped to the line. He had sixteens closed and could have moved to the fifteens. Instead, he returned his focus to Sebastian's open sixteens. He hit a triple and banged Sebastian for forty-eight points.

Sebastian glared at Marc. "You pointin' mother—"

"Sorry about that, Sea Bass," said Marc. Emily stifled a smirk and checked to catch Sebastian's reaction to the nickname.

The whites of Sebastian's eyes flashed. His jaw clenched.

"Oh, it is about to get *ugly* in here," muttered Sebastian, stepping to the line.

Sebastian didn't usually compete with such bloodlust. Generally, he was reserved to the point of appearing bored; nothing could ruffle him.

Marc, too, seemed transformed. He'd traded his goofy demeanor for the stony countenance of one of his favorite movie gunslingers.

Emily peered through the bar's front window and noticed Greta hustling by, partially concealed behind her friend. She recognized the bright orange purse. Her skin prickled with nervous dread.

Greta didn't come in.

Emily glanced at Sebastian to see if he'd noticed his girlfriend outside. He hadn't. He'd just hit two bulls-eyes and a sixteen to win.

"*Bam!*" he barked at Marc. "*Bring it.*"

Marc gritted his teeth and erased the chalkboard to prepare for a rubber match to break the tie.

Intrigued by the way Greta had scuttled past the bar, Emily put down her drink and walked outside. She peered down the street in the direction Greta had headed.

Half a block away, she saw two girls.

The one shaped like Greta was kissing a man.

The object of Greta's smooching was standing outside the open passenger door of a dark car parked at an odd angle in front of a parking lot. The headlights were on, and the engine running. Emily stepped back into the Rover's entrance nook and peered around the corner like a spy. The group would be less likely to see her tucked inside the doorway, though if they *did* spot her, she'd look *crazy*.

She worried about looking crazy a little less every day.

Emily saw well enough to confirm it *was* Greta kissing the man. Her large orange purse was the visual equivalent of a safety vest. She couldn't have been more obvious if she'd been wearing a traffic cone as a hat.

She couldn't see the face of the man; it spent most of its time smooshed against Greta's. He had an average build and height and wore shorts. He could have been anyone.

The driver of the car called out. The man smooching Greta returned to the car's passenger seat, followed by Greta herself, who squeezed in to sit on his lap. Her friend opened the back door and slipped inside.

Emily waited for the car to pass, hoping she'd see the men in the front seats, but the car nosed out, waited for another vehicle to pass, and made a U-turn to head in the opposite direction.

Damn.

She stood there a moment longer, processing this new information.

Greta was having an affair.

The kiss she'd shared with the man wasn't a peck with a friend. It was the sort of kiss that led to naked people.

She stared through the glass at Sebastian and realized the awful truth.

I can't tell him.

A girl with a crush catches the rival girlfriend cheating? How *convenient*. No one would believe her. Even if Sebastian *did* believe her, the reveal would invade his privacy and stir drama. He might resent her. Kill the messenger.

She couldn't tell him.

She wanted to scream.

Maybe I could send an anonymous letter, wear gloves as I wrote it, buy the paper in another state and mail it from yet another...

"Emily!"

Hearing her name, she turned. A girl walked towards her and stepped into the light, revealing a head of bouncing curls.

124

Kady.

Emily grabbed her arm. "You will never guess what I just saw—"

"Joe is cheating on me," said Kady.

Emily shut her mouth with a click of teeth. Kady didn't look like she'd been crying, but she didn't look happy.

"Why do you say that?"

"I know it. I was hoping you were here to get my mind off it. I—" Kady glanced through the window of the Rover. "Holy hell. Who is that with Sebastian?"

"That's Marc. My car part buddy."

Kady shot Emily a look. "*That's* the guy who asked you out, and you turned him down?"

Emily nodded. "We're friends now, though."

Kady gaped at her.

"Are you *insane*? He's *gorgeous.*"

"Yeah, by the numbers. He's just not my type. I like them a little taller, a little—"

"A little more Sebastiany," added Kady, smirking.

"Exactly. Do you want to go somewhere and talk about Joe?"

Kady was still staring at Marc. She didn't answer.

"Or, maybe you'd like to come in for a bit and cheer up?" suggested Emily.

"Yeah, I'll go in for a bit," said Kady, already halfway through the door.

Marc and Sebastian sat at the snug bar.

"It's over?" Emily asked.

Both boys nodded.

Marc sighed. "He beat me. He always did."

Sebastian patted him on the shoulder. Marc jerked away, scowling.

"This is my friend, Kady," said Emily introducing her to Marc.

"Hey," said Marc, turning on his million-watt grin as if the fierce dart battle had never happened.

"Hey," said Kady, shaking his hand. Emily saw cartoon hearts in Kady's eyes.

"You play?" asked Marc.

Kady nodded. "But I didn't bring my darts."

"You can borrow mine," said Emily.

Kady snatched the darts from the bar.

"Let's diddle," she said to Marc.

Marc winked at her.

Kady giggled.

"Jeez, get a room," mumbled Emily.

At ten o'clock, Emily hit the wall and wanted to go home. She hadn't planned to stay out so late. Marc and Kady were playing their fifth game, and she'd remained to be a good wingman. It made her happy to see Kady happy.

Sebastian had disappeared. She assumed he'd gone home. She hoped he was walking in on Greta and her mystery man at that very moment. It wasn't a *nice* thought, but poor Sebastian had to find out sooner or later and *sooner* worked for Emily. It was like peeling off a Band-Aid. Or makeshift nipple tape. Whatever.

Emily left the snug and weaved toward the ladies' room through the bar crowd. She'd gone twenty minutes earlier for the first time since arriving, and now she'd have to go every twenty minutes for the rest of the night. That's the way drinking and going to the bathroom worked. She hated when she broke the seal.

Mission accomplished, she headed back to the front of house and felt someone touch her shoulder as she neared the snug. She turned to find Sebastian bleary-eyed and buzzed. She wasn't the only one who had stayed too late.

"You're here—hey," said Sebastian.

"I am. Hey," she answered.

Sebastian paused to steady himself and then pointed at her with the hand gripping his cocktail. The pink liquid sloshed, each wave cresting at the lip of the glass but never spilling. He was a professional.

"We should talk," he said.

"Yeah?"

With his free hand, he raised his middle and index fingers into a "V" shape, like a backwards peace sign. He used it to point 126

at his own two eyes, one finger for each eye, and then directed the fork back at Emily.

"I've had my eye on you," he said.

She laughed. "Who, *me*?"

He straightened to his full height and stared down at her.

"You're short," he said.

"I'm not short. I'm five-five. That's *average*."

He patted Emily on the head.

"You're cute. Like an adorable little Oompa Loompa."

"You better watch it, bub. You're about to get Oompa Loompa'd." She balled a fist.

Sebastian snickered.

Around them, people yelled to be heard over the music and other screaming drunks, oblivious to the magic happening in their midst.

"Are you dating Marc?" Sebastian asked.

"What? No, I—"

Sebastian cut Emily's protestations short by putting his index finger against her bottom lip as if to hush her. Gently, he pushed her upper lip against her nose. He pushed her lips around with this finger until she started giggling.

"What are you *doing*, weirdo?"

"Chh!" said Sebastian.

"Sebastian..."

"Cchh chh! Hush now. You hush."

He was being a total goofball.

It was *adorable*.

Unable to contain herself any longer, she slapped away his hand.

"You're drunk," she said.

"Me? Drunk? Nooo..."

"Lil' bit," said Emily, pinching the air with her forefinger and thumb.

He imitated her gesture inches from her nose.

"Lil' bit," he echoed.

He wiped his face with his hand and shook his head like a wet dog.

"We should talk," he said. He looked around the bar. "You want to go somewhere quiet?"

Emily nodded. "Okay. I need to get my dart pack. It's behind the snug."

"Okay. Pack it up!" He thrust a finger into the sky like a king directing his minions.

Emily pushed through the crowd to the front of the bar. It was like squeezing into a Japanese subway car, and it didn't help she was *shaking* with giddiness.

This was it.

This was the moment.

Sebastian was going to tell her he and Greta were breaking up, and they were a green light.

Maybe the expensive, day-glow handbag had been a consolation prize?

She grabbed her dart pack and paid her tab. She battled back to where she had left Sebastian.

He was gone.

Noooo...

She stood on her toes and scanned the bar. Sebastian was tall; surely, she would spot his head bobbing above the crowd?

Nothing.

Maybe he followed her to the front? Maybe he was standing outside waiting for her?

Steeling her resolve, she cut through the crowd until she spotted Benny.

"Benny!" she said, grabbing his arm. He was drooling over a girl in a red tank top. She didn't seem impressed, but Emily didn't have time to give Benny pointers.

"Have you seen Sebastian?" she screamed over the noise.

Benny pointed to the door. "He left."

Emily looked to the front door to confirm Benny had pointed to the *exit*.

"What? *When?*" she screeched.

"A minute ago. He does that. Once he hits a certain level of drunk, he disappears. He pulled a runner. The ol' Irish goodbye."

Emily gasped.

"No!"

She burst out of the bar, certain she'd find Sebastian waiting outside.

The sidewalk was empty except for one stumbling couple weaving their way home.

No Sebastian.

Emily threw her back against the wall.

Sonovabitch.

CHAPTER NINETEEN

Sebastian pulled his phone from his pocket and called his brother Garrett.

"Hello?" answered a sleepy voice.

"You awake?"

Garret groaned. "I *wasn't*. I guess I am now. What's up?"

"I'm walking home from the Rover. This part of town is a little sketchy, so if I drop the phone and you hear gunshots, come get me."

"Got it." Garrett yawned. "You drunk?"

Sebastian nodded and then realized his brother couldn't hear his nod.

"Yeah. What was your first clue? That it's midnight or because I left my truck at the bar and I'm walking home?"

"Yep. Those."

Sebastian heard the sound of a door opening as he passed a house and quickened his pace. He glanced behind him. No one followed.

"Don't you work tomorrow? Why are you out so late? Is Greta with you?" asked Garrett.

"No. We're done. Been weeks."

"Oh, right. That's why you keep showing up here. Sorry to hear that."

Sebastian scowled. "Really?"

"No. I couldn't stand her."

Sebastian hesitated, trying to decide how much he wanted to get into his story. He still had a long walk ahead of him.

"There's this other girl," he began.

"Uh oh. You got caught?"

"*No*, I've never cheated on anyone in my life. Unlike *Greta*."

"She was cheating on you?"

"Yeah, pretty sure. Not that it mattered. We have *nothing* in common."

"No kidding. I could have told you that months ago and
130

saved you some time."

"Whatever."

Sebastian weaved too close to the edge of the curb and slipped. He caught himself and looked around to see if anyone had noticed. It was dark. He walked faster.

"Hello?" said a voice.

Sebastian looked at his phone. Someone was on his phone.

"Hello?"

"So, who's the new girl?"

"Oh, hey, Garrett. What new girl?"

"The new girl you like."

Sebastian remembered now. *Emily.*

"She's—I dunno. I mean, I *know*... I know who she is—her name's Emily. She's just...I like her. I *really* like her. She's smart. And cute. And when she laughs, her eyes do this thing—"

"I get the picture," said Garrett, cutting him short.

Sebastian rubbed his face with his hand. Suddenly, he had the weird feeling he'd forgotten something—like he was supposed to *do* something.

Maybe something at work? Was that it?

He continued. "Problem is, though the Greta thing is dead, I'm still in her house. I need to find a place. I don't want to move into this new girl's place like a loser. I mean, not that she asked or anything."

"She has a place? Dude, move in there. Just to get out of Greta's."

"No. I'm not a damn giggle low...er, jigaglo... dammit...I mean, *gigolo.* And I just met her. We've sort of been hanging out, but I don't have a clean break yet, and it's just—I dunno. I don't want to mess up everything. I have to get out of Greta's house. She's, like, always trying to seduce me."

Garrett laughed. "Oh, that sounds *awful.*"

"Shut up. Greta and I never really gave a damn about each other, and now that we *officially* don't give a damn about each other, nothing has changed. That makes it hard to say no sometimes, you know? That stuff's confusing."

Garrett yawned again. "Dude, *you're* confusing. You're making no sense."

"She keeps pushing for sex. It's a pain in the ass."

"I'm not touching that."

"I should have been gone a long time ago. But every time I almost went, something came up, and I got sucked back in."

"Just when I thought I was out," said Garrett, in his best Michael Corleone voice. "*They pull me back in.*"

"I *really* like this Emily chick," said Sebastian, ignoring him. "But I'm not ready to do this all over again. I'm tired. I feel like I need to be by myself for a while. I need to find a place...and on the other hand, I think she might like this guy Marc I know from high school, which is weird, and I'm afraid I'll miss my chance with her."

"You're overthinking. Get the hell away from Greta; go move in with Cecily."

"Emily."

"*Emily*. Whatever."

Sebastian sighed. He looked up, surprised to find he was home. "I'm home. I'll let you go. You were no help, thanks."

"No problem, anytime. You can stay here for a while if you want, y'know."

Sebastian considered this as he walked up the steps to Greta's apartment. Living at his brother's would be a pain, but it might be time to bite the bullet.

"Thanks, man, I appreciate it. I'm going to do some hardcore apartment hunting, and if I can't find anything, I'll take you up on it. I gotta get out of here."

"Yup, 'night. Call me again this late, and I'll kill you."

He hung up.

"Night," said Sebastian to the dead phone. He felt his pockets for his keys. After a moment of panic, he found them and let himself in.

Greta wasn't there. Binker stretched out on the bed, sound asleep and snoring. He didn't flinch when Sebastian bumped into his boxes, and the kitchen items inside clattered. In addition to being fake blind, the dog was nearly fake deaf.

Sebastian stripped to his boxer briefs, grabbed a blanket, and went to the sofa to sleep. He lay there staring at the ceiling for a few minutes. Something was nagging him.

He was supposed to have done something.

He couldn't remember what.

Sebastian hummed as he fell asleep.

"Oompa, doompa, oopity doo... I got another drinky for you..."

Things went dark.

Then he woke.

"Where am I?" he said, looking around the living room.

He spotted Greta standing near the door.

Ah. Sofa. Got it.

"You just getting home?" he mumbled, looking at his watch. He squinted until his eyes closed.

It was four a.m.

"I passed out at Sydney's for a while," said Greta.

"Mm."

"You look drunk."

"*You* look drunk," he said without opening his eyes.

"You know you don't have to sleep on the sofa."

"We broke up," said Sebastian, barely moving his lips. His face was pressed into the pillow. He couldn't breathe. He turned on his back, gasping for air.

"I know. That doesn't mean you have to sleep out here."

Greta sat on the edge of the sofa and ran her fingernails through Sebastian's hair, scratching his scalp.

It felt good.

Maybe I can let her do that for a little bit longer...wait—

"*No,*" said Sebastian aloud, swatting at Greta's hand as if it was a bothersome fly. "Bad Greta. *No.* I'm not falling for your womanly willies anymore. No more touchy. Go away."

"I think it's feminine *wiles.* Not womanly willies."

"That too."

"Come on, come to bed," breathed Greta. "You'll hurt your back sleeping on this crappy sofa."

"*No.* Go away, She-Demon. Go. Shoo."

Greta stood.

"Come on, Sebby..."

"No means *no,*" said Sebastian, lifting his hand high enough off the sofa to snap his fingers to his palm, waving. "Buh-bye."

Greta huffed. Sebastian opened his eyes a slit and saw Greta standing over him, her hands on her hips. He closed his eyes again.

"Whatever," she said.

"*Whatever*," Sebastian echoed into his pillow.

He heard her go to the bathroom and rolled onto his back. He stared at the ceiling for a few minutes.

"Nice try, trying to seduce me when I'm drunk and sleepy," he called out to her.

There came no reply.

"We're broken up."

Silence.

"It's official, no confusion."

More silence.

"Line in the sand. Done. Splitsville. Over and out!"

Greta slammed the bedroom door.

Sebastian smiled.

"Exactly," he mumbled, rolling onto his opposite side. "That's what *I* said."

He closed his eyes and released a long, sleepy sigh.

CHAPTER TWENTY

The next night was Dart Night at the Irish Rover, and Sebastian appeared in good spirits. Emily didn't bring up the meeting that never happened or his sudden disappearance.

He'd been drunk.

He'd made a mistake.

Moving on...

She was partnered with Tompkins, the best dart player in the house. They'd won, no thanks to her, and she was ninety-five dollars richer after splitting the winnings. She'd nearly forgotten about Sebastian until she heard a voice from across the bar.

"Hey, *Emily*."

He sat by himself in the back. He and Benny had been knocked out of the running early.

Sebastian patted the bar stool next to him as she approached.

"Have a seat," he said.

"Poor you," she said, hopping on the stool. "I'm *so* sorry we had to kick your ass earlier."

Tompkins and Emily had *crushed* Sebastian and Benny early in the evening, and it felt good. She only had a couple of angry thoughts about being ditched by him during the game. Quick little thoughts. Hardly anything.

At least she'd beaten him.

Sebastian was good but not good enough to carry Benny past Tompkins. Emily was grateful for Benny; his presence ensured she wasn't the worst player in the house. Her game improved while his never did.

"You won. I mean, *Tompkins* won—Congrats," he teased.

She chuckled. "Fair enough. I know he gets the credit. But I *did* hit the closing bull's eye."

"Cheers."

The two of them clinked Chicken Clubs.

"So, you want to go somewhere quiet?" he asked after taking a sip.

Emily frowned.

"I'm not falling for *this* again."

"Falling for what?"

"I'm going to get my darts together and pay my tab. And you're going to disappear."

Sebastian's brow knit.

"Why would I do that?"

"It's what you did last night."

"I did? When?"

"Last night."

Sebastian snapped his fingers. *"That's* what I forgot to do. I knew there was something; it's been bothering me all day."

Emily looked up at the ceiling. *"You forgot me.* Wow. You sure know how to make a girl feel special."

He shook his head. "I'm sorry. I didn't mean it. I had a weird night last night."

Emily peered into his blue eyes.

He leaned forward until their noses touched.

"So you want to go somewhere?" he asked.

"Um..."

Emily looked from his left eye to his right, trying not to laugh.

"Hmmm...?"

He looked from her left eye to her right five times very quickly.

She pulled back, worried she'd burst out laughing and shower his face with spit. Not that he didn't deserve it.

"So, if I go get my pack, you'll be *here* when I get back?"

He nodded. "I am like a tree, grasshopper, rooted to this spot."

"Fine. You better be."

Emily strode to the front snug to grab her pack. She'd settled her bar tab earlier. She'd been testing a new theory; playing darts with only two drinks in her blood. Experimentation had identified a sweet spot for darts and drinking. She had to drink enough to relax but not *so* much that her game began to suffer.

She'd had two Chicken Clubs earlier in the evening and then stopped, and her game had been better than usual.

136

Science.

As Emily entered the snug, she ran into Benny. It felt like running into a rhinoceros.

"Hey," he said.

"Hey."

"What are you up to? You look crazy happy."

"Sebastian wants to go somewhere quiet," she whispered to him.

Benny laughed. "Oh, jeez, don't let me get in your way then. Run woman! Run to him!"

Emily laughed and trotted back to find Sebastian still sitting at the bar, staring into middle distance.

"Ready?" she asked.

He snapped from his thoughts.

"Yep."

He stood.

The two left the bar.

"Where do you want to go?" he asked.

"I don't know. I thought you had a spot in mind."

"Not really. I probably should have thought a little farther ahead."

"What were you thinking about when I came back? You looked deep in thought."

He sniffed. "You know how there's that candy called *Smarties*?"

She nodded.

"Well, they should make another one called *Dummy Bears*."

"So you *were* deep in thought."

"Yep. It's what I do. Someone has to."

Emily thought about his idea.

"There are lollipops called Dum Dums," she said.

"Ooh, I've seen those. Damn. Barely off the ground, and I already have competition."

"The makers of Gummy Bears will sue you into next year, anyway."

"Details for lawyers," said Sebastian, closing his eyes and shooing at the air.

They stopped walking in front of an alley a few doors down from the Irish Rover.

"Do we know where we're going?" she asked.

He stepped toward her, so close she needed to take a step back to keep from falling backward.

"I have an idea," he said in a conspiratorial whisper. He guided her gently to the alley.

"You're not going to mug me, are you?" she asked.

"Something like that."

Tucked in the alley, Emily's back to the wall, Sebastian kissed her, his lips lingering against hers, his body drawing closer. She felt the touch of his fingers on the back of her shoulder sliding downward along her naked arm. He took her hand in his and pulled back, searching her eyes.

"Okay?" he said.

Emily licked her lips.

"If I'd known you mugged like this, I'd have wandered outside your house at night wearing *all* my best jewelry."

"And nothing else?" asked Sebastian leaning in and kissing her neck.

She reached up to cradle his head, praying he'd never stop.

"I didn't say *and nothing else* because I thought it'd be corny," she mumbled.

"It was," Sebastian whispered between kisses. "I deeply regret saying it."

He worked his way back to Emily's mouth, and they kissed until she had to pull away to breathe.

"I have a pool table and a dart board," she said.

"Congratulations." He left a trail of kisses along her collarbone. "I have bad knees and a nine iron."

"No, I mean we could go to my house. It's quiet, the booze is free, and I have a pool table and a dart board."

Sebastian stopped. "I don't know how I can argue with that."

He took her hand and led her towards their cars. She had to break into a trot to keep up with his long strides until they reached the Rover parking lot.

"You can follow me in your truck," she said.

"Okay."

They walked toward their respective cars.

"Wait. How did you know I have a truck?"

Emily bit her lip.

Because I've been stalking you for months didn't sound right.

"I've seen you pull up before," she said, shrugging.

138

She slipped into her car and waited for Sebastian to pull out, then headed for her house, checking her mirror every few seconds to be sure she hadn't lost her tail.

She didn't turn on any music. She just chanted in her head.

Ohmygodohmygodohmygod..

Emily pulled into the driveway of her modest ranch house and stepped out of her car. She drew a calming breath.

Sebastian pulled beside her and met her on the walkway from the driveway to the door.

"This is your house?" he asked.

"No, but it looks easy to break into."

"Ha ha. No, I mean, it's nice."

"Thank you, it isn't anything special, that's for sure, but it works."

Emily opened the door, and Duppy walked over to say hi to the stranger.

"Hiya, puppy," said Sebastian, petting the old man.

"That's Duppy."

"Hey ya, Dupster, Duparama." Duppy leaned into Sebastian's ear-scratching, loving every moment of it.

"He seems nice. Nicer than some dogs I know," he added, muttering.

They stared at each other. The sudden passion in the alley had felt so natural, but now, in the glare of her kitchen lights, things grew awkward.

"You want a drink?" she asked.

"Is a bear Catholic?"

Confident scratching time had ended, Duppy padded back into the bedroom.

Emily kept cranberry in the house for homemade Chicken Clubs, and mixed two in pint glasses, the same way they served them at the Irish Rover.

She handed Sebastian his drink and gave him the nickel tour. Rather than walk him to the bedroom, she pointed down the hall and said, "Bedrooms and my office are back there."

She feared standing in the hallway, staring at her bed with Sebastian, would make her head explode.

"What happened to your wall?" asked Sebastian, pointing to the end of the hall and the drywall patch. Marc had fixed the wall, but she hadn't repainted.

Emily blushed at the memory.

"Oh, just an accident. Tripped over the dog." She chose not to share *who* tripped or the difficulties of walking with a girl wrapped around your waist.

Sebastian followed Emily to the basement, where she kept her new dartboard and the pool table.

"My parents moved to a smaller place and had nowhere to fit our old pool table, so I ended up with it."

"Nice," said Sebastian. He walked to the sliding glass door that led to the backyard and peered outside. "Okay if I go outside?"

"Sure," she said.

He tugged at the door, but it didn't move.

"I'm weak," he said.

Emily laughed, removed the half broom handle that served as her security system, and slid open the door.

"Now I feel a little better," he said.

They walked outside. The temperature was perfect, and the humidity had eased. The sky was clear, but for a few wispy clouds illuminated by the light of the nearly full moon.

She walked to the large free-standing hammock sitting on the brick patio and sat in it. Sebastian looked at the patio chairs and then joined her. They fell together, hips and shoulders touching, the sag making it impossible to separate.

Emily wanted to know so much about his feelings for her and his situation with Greta, but she knew poking him for answers would only make him more reticent to share. Instead, they sat there, sipping their Chicken Clubs, reclined, and staring at the stars.

He lifted his left arm and put it above Emily's head. Gently, he rested it against the top of her skull until she leaned forward and slipped it behind her. He used his feet to rock them back and forth. Emily appreciated the help; she couldn't reach the ground.

They swayed, silent, Emily's head nestled in the crook of his arm. After a while, she looked up and found Sebastian's eyes closed.

"Don't you have to go home?" she asked, her voice soft and sleepy. She, too, was tired.

She felt him shake his head before she heard him.

140

"No," he said.

She braced herself.

It was time to ask.

"What about Greta?"

He answered without hesitation.

"Greta and I broke up. I guess I thought you knew."

"You broke up?" she said, lifting her head to look at him. Suddenly, she felt very awake. "I don't get the Sebastian Newsletter. When did this happen?"

He shrugged. "Like a month ago. More than that, technically, but it's complicated. I still need to move out. It's a weird situation."

Emily stared at him.

"Over a month ago?"

He nodded.

"But you bought her an expensive handbag?"

"Hm?"

He seemed genuinely confused, and Emily began to doubt her eavesdropping skills. She also doubted the wisdom of continuing her story. She might look crazy, obsessing about the origins of a handbag.

"Greta was in the bar with an expensive orange purse. She said you bought it for her."

"*Me*? That's hilarious on several levels. I know the one you're talking about, but I assumed she bought it for herself. It wasn't me. I didn't even know it was expensive."

"Huh," said Emily.

They rocked again. Emily returned her head to his shoulder.

"You know, I could help you find a place."

He looked at her. "You know an apartment?"

"No, but I could help you find one. Heck, I could never *rest* until you found one."

Sebastian chuckled.

So much for playing coy.

Emily snuggled and placed her head and left hand on

Sebastian's chest. She felt Sebastian kiss the top of her head.

She tilted her head back; the light spilling from the basement was bright enough to see Sebastian staring back at her.

Tentatively, their lips brushed. Emboldened, they leaned into each other, kissing more desperately until they gripped at each other like lost lovers reunited. Sebastian rolled toward her, the weight of his body on hers enflaming her passion. His hand ran down the side of her body, and she felt him stroke her hip, grabbing her buttocks and pulling her closer to him. Feverishly, she began to unbutton his white work shirt.

"Wait, wait," Sebastian said.

He rolled back to lie beside her, both of them breathing heavily.

"What?" She'd waited for this moment for so long stopping didn't feel like a viable option.

He slipped his arm out from behind her and rubbed his face with both his hands. "I want to do this right."

She scoffed. "I thought we were doing a pretty good job."

Sebastian smirked. He gave her a quick kiss.

"Can I sleep here?"

She squinted at him. "Are you asking yourself or me?"

"You. Do you mind if I crash here tonight?"

"No. Now can we get back to our regularly scheduled programming?"

Sebastian stroked her cheek, and Emily closed her eyes, drinking in the feel of his touch.

Then, nothing happened.

She opened her eyes. He was still looking at her.

"Let's go to bed. Is that cool?"

Emily paused, wondering if it was a trick question.

"Yes."

She rocked out of the hammock and held out a hand to help him. He stood, groaning with the effort of pulling his lanky frame from the depths of the sagging netting.

He picked up his glass, and she grabbed hers. They went upstairs, and she led him to her bedroom.

"Can I borrow your bathroom?" he asked.

She turned on the bedroom light.

"You want to sleep over, and now you want to use the bathroom, too? I never dreamed you were so high-maintenance."

He chuckled.

"Oh, you have no idea."

He entered her en-suite and closed the door.

Emily burst into action.

142

She stripped her clothes and threw on a simple chemise made from t-shirt material. She thought it would appear sexy but casual. If Sebastian came out of the bathroom to find her squeezed into a black teddy, it would look desperate. She jogged down the hall to the spare bathroom, washed her face, and brushed her teeth with the new toothbrush and toothpaste she kept for guests. As she scrubbed, Emily realized they'd done everything wrong. He should have used the guest toothbrush. Now it was too late.

Emily ran through her nightly ritual as if timed for speed. She bolted out of the guest bathroom, trying hard not to sound like a herd of cattle galloping down the hallway, and found her purse. She rummaged inside for her travel makeup and bolted back down the hall.

She poked her head in her bedroom.

Sebastian was still in the bathroom.

Excellent.

She spun and reached the guest bathroom with one leap and re-applied mascara, blush, and lipstick.

Hm? No, I always sleep in full makeup. Why?

She heard the toilet flush in the other bathroom. Panicking, she placed the makeup in the spare tub and pulled the curtain to hide it; no time to return it to her purse. She ran to the bedroom, bouncing off the hallway wall, and dove into the bed, thankful Duppy had chosen the dog bed in her office over her bed this evening. She arranged herself on the bed like a bouquet of flowers for maximum beauty.

Emily looked up sleepily as Sebastian walked out of the bathroom like Sleeping Beauty rising from her long slumber.

"I borrowed some toothpaste. Just on my finger," he said.

She opened her mouth to mention the spare toothbrush in the other bathroom and then remembered she no longer had one.

Sebastian walked to the bedside opposite hers.

"I'm going to sleep in my underwear," he announced,

pausing a moment before undoing his belt and letting his khakis drop to the ground with a jangly thud. His pants slid from his skinny frame as if they'd been straining to stay on his hips.

Emily didn't say a word. She rolled over and turned off the light on her nightstand.

Sebastian removed his half-unbuttoned work shirt and undershirt and slid into bed beside her.

She rolled on her side to face him.

He rolled to face her.

He leaned in and kissed her on her forehead.

"Good night," he said, patting her hand.

Emily lay there, stunned

Did he just pat my hand?

Two seconds later, she heard his breathing grow heavy.

He was asleep.

Asleep.

She wanted to scream.

Excuse me, sir, but could I draw your attention to the half-naked girl beside you?

CHAPTER TWENTY-ONE

Emily awoke to find a man in her bed.

The kitchen light at the end of the hall provided enough illumination for her to confirm she wasn't alone. She ogled the sleeping Sebastian, her eyes following the curve of his tanned neck and watching his chest rise and fall as he breathed. She liked the little tuft of dark blonde hair on his perky pecs. She liked the little scar on his left cheekbone.

She liked that he was in her bed.

She studied him until it occurred to her that, should he open his eyes and find her staring at him, he would *freak out.*

She looked away and stared at the ceiling. She breathed into her hand and smelled her breath.

Yikes.

She eased a leg off the bed to the floor. The old hardwood floor creaked beneath her weight. Sebastian grunted in his sleep.

She froze.

She tiptoed into the hall bathroom when he fell still again, shut the door, and turned on the light.

She brushed her teeth with the guest toothbrush a second time. She fixed the smeared mascara under her eyes and searched for beauty products in the mirrored cabinet. *Nothing.* Why had she never thought to keep an emergency beauty kit in the spare bathroom? Sneaking into her en-suite bathroom would mean more creaking floorboards.

Emily pinched her cheeks to raise their color and then bit at her lip, thinking the same trick might apply. She took a step toward the mirror and accidentally kicked the metal trashcan, which clattered to its side and bounced back and forth like an infernal clock pendulum.

The noise was *horrendous.*

She dove to stop the can from clanging and clipped her forehead on the sink as she dipped.

She barked a low, guttural grunt.

The blow sent her arching back in the opposite direction as if struck by an uppercut to her jaw. Her left hand clutched her throbbing forehead. Her right slapped across her mouth to stop herself from howling in surprise and pain. She stumbled back from the sink, her heel jamming against the tub, clipping her legs from beneath her. Tumbling backward, she grabbed for the shower curtain to stop her fall, ripping it from the rod with a jangling succession of snapping clasps, punctuated by the hollow thuds of her elbows and head smacking the shower insert.

She lay perpendicular across the tub, covered by the shower curtain and rod, her legs over the edge, dangling above the floor.

"Emily?" called a voice outside the door.

She lifted her chin and smacked the back of her head into the wall a second time. She was out of breath. Who knew trying *not* to die in a tragic bathroom accident was fantastic exercise? Funny, she'd never seen *that* workout video.

She noticed a compact sitting in the tub beside her. She'd forgotten she'd hidden her beauty products in the tub the night before.

"Emily?" called Sebastian again. "Are you okay?"

"I'm fine," she called as cheerily as possible. "I'm sorry I woke you. I knocked over something."

"Uh, okay..."

He sounded dubious. She knew, short of pushing a grandfather clock into a pile of china dishes, noises like the one she'd made didn't exist in nature.

She hauled herself out of the tub to the music of clattering plastic clasps. She re-hung the rod and curtain and inspected her head in the mirror. A small egg had already appeared near the hairline of her left temple. She touched it and winced.

She used the makeup in the bathtub to perform rapid maintenance on her face *and* the lump.

She righted the trashcan, took one last look in the mirror and opened the door to make her way back to the bedroom.

Sebastian sat up in bed.

"Decide to do a little home remodeling?" he asked.

Emily laughed. "I fell. I'm sorry if I woke you."

146

She left out the part where she probably had a concussion.

"I woke up in a strange house to the sound of the roof caving in. Happens all the time. You okay?"

She nodded and crawled into bed. He turned on his side to face her.

"Come here," he said, lifting his arm. "Tuck in."

Emily turned to her opposite side to spoon. He draped his arm over her and pulled her close to him.

She lay there tucked against him, his hand close to her breasts. She shifted so her right breast would bump against his fingers. It was like dipping bait in the water and waiting for a bite.

She felt a nibble on her neck.

The nibble turned into kisses.

Here we go...

She felt Sebastian's hands slip under her chemise, warm fingers dancing across her nipple. She turned to him, and they kissed.

Yes, yes, yes...

He slid her chemise towards her chest and kissed her belly. Sliding his fingers under the hip of her thong, he pulled it gently so she could feel the tug between her legs. She moaned and rolled towards him. Sliding her hand down his side, her fingertips slipped beneath the elastic of his boxer briefs.

That's when the phone rang.

Sebastian's phone.

Emily froze.

No, no, no...

"I better get that," he said, his breathing erratic. He shifted his hips away from her and threw one of his long legs over the bed.

She closed her eyes.

Two seconds. Two seconds longer, and at least, I would have known what he brought to the party.

"I'll be right back," said Sebastian.

"Okay."

What else could she say?

She swallowed, her blood racing.

Sebastian snatched his discarded pants from the floor and pulled his phone from the pocket as he disappeared into her ensuite bath.

Emily lay in bed, staring at the ceiling.

No conversation drifted from her bathroom.

Weird.

A moment later, he emerged, *wearing his pants.*

"I borrowed some mouthwash this time," he said.

She tried not to panic.

Keep it light. He doesn't know it's been two freakin' years...

"I'm keeping a list. So far, you owe me four ninety-eight," she said.

"What do you want to do today? I don't have to work."

"Uh..." Emily sat up, her eyes tracing every curve and contour of his bare chest.

Several ideas came to mind, all too crude to say aloud.

"I kinda liked what we *were* doing."

"Can't," said Sebastian running a hand through his hair and looking for his shirt.

Emily tried to read his expression.

Is he kidding?

"*Can't?*" she asked.

"Not until I'm out of Greta's house. I almost messed up there. You're so damn gorgeous—"

"So you *are* still dating?" Emily scrambled to sit higher.

"*No,*" said Sebastian, waving his hands in front of him to emphasize his answer. "Not at *all.* That's been over for over a month, like I said. It's just..." Sebastian bobbed his head from side to side, trying to find the words to finish his sentence.

"You need a clean break first?" prompted Emily.

Sebastian nodded. "Right. It doesn't feel right to be here and then be there... It feels *creepy*, you know?"

"Creepy," echoed Emily, rolling the word around her brain.

Emily released a loud sigh and flopped back down into her pillows.

"I guess. But I don't know how you were able to stop."

"Practice," muttered Sebastian.

"What? Did you say *practice*?"

"Nothing. It wasn't easy." He slid his hand across Emily's flat stomach and kissed her cheek.

"You better cut that out," she warned.

He chuckled. "So, what *do* you want to do today?"

148

"Besides jump your bones? For starters, I make some mean French toast."

"Really?"

She perked. "You like French toast?"

"No."

They laughed.

"Hm. Well, I'm glad we're both morning people. We have that in common."

He nodded. "I've always been a morning person. It drives me crazy when people sleep in."

"Ooh, I know—we can go out in the boat. Float around, get a tan."

He pointed at her. "Nice. Perfect. Public. I can't be trusted alone with you here."

"Or we could stay here... you look *hungry*," she purred.

He sighed.

"Maybe we *should* stay here," he murmured, tracing her hipbone with his finger.

She took a sharp breath, and he patted her rump—two quick taps.

"Nope, get up!" He clapped his hands together. "Let's get this party started."

Emily found her cooler and put ice and iced tea into it. She threw herself into chores to keep from dragging Sebastian back to bed. His plan to start their relationship "right" was romantic, sweet, and *incredibly frustrating*.

While she searched her cabinets for snacks, Sebastian found his cell phone and checked it.

"Nine messages," he muttered.

"Nine? Work emergency?"

Sebastian took a closer look. He shook his head and put the phone in his pocket.

"No, nothing important."

Emily opened her mouth to ask who'd called that morning, but she thought she knew. She chose not to invoke that specter.

They took Sebastian's truck to the dock where Farker the Parker sat, bobbing in the water, patiently waiting for Emily to ram it into something.

They tooled into the Severn River and found a large cove where they could drop anchor and float. She produced a small radio from the storage beneath the steering wheel and turned it to a local station.

"I can't believe it's so warm," she said, removing her shirt. She'd spent half the morning deciding which bikini did her cleavage the most justice. She tilted her head back and adopted a sexy sunning pose.

Sebastian sat on the rail of the boat and took his shirt off. He crunched, and Emily watched as the skin on his stomach tucked into a dozen rolls of skin, each barely thicker than a pencil—not an ounce of fat on him. She found herself trapped somewhere between aroused and jealous; the bastard probably didn't even diet.

"Yeah, this is perfect," he said.

Emily peeked at his chest, remembering fondly her head nestled there.

Sebastian's phone rang. He pulled it from his pocket, glanced at it, hit *ignore* and put it back into his pocket.

He stretched and rubbed his eyes.

"I shouldn't be out here," he said, putting his hands on his hips as he scanned the shoreline. "I should be looking for an apartment. I don't have time to search on work days."

"You know," Emily said, slipping off the boat's rail. She wrapped her arms around his waist. "You *could* move into my house. As a roommate."

Time froze as Emily waited for him to answer. She felt crazy for suggesting it. It was much too early in their relationship for him to move in, but she couldn't stop from entertaining the idea. It would also be nice to take a bite out of her mortgage.

He shook his head. "I can't do that. I can't bounce from one girl's house to another's."

"Oh, I mean in the spare room," she said, pressing herself

against him. "I have a guest room for hot, visiting monks."

He snickered and draped his arms around her shoulders.

"Riiight. That could work. We could station our moms in the hallway to keep us from sneaking into each other's rooms."
150

She tilted her head, and Sebastian kissed her.

"And I promise you, I am *not* a monk," he added.

"I wish I were taller," said Emily. At six-two, Sebastian had to hunch to reach her lips.

He waggled his eyebrows. "I know where you can get another three inches, baby."

"Oh *baby*."

Emily burst into giggles. She must have sensed this silly side beneath his cool-guy-at-the-bar exterior. Maybe that was her mysterious connection to him.

Sebastian pursed his lips and sucked in his cheeks, aping a male model. "No, I change my mind," he said in a terrible French accent. "You cannot have me. I am too beautiful."

"Oh Se*bas*tian," she begged. "Please, please pity me, a poor peasant girl..."

"Alright. I will do this for you," he said, wrapping one of his ridiculously long legs around her body as if he were a monkey and she was a tree. His eyes grew wide and crazy as he moved his hips.

"I'll fly you to the moon and back in my jet-powered love machine," he murmured, petting her hair into a tangled mess. The more she laughed, the more he poured it on. She felt like she was being leg-humped by a Great Dane; only her whole body was the leg.

"You want to be one with me? You want I should pour a bucket of love potion number ten on you?" he asked, holding her so tightly she could barely breathe.

"I think that's love potion number nine," she croaked.

"I'm out of nine. We're on ten now."

They tumbled to the deck, rolling like giggling teenagers.

"You're an idiot," said Emily.

"*You're* an idiot," said Sebastian.

"No you aaahh," she said in a Boston accent, imitating an old *Saturday Night Live* skit.

"No you aaahhh," he echoed, catching the reference.

They looked at each other, uncontrollable grins on their faces, when Sebastian's phone rang.

He huffed, climbed to his feet to look at his phone, and shut off the ringer.

Emily pulled herself up and sat on the side of the boat.

"We should have grabbed some food," said Sebastian.

She nodded. "Hm. I am getting hungry."

"Hey, Ms. Trivia, do you know why McDonald's fries are so good?"

Emily shook her head.

"Because they add a tiny bit of sugar to the salt."

"Really? I didn't know that."

Sebastian nodded. "Put that in your trivia pipe and smoke it."

They sunned for another hour until their hunger drove them back to Emily's for lunch. As they walked in, Sebastian paused and looked toward the back of the house.

"I'm going to get a shower if that's okay."

"No problem."

"I'd ask you to join me, but I'm only human," he said, pulling her to him and kissing the top of her head.

She collapsed against him. "That's okay. I'll make lunch."

"Are you sure? I don't want you to have to make something—we can go out?"

"No, I love to cook, and I have a camera in the shower to record you, so I won't miss anything."

"Excellent. I'll remember to flex."

As soon as Sebastian closed the bathroom door, Emily ran. She made hamburgers for lunch and, for the pièce de résistance, reproduced McDonald's fries.

She julienned three potatoes and fried them in a pan with olive oil. She guessed McDonald's didn't use olive oil in their deep fryers, but she didn't have any vegetable oil or a deep fryer. While she waited for the potatoes to turn golden, she defrosted burgers she'd made a few days earlier and put them in a pan. When the potatoes were ready, she put them on a paper towel and patted the oil from them. She arranged the fries on a cookie tray, sprinkled them with salt, added a pinch of sugar, and put them in the oven.

Sebastian walked into the kitchen, his hair wet.

"Whatcha makin'? It smells awesome out here."

"Hamburgers and fries."

"Oh perfect."

With Emily's guidance, Sebastian found the plates and set the table. She showered, and by the time she returned, things were ready. She brought the food to the plates, and they sat

152

down, starving.

Sebastian took a bite of his burger, raved that it was delicious, and then popped a fry into his mouth. Emily laser-focused on his face, waiting for him to erupt into euphoria over her authentic McDonald's fries.

Sebastian's chewing slowed. He swallowed. He slipped another fry into his mouth. He chewed.

He scowled.

He looked confused, but she wasn't sure; it might have been the face people made when fighting a gag reflex.

Sebastian swallowed hard and looked at her.

"Did you put *sugar* on these?" he asked.

Whoops.

"You said McDonald's put sugar on their fries?"

"I might have remembered that wrong," said Sebastian, laughing. "I'm sorry, you were so sweet to cook, but these are *terrible.*"

She offered him a sheepish smile.

Sebastian's phone buzzed, and he reached for it. He sighed.

"I'm sorry. This is like the twentieth message. I should probably check them."

"No problem."

She stared at the fries on his plate. They were terrible. Too much sugar.

Damn.

Sebastian wandered into the other room as he listened to his messages. He paced. He wandered out of the kitchen and wandered back. Finally, he sighed and pulled the phone from his ear.

"I have to go," he said.

"Really? Work?"

He shook his head.

"Worse. Apparently, Greta was robbed. Or carjacked. I don't know. It depends on which message you listen to, but she's freaking out. I have to see if she's okay. She sounds hysterical."

Emily felt a stab of jealousy.

"Oh," she mumbled.

"This is why I said I needed a clean break."

She nodded.

He hugged her, gently rocking her back and forth as he squeezed. "I know she isn't technically my problem, but she's upset and crying and might be hurt. This is the stuff I worried about—as long as I'm at her house, I'm the first person she calls."

Emily nodded. "I know; you're right. You're doing the right thing." She tried to think of several other ways to sound understanding but ran out of synonyms and the urge.

Sebastian took two huge bites from his burger, nearly finishing it. He walked to the front door and paused as Emily followed. He gave her a quick kiss on the lips.

"I'm sorry," he said, wiping a dab of mustard he'd left on her mouth. "She's not a strong person like you."

Emily offered a crooked smile as Sebastian went to his truck and pulled out of her driveway.

"*Yea* for strong women," she said, closing the door.

154

CHAPTER TWENTY-TWO

Sebastian entered Greta's apartment, empty but for Binker, who was asleep on the sofa. Everything felt normal; the house was messy but not ransacked. It didn't appear anyone had robbed the house.

Sebastian called for Greta. No answer. He checked his phone. Her last message had arrived an hour previous. The last message he'd heard beeping at Emily's had been his mother, but the nineteen before that had been Greta. Had she been calling from the hospital? Her texts made no sense but implied robbery and injury.

He dialed Greta's number, but she didn't answer.

He called her sister but couldn't reach her or her mother. He kicked around the apartment, becoming more and more agitated. He didn't know whether to be angry or worried.

After two hours, he tried Greta's phone a fifth time. She answered.

"Where are you?" he asked.

"I went to my sister's. Where were *you*? I called you, like, a thousand times."

Sebastian paused. It sounded as if Greta was out of breath. "You're at your sister's now? I just ran home to see if you were okay. Are you okay?"

Sebastian heard a succession of muffled rustling noises. It sounded as if Greta had covered the phone and said something. He thought he heard a car door.

"I said are you okay?"

"No," said Greta, her voice cracking. "I'm not okay. Where

were you?"

Sebastian decided now was not the time to get into his new relationship with Emily.

"I'm at home. Do you need me, or are you okay? What happened?"

Sebastian heard music rise in the background.

"Are you in your car?"

"Yes. I'm coming home. Are you there?"

"Yes. I just told you I am."

"I'll be there in a second. Wait for me, please, baby?"

Sebastian sighed. "I'm here."

He sat next to Binker, who crawled into his lap. He stroked the dog until he heard a series of dull thuds on the front door. He stood slowly, giving the dog time to scuttle off his lap, and opened the door.

Greta stood perched on crutches, a large brace around her knee.

"What *happened*?" he asked.

As soon as Greta saw him, her eyes welled with tears.

"Oh baby," she said, hobbling into the house. "I'm so glad you're here. I feel so much *safer*."

"What happened to your leg? You said you were robbed? What's going on?"

Greta shook her head and waved her hand at him.

"I'm *freaking* out. I'll be right back. I have to relax. Can you order us a pizza or something for dinner? Please?"

Sebastian opened his mouth and then shut it.

"I'm *starving*. Please?" she pushed.

"Fine. I'll call. Pepperoni, okay?"

Greta nodded and crutched her way into the bedroom. He heard the shower and stared angrily at the closed bedroom door.

Why did she need to take a shower before she answered his questions?

He made a delivery order and reclaimed his waiting spot on the sofa. After fifteen minutes, Greta reappeared on her crutches, wearing only a kimono and her knee brace. When she moved the crutches forward, the robe opened at the bottom, giving Sebastian a view of her naked body.

"Could you put some clothes on? The pizza guy is going to be here."

She flopped onto the sofa. The top of her robe fell open,

exposing one breast. She eased her bum leg on the table and then leaned back, panting.

"*You* try and get dressed with this thing wrapped around your knee. What, am I supposed to pull yoga pants over it?"

"*No*, but you could put some freaking shorts on," said Sebastian. "And your boobs are hanging out."

Greta looked down at her chest and adjusted the robe.

"Like you've never seen me naked before. You're so *mean*."

"I'm not *mean*. I'm just *not your boyfriend*. Do we have to go over this every day?"

Greta's eyes welled with tears again as she glared at him.

"Oh, do you mean we have to go over it every day that *you're living in my apartment*?"

Sebastian closed his eyes and calmed himself.

"You're right. You're totally right. I need to move out. I know. I'm trying."

"*No*." Greta groped at him, looking for a hug. "I didn't mean it. I told you to take as long as you need to find a new place, and I want you here now."

She sobbed. He lightly patted her back, staring at the ceiling, imagining this was what new parents felt like at two in the morning, waiting for a baby to calm down.

"Don't cry. Tell me what happened."

She took a ragged breath. "I drove to work to do a few things, and I was walking back to my car, and this guy came out of nowhere and grabbed my purse and knocked me down. Some other guy saw him and screamed out 'Hey!' and he got scared and ran away, but I twisted my knee really bad."

Greta pointed to her knee, sniffling.

"Otherwise, you're okay?"

"I guess. But I'm so scared to be alone now. Please promise me you'll stay. Don't move out."

He sighed. "Greta, I can't stay here forever. You have to get on with your life, and so do I."

She heaved a mighty sob and fell against him. "I don't want to get on with my life. I want us to be together again."

She took his hand and led it beneath her robe to her breasts. She kissed his neck.

He recoiled. "Greta! I'm sorry about your knee. I feel terrible for you. I do. But I can't—"

He wanted to tell her about Emily. It might force her to face the reality of their situation. But, as she sat there, robe akimbo, eyes swollen with tears, he couldn't bear to upset her any further. He couldn't stand the tearful, moaning conversation his confession would inspire.

Someone knocked on the door. Sebastian grabbed a blanket from a nearby chair and threw it on top of her.

"Cover up. Pizza's here."

"You'll stay tonight?" begged Greta. "Please? Please?"

"Well, yeah," said Sebastian, opening the door. "I haven't found a place yet."

"*Yea!*"

Greta's happy yelp drew the attention of the pizza guy.

"Everybody loves pizza," said the delivery man, ogling her.

Sebastian took the box.

"Yea," he muttered.

158

CHAPTER TWENTY-THREE

Ten minutes after Sebastian left, Emily grabbed her phone and called Kady.

"He stayed over?" asked Kady.

Emily grinned so hard she thought her cheeks would break.

"Yep!" she squeaked.

"And did you..."

"No."

"No?"

"He says he wants to wait until he's got his own place and a clean break from Greta."

"So he's still dating Greta?"

"No, they broke up a month ago, but he feels weird because he's still living in her house... I dunno. We had a good time otherwise."

"It's sweet, I guess. He must really like you if he wants to do things right."

"I don't disagree, but try explaining that to my hormones when he's lying in bed with me."

Kady snickered.

"Greta has some hold on him," Emily added. "She worries me."

"What do you mean?"

"I think she's trying to get him back."

"*Ooh.* That's not good. Not when he's in her house."

"Gives her home-field advantage."

"Exactly."

Emily grimaced. "I mean, there's no sign he *wants* to be with her anymore. But she could muddy his path to me, if you know what I mean."

"Yeah—Hold on a second."

Emily heard Kady and Joe talking. It sounded as if Joe was going out, and Kady was wondering why and where.

She heard the slam of Kady's screen door.

"Em? You still there?" asked Kady, returning to their conversation.

"Yes. Something wrong with Joe?"

Her friend sighed. "He came downstairs with his hair all done, smelling like cologne. Says he's going to help a friend pick out new bar furniture or something."

"Cologne?"

"That's what I'm saying."

Emily sighed. "Screw this. Hang up with me, right now, and follow his ass."

"What?"

"Get in your car and *follow* him. You can't sit around wondering if something is up all the time. Just *follow* him."

"Oh, that's a good idea," said Kady, whispering.

"*Go.* Call me when you can and let me know what's going on."

"I *will.*"

The phone went dead.

Emily sat staring at her phone.

What is wrong with the world? Why are relationships so hard?

She heard a knock and jogged to her door, hoping it was Sebastian.

It was Marc.

"Oh, it's you," she said.

He scowled. "Don't be too excited."

"Sorry. What's up?" she asked, letting him in.

"I'm bored. I was wondering—"

Emily's phone rang, and she held up an index finger to put his thought on hold. He immediately wandered to her kitchen and started picking at the fries scattered on the cookie tray.

Kady's name appeared on her caller ID.

"Where are you?" answered Emily.

"I'm in the parking lot at the Mexican restaurant on Route 2. Joe went inside."

"Did you see anyone else?"

"No, that's the problem. The windows are dark, and if I go in, he'll see me the second I walk in the door. I don't want to give him a chance for a cover story. I want to catch him *cold*."

"Hmm..." Emily mulled the situation while she watched

160

Marc demolish the half-eaten hamburger she'd planned on finishing.

"I have an idea. Marc just showed up. We'll drive there, and Marc can go in. Joe doesn't know him."

Kady gasped. "That's *brilliant*. I'm parked across the street at the car wash."

"We'll take Marc's truck." Emily watched Marc as he opened the refrigerator and drank orange juice directly from the jug.

"Seriously?" she asked.

He peeked at her from behind the inverted bottle and lowered it.

"Sorry. You always have such good orange juice."

"Did you bring your truck?" she asked.

"Yeah. You need me to haul something?"

"No, I need you to run a secret covert operation for Kady."

Marc straightened. "Kady from the Rover?"

Emily nodded.

"She's a cutie. Whatever you need."

Emily put the phone back to her ear. "Okay, he's in. We'll meet you at the car wash parking lot, and Marc can drop me off with you and then go over to the restaurant."

"Great, see you in a bit," said Kady.

Emily took a moment to freshen up, and then she and Marc headed off in his enormous truck. Luckily they didn't need to sneak up on Joe—the truck was about as subtle as a jackhammer.

"Those fries were weird," said Marc as they drove.

Emily scowled. "You ate them all."

"Well, *duh*, but they were, like, sweet or something—?"

Emily didn't want to talk about the damn sugar fries anymore. She cut him short by explaining Kady's problem and what he could do to help.

"You'll go in, find out who Joe is meeting with, maybe take a picture of the situation if you can, and then report back to us."

"Kady thinks her boyfriend is cheating on her?"

She nodded.

"Do girls spy on their boyfriends like this all the time?"

Emily shrugged. "Only if you idiots force us to, I guess."

Marc grimaced. "Yikes." He fell silent for a few minutes and then asked, "You think Kady's going to be single soon, then?"

She looked at him. "I don't know if I want to do that to her. She already has one horndog."

"What? I told you I'm looking for *love*. I haven't cheated on anyone in like, I dunno... like two or three months."

Emily put her hand on her chest.

"Wow. What a show of restraint."

"I know. See?"

She sighed. "You guys do what you want, but you can't hit it and quit it. You have to *promise* me."

Marc held up his hand. "Scouts' honor."

Emily eyeballed him.

"Were you ever a Boy Scout?"

He twisted his lips and looked away. "No."

They pulled up to Kady's car. Emily hopped out and ran to Kady's passenger door, opening it wide enough to poke in her head.

"What's Joe wearing?" she asked.

"Oh, a light blue polo and khaki shorts."

Emily closed the door without latching it, and Marc rolled down his window.

"The guy you're looking for has brown hair, medium build, medium height, and is wearing a light blue polo and khaki pants."

"Got it. Hi Kady!" he screamed at Kady's car.

Kady leaned into her passenger seat and looked up, waving.

"Hey, Marc!" she called back.

Emily shok her head.

This won't end well.

No time to worry now.

"Okay, *go*," she said, slapping Marc on the shoulder.

Marc saluted her and rolled up his window. As his truck pulled away, Emily settled herself in Kady's car.

"This sucks. I'm so sorry, Kady."

Kady shrugged. "I don't know. I know it's over. In a way, it's good. We've been falling out of love for a while now."

"Why don't you break up with him?"

"I guess I want there to be no question. If I prove he's a cheat, we don't have to have long conversations about what ended us."

"That's true, I guess."

"Every time I break up with someone because it doesn't feel

162

right, I question my feelings the second they're out the door. Just once, I want to have things nice and clean."

Twenty minutes later, the girls saw Joe's truck pull out of the Mexican Restaurant and turn left. He made a U-turn around the median and returned to where the girls waited.

Marc hopped out of his truck and jumped into Kady's back seat.

"Okay, whatcha got?" asked Emily, turning to face him.

He clapped his hands together.

"This is so *cool.*"

Emily scowled. "What. Do. You. *Have*?"

"Right. Okay. There was a guy in a light blue polo sitting at the bar. I wasn't sure it was Joe because, you know, lots of people wear polos."

Marc sat between them, hunched at the end of the seat, his face inches from theirs. He fell silent until Emily couldn't take it anymore.

"So...*was it?*"

"Was it what?"

"Was it *Joe.*"

"Oh." He grinned. "That's the *smart* part. I went up, kind of close to him, and called out *Hey Joe!*"

Emily gaped. "Oh no. You didn't *talk* to him, did you?"

He shook his head. "He looked at me, but I pretended to wave at someone on the other side of the restaurant."

"Aahh," said Kady. "*Nice.*"

Marc tapped his forehead. "That's some *spy* stuff, right there."

"Okay, so we know it's him. Was anyone with him?" asked Emily.

"Well, yes and no. When I first walked in, a girl was walking away from where he was sitting at the bar. After she left, he sat at the bar with half a glass of white wine, and there was another glass next to him like someone had been there, so I'm pretty sure the girl walking away had been with him."

"She never came back?" asked Kady.

"No."

Emily groaned. "Did you see what she looked like?"

Marc beamed. "I took a picture of her."

Kady's eyes popped. "Show us!"

Marc flipped to the photo and held it up for them see.

They peered at his phone. The bar appeared to be traveling eighty miles an hour; the photo was barely more than a series of colorful streaks. A dark, blurry figure in the center of the picture walked away from the camera.

Emily squinted at Marc.

"That could be *Big Foot*."

"I told you, I only saw her for a second and only from behind," he said, yanking away the phone. "She had dark hair."

"Okay. Then what?"

"Joe waited a minute or two, finished his white wine, and then walked off in the same direction she went. So, there's big problems right there."

"What are you talking about? What big problems?" asked Emily.

He shook his head with disapproval.

"What kind of dude drinks white wine?"

"Oh, for godssake," said Emily. "Where did he go?"

"I followed him. He went out the back of the restaurant. There was a fire exit back there that was propped open."

"Weird," said Kady.

"He went to the far end of the parking lot and got into the back of a black car. A Hyundai I think." Marc grimaced and looked at his phone. "I'm better with trucks."

He flipped to the next picture.

"Then this happened," he said, holding up the photo.

The girls looked at the phone. It was another blurry photo, though not as blurry as the first. The license plate of the car was readable.

"It's a car," said Emily.

"Yeah, but that's not the important part," said Marc.

He paused, waiting for the girls to guess. When it became clear he was on permanent pause, Emily pushed the phone aside so she could look him in the eye.

"What's the important part?"

He moved the phone back in front of Emily and smiled.

"It's *moving*," he revealed.

"What's moving?"

"The *car*. It's rocking."

Emily looked at the phone and then back at Marc.

164

"How can we tell the car is rocking from a photo?"

"Yeah. I probably should have taken a video."

Kady frowned. "I don't understand. The car was moving?"

"*Rocking.* I'm so sorry, Kady," he said, leaning forward to put his hand on her thigh. "He was having sex with someone in the car."

Emily watched his hand and rolled her eyes.

Kady's jaw fell slack.

"*No.* You're *kidding* me." Kady looked at Emily. "He's having sex in a car like a teenager? In the parking lot of a Mexican Restaurant?"

"Gross," agreed Emily. She looked at Marc. "Are you sure?"

He nodded. "I can't prove it, but unless they were wrestling or something—the car was a rockin' so I didn't go a knockin'."

He glanced at Kady with puppy dog eyes.

"I am so, so sorry, Kady." He reached to touch her thigh again, and Emily slapped his hand away. He scowled and rubbed the back of his hand.

Kady shook her head, staring at the center console.

"This is unbelievable. So who was it?"

Marc flipped his palms toward the roof. "I don't know. He got out, went to his car, and drove off. I *can* tell you he was, like, *fluffy*."

Emily scowled. "*Fluffy*?"

"You know," said Marc, motioning to his hair. "His hair was all fluffy and messed up, his shirt was untucked. He was all deviled."

"*Disheveled*," corrected Emily.

Marc nodded. "Yep, that."

"What about the girl? Any info that might help us figure out who *she* is?"

"No. She left, too."

"Shoot. We could have followed her," said Emily.

"I didn't even think of that." Marc slapped the seat beside him and looked up, his eyes wide. He pointed at his phone.

"Hey, I have her license plate."

Emily shook her head. "Unfortunately, that's useless unless you have connections at the DMV."

"What about a cop? Anyone know a cop who owes them favors?"

The girls shook their heads.

Marc scowled. "Really? When people spy in the movies, someone always has a friend who knows someone who can look up a plate number."

Emily offered Kady a withering glance.

"You know what—Joe headed toward home. You should go. You need to ask him where he's been so we can see how ridiculous his lies are."

Kady frowned. "But why? I know he's cheating on me."

"It's ninety-eight percent probable, but first, a shaking car isn't one hundred percent for sure, and second, you said you wanted irrefutable proof to make sure this breakup was as simple as possible. We don't have that yet."

Kady nodded. "Okay."

She turned her ignition, and Emily and Marc climbed out. Emily held her hand to her face as if she was speaking into her pinky and listening to her thumb, the international symbol for *call me* as Kady drove away.

"Why doesn't she just leave him?" asked Marc.

Emily shrugged. "Once you've loved someone, it's never that easy."

166

CHAPTER TWENTY-FOUR

The next day, Sebastian called Emily.

"I need to find an apartment," he said.

It was only eight o'clock, but Emily had been up for *hours*. To her, the answer to Sebastian's housing problem seemed as obvious as the empty drawer in her bureau, which didn't exist, but *could*.

She didn't want to help him find an apartment; she wanted him to move in with her.

Too soon? *Absolutely.*

She didn't seem to care. It wasn't like they'd be getting married. If every instinct in her body was wrong and they didn't fall madly in love, he could always move out.

"Seriously—why don't you just move in with me, *temporarily*?" she asked.

She used the word "temporarily" seven times during the next ten minutes of negotiations—Smitten Kitten-speak for "forevs."

"Every night, I make huge dinners and have no one to eat them. You'd be doing me a favor."

He laughed. "Every night you're sitting there with a Thanksgiving turkey and no one to eat it?"

"Yep. It's a terrible waste of food. I pack it up and send it to starving kids, but the postage is killing me."

"I imagine the packages are pretty greasy, too. By the way, I'm at your door."

"Oh." Emily jumped and scanned the room. She had nothing she could use to make herself look any less slouchy.

She jogged to the front door, the phone at her ear, unlocked it, and then bolted to her bedroom.

"It's open," she said into the phone.

She heard Sebastian enter. Duppy offered one bark and then considered his home defense program complete.

"Where did you go?" he asked.

"Coming," she called from the back of the house.

She returned a moment later, wearing a summer dress, slightly out of breath. Sebastian had wandered into the living room and now sat on the sofa in front of the television.

"Kind of dressed up for eight o'clock, aren't you?" he asked.

"This old thing?" asked Emily, flopping on the sofa beside him.

"Got any turkey left?"

She shook her head. "Already shipped last night's, but here's another bit of trivia for you. I read a book that said giving nightly back rubs can improve a person's health. Who will I give backrubs to if you don't move in?"

She pushed on him until he collapsed to his side.

"What are you doing?" he asked.

She kept pushing him until he rolled onto his stomach, allowing her to straddled his back. She gave him the best back rub she could muster.

Sebastian groaned. "You're making this very difficult."

"That's the idea."

"But I *really* need to find an apartment."

She rubbed harder.

"Oh, sure. Hey, how 'bout those Orioles?"

"I don't watch baseball much," mumbled Sebastian, his face pressed into the cushions.

She felt a spike of happiness. She loved football but despised baseball. He really was her perfect man.

"I don't like baseball either. There's another thing we have in common."

"Another thing we could have in common is we both have our own places."

Emily grabbed the back of his neck and pinched the muscles on either side.

"Hey, is that a hummingbird outside?" she asked.

"I'm not going to *forget* I need an apartment. I'm on to your distraction techniques."

Emily's fingers slid around his neck, and she pretended to

choke him.

"This is the worst happy ending *ever*," he croaked.

"Fine. We'll go look."

168

They searched the weekend papers for apartment ads and found a few places to investigate.

The first promised a large bedroom and porch. His truck barely slowed as they rolled by the dismal brick box in one of the sketchier neighborhoods. Rust stains oozed down the walls, and the stairwell sported drying clothes draped over the handrails.

She knew what building this was when she circled the advertisement. It was perfect for *her* needs because it was a *nightmare* for Sebastian's. A few more pieces of prime real estate like it, and he'd be *begging* to move into her house.

"I'm afraid most apartments in your price range look like this," she said, punctuating her bad news with an exaggerated sigh.

He rolled his eyes but didn't ask to inspect the apartment.

The next spot sat on Main Street in Annapolis' historic district. The idea of downtown living had him giddy, and he chattered about living in the middle of the action. The more he gushed, the more Emily scowled.

They parked and mounted a set of stairs to the second-floor apartment, situated over a store that sold kids' clothing. The building was brick and very *historic* feeling—small, but doable. The rent was *large* and *not* doable.

"Maybe I could make it work?" he mumbled, looking out the window at the busy pedestrian street below.

Emily shook her head. "It's *way* out of your price range. Shame. I should have never brought you here."

"We could maybe drop the price a little," said the landlord, who'd let them in.

Emily's attention snapped to the man.

Shut up.

She said it in her head, straining to become telepathic.

Shut. Up.

"Like how much?" asked Sebastian.

"Maybe a hundred dollars?"

Emily breathed a sigh of relief.

That won't be enough.

Sebastian pouted.

They thanked the man and headed back to the truck.

"I could maybe do it," said Sebastian.

"There was no closet space."

"But it's right *here*."

"And I think there was a leak under the sink. It didn't look good. Probably full of mold."

His shoulders slumped.

"It's probably haunted, too. You don't want to end up in a haunted apartment," she added.

"You just want me trapped in your sex dungeon."

"Better a sex dungeon than the spirit of a murdered innkeeper molesting you at night. I mean, I assume. Depends on the innkeeper, I suppose."

"It wasn't *haunted*."

Emily shrugged. "I'm pretty sure that place is on the ghost tour."

The last apartment sat atop a garage behind an old lady's home. It was August, but Sebastian's potential landlady had more glowing reindeer on her lawn than the entire herd population of Norway. By the time they started up the stairs to the apartment, the blinking multi-colored lights on the porch had burned starbursts on their retinas. Emily was sure she'd have nightmares about the gyrating Santa for a week.

Unlike the landlady's taste in holiday decorations, the apartment was perfect. It was close to work and downtown. It was in Sebastian's price range.

Emily grew nervous.

"It seems pretty nice," said Sebastian.

She grunted, searching for reasons to hate the place.

He opened a closet. "It has everything I need. It's in a great location..."

Emily opened the cabinet under the sink, praying for mice.
Nothing.

"Oh, you'll love it," said the elderly owner, lurking at the door.

He agreed. "It's pretty much what I need."

The woman clapped her hands with glee. "And here's the best part—I'll be right *there*."

170

She pointed to her home, a few steps across the driveway, holiday lights glowing like the sun.

Landlady House, brought to you by Christmas.

Emily felt a pin-light of hope pierce her heavy heart.

"Go on," she said.

"You remind me of my son," the landlady continued. "I can bring you dinners when I make the crock-pot meals. I always make too much."

Emily covered her mouth to keep from yelping with joy. Fear flashed in Sebastian's eyes.

"I wouldn't need dinner—" he stammered.

"No trouble at *all*. I can stop by any time—I'm right *there*."

Emily fought the urge to high-five the woman. The old gal couldn't have ended the interview faster if she'd confessed to being a serial killer in the process of building herself a Polish Guy skin suit.

She already knew Sebastian well enough to know he'd *never* live in an apartment where a crock-pot-armed, house-coated woman could appear at his door at any moment.

"We'll get back to you. Thanks so much," he said, moving toward the exit. The woman followed.

"Thank you," Emily said, shaking the landlady's hand as she passed. "Seriously. *Thank you*."

Back in the truck, Sebastian turned to Emily, his eyes wide. They burst into laughter.

"Let's go get lunch," he grumbled.

"I could make fries."

"No, thank you. Let's go *out* to lunch. I'll buy if you promise never to make those fries again."

She chuckled. "Deal."

"Those apartments were awful. You did this on purpose," he said when they were on the road.

Emily looked away and grinned to herself.

"Did what?" she asked.

CHAPTER TWENTY-FIVE

After apartment hunting, Sebastian and Emily spent the rest of the day together, a wonderful day regularly punctuated by the sound of Sebastian's phone. He'd look at it, hit ignore, and put it away. Emily suspected she knew who it was and refused to ask.

They were playing darts in the basement when Sebastian excused himself to go to the bathroom.

The moment he left the room, her gaze fell on his phone. He'd left it sitting on the pool table.

It was just *lying there.*

She glanced toward the bathroom.

She looked at the phone.

She glanced toward the bathroom.

She *grabbed* the phone.

It wasn't locked. There were several missed phone messages. She wanted to listen to them, but feared the phone would Marc them as "listened to."

I am going to girlfriend hell for this.

She moved to the text messages. They were all from Greta.

"Where are you?" said one from the night Sebastian stayed at Emily's house.

"I was robbed! I'm hurt!" said another.

Emily stepped away from the direct view of the bathroom to give herself additional reaction time should Sebastian burst through the door. She checked his mail. One particularly long email caught her attention. Greta had written it a month earlier, packing the note full of dramatic flair and claiming she wanted to be a better girlfriend.

"I know we're supposed to be separated, but I know you still love

me. That night last week couldn't have been a mistake. You were so sweet to me when I was crying. We belong together..."

Emily's stomach lurched. She scrolled to the end of the email and found Greta's boilerplate footer featuring a cartoon kitten 172

surrounded by colorful butterflies and flowers. Beside it in script font, it said, *Kitty says: Take time to smell the roses!*

Gag.

Emily closed the email and moved to another entitled *I need you.*

The email said, *"Sebastian, this is serious, please call me!!"* followed by the same damn kitten.

She closed it and scrolled until she found the last email. The subject was 'Help.'

The body said, *"Sebastian I was attacked tonight!!!! I'll tell you the details later – I just got back from the hospital, and I need your help!! I am still so scared!!!!! I messed up my knee and he stole my wallet!!!! Please come home!!!"*

Emily scowled. *Was Greta paid by the exclamation point?*

And why is she *emailing* him?

She heard the toilet flush and jumped, nearly tossing the phone into the air. She set it on the pool table where she'd found it and then leaped away from it like it had teeth.

"Okay, where were we? Oh yeah, I was kicking your butt," said Sebastian as he exited the bathroom.

"Pretty much," said Emily, with a weak smile. Her stomach felt sick.

Greta would never let Sebastian go.

After the dart game, Sebastian announced he needed to leave.

"Why? Why don't you stay here?"

"I don't have work clothes for tomorrow," he said, gathering his keys and phone. "And I'm not sure how much longer I can keep from ravishing you."

"I don't see that as a problem."

Sebastian looked at his phone, and Emily froze, terrified she'd left evidence of her spying. He slipped it back into his pocket. She relaxed.

Emily's lip curled as she thought about the emails, texts, and constant ringing. *Stupid phone.* She couldn't help but think if it hadn't been ringing all afternoon, he would have stayed.

They said their goodbyes. He kissed her and thanked her for a wonderful day.

"My pleasure," she said.

"Well, that goes without saying," he said.

"Ha," she said, not feeling as playful as she had earlier. She still felt like throwing up. She deserved to feel queasy for prying. She felt guilty for looking at his phone and sick over what she'd read. If she hadn't looked at his messages, she'd feel fine.

She also knew she'd check for new messages the next time she had the chance.

She closed the door behind him and wandered into her living room to flop on the sofa. Now she felt depressed. Maybe she should text Sebastian something like, *"Help Sebastian!! I am depressed, and I need you!! Let your smile change the world, never let the world change your smile! You are special!!!!!!!!!!!!"*

The worst part was she knew she couldn't blame the situation entirely on Greta. Sebastian lived in her house. He could leave any time he wanted.

She suspected he didn't want to hurt Greta, but someone like her easily manipulated soft-hearted men. Sebastian was on his way home, where Greta would sit, fragile and teary-eyed, her huge knockers heaving... *Anything could happen.*

She felt like, even though they hadn't been together yet, there was an understanding he wouldn't be sleeping with Greta again.

But was there?

If he did, not only would she feel betrayed, but he wouldn't be the person she thought he was.

She huffed. Nothing felt fair to him, her or maybe even Greta.

What have I done?

She'd put herself in the middle of this confusing emotional gray area.

Did Greta know about Emily and their blossoming

relationship? Had he told her? If she knew, she might double her efforts out of spite—do almost anything to keep him so she could declare victory.

It wasn't a battle. She had no beef with Greta.

174

Could she blame Sebastian's unwillingness to commit? He barely knew her. Given the time to grow, she felt confident their bond would strengthen, but between Greta and his housing situation, he might run screaming from everything to clear his head.

Bad timing killed love all the time.

She fell back on her sofa and stared at the ceiling. She hated seeing both sides of a story. It immobilized her; kept her from forming solid opinions and acting on them. Other girls might demand that Sebastian commit. That didn't seem fair and might push him away. She wouldn't want ultimatums thrown at *her*.

He had to come to his own decisions.

She had a choice. She could end things until Sebastian moved from Greta's, or she could be herself and continue her course. If her heart was broken in the end, at least she'd have fought for what she wanted.

Feeling a tear slide down the right side of her face, she refused to wipe it. She tilted her head to encourage another tear to fall down the *left* side of her face in the interest of symmetry. She forgot about her problems for two minutes while racing one tear against the other until one dripped into her left ear.

Mission accomplished.

She returned to dwelling on her plight.

The smart move was probably to let Sebastian go until he returned to her. The old, *if you love something, let it go. If it comes back to you, it's yours.*

Did that crap *ever* work?

She sighed.

She sighed a more ragged sigh.

Much better.

She made her decision.

Screw it.

She sat up, teeth gritted.

It's on.

It's on like Donkey Kong.

176

CHAPTER TWENTY-SIX

Sebastian didn't show up at the Rover the next night. Emily left the moment the competition ended. She was sick to her stomach with worry. She imagined the worst.

Greta had re-seduced him.

Emily pulled into her driveway and sat in the car, staring at her steering wheel, overcome with sadness. Her phone rang. She picked it up and read the caller ID printed in bold across the screen.

Sebastian.

Her heart flipped like a pancake.

"Hey! You didn't go to darts," she answered.

"You home?" asked Sebastian.

"Yes."

"Stay there."

The phone went dead.

Emily ran inside to primp and let the dog out. Should she change into something more comfortable or stay dressed?

Fifteen minutes and an outfit change later, an old Mercedes flew into Emily's driveway. Sebastian hopped out of the passenger seat, spotted Emily peering through her bay window, and motioned for her to come outside as he walked toward her house.

"Come on," he said as she opened the door and popped out her head. "We're going to look at an apartment."

"Now? It's nine-thirty."

"Ryan knows a guy. He's got some big house on the water he inherited from his mom, and he's renting a room."

Sebastian bounced on the balls of his feet, rushing Emily

towards the car. He opened the driver's side back door, and she stepped in. He closed the door and jogged to the other side of the car.

"Let's go," he said, sliding into the passenger seat.

"Hey Emily," said Ryan, twisting to see as he backed out of her driveway.

She waved to him. She tucked her feet to her knees. She couldn't drop them to the floor; it was littered with empty beer cans.

"Are you big into recycling?" she asked.

"Passenger leavings. They're animals."

"Oh, I am so going to die," Emily whispered under her breath. She found a seatbelt amidst the fast food wrappers and aluminum. "So, What have you boys been up to tonight?"

"Makin' plans, movin' mountains," said Ryan.

"Okay. That makes no sense."

"Oh, it *totally* makes sense," said Sebastian.

"Right. Would you mind pulling over so I can get out?"

Sebastian twisted to look at her. "He's not drunk."

She grimaced. "Really?"

He nodded and put his hand over his heart.

"I'm not drunk, I'm the double D! The designated cabbie!" said Ryan.

Sebastian nodded. "He's high on life. And about eight Cokes."

Ten minutes later, Ryan pulled into a long, winding driveway. A single light glimmered at the end of a pitch-black dirt road, silhouetting the shape of a man standing like a sentry in front of his garage.

He held a shotgun diagonal across his chest.

"Whoa," said Sebastian. "Ryan, are you sure you know this guy?"

Emily slapped her pockets, looking for her phone. She wanted to tell her mother if she went missing, she was dead at the end of a lovely tree-lined driveway.

Ryan didn't hesitate. He pulled beside the armed man and rolled down his window.

"Hey, you know where they keep the women around here?" he asked.

"Haw!" The giant with the shotgun released an ear-deafening laugh. "What's up Ryan, I forgot you were coming."

"He *always* greets strangers with a shotgun?" Emily

whispered to Sebastian.

He grimaced. She suspected he wouldn't be finding the apartment of his dreams tonight.

"Come on in," said the man, lowering the gun to his side.

178

Ryan turned off the engine and they got out.

"So Teddy, this is Sebastian, the guy looking for a place," said Ryan.

The two men shook hands. Sebastian's hand looked like a child's, wrapped in Teddy's beefy paw.

"And this is Emily, Sebastian's, uh, friend," said Ryan.

Teddy nodded and bowed in her direction.

"Hello, Sebastian's uh-friend," he said.

"Uh, hello," she said.

"C'mon inside, people," the giant roared, turning on his heel and walking to the house. "Quit gawkin' and start walkin'."

The house was huge. They rounded the garage and left the glaring driveway light. A softer, yellow glow shone through the windows facing the river, providing enough illumination for Emily to see the house's gray shaker siding, spotty with wear and missing pieces. The garden lining the side of the house, brimming with plant husks and skeletal bushes, looked like a graveyard where chrysanthemums went to die.

Teddy pushed open his front door, enveloping the group in a fog of stale air. The entrance hallway featured a coat rack with two missing hooks and six pairs of huge shoes scattered against the wall. A staircase led to darkness on the left. Teddy led them straight ahead and through a doorway on the right into his kitchen.

Towers of paper, used plates, and silverware merged to create the ragged landscape of the countertops. Emily had seen post-party frat houses with better housekeeping.

"This is the kitchen. It could use a little straightening," said Teddy

Emily nodded.

It could use a flamethrower.

She thought she spotted something scuttle beneath a plate and touched Sebastian's arm. He glanced at her, and she saw the horror in his eyes. Once at a Dart Night, someone had splashed a drink on his pants. He'd fought the urge to leave but finally left to change and return pressed and spotless. If a drink spill sent him into a tailspin, this kitchen had to be fodder for nightmares.

"You got a beer, Teddy?" asked Ryan.

"Don't drink. Not for five years."

Everyone in the group offered the obligatory nod of approval.

"Good for you, Ted. Not my thing, but good for you," said Ryan.

Emily thought a guy who met people in his driveway with a shotgun was probably a good candidate for sobriety.

"Let me show you the room," said Teddy.

He led them through a surprisingly formal living room. In the dim light, Emily saw old-fashioned furniture, Hummel-like statues, and giant doilies draped over the backs of chairs. It looked like the home of someone's spinster aunt, not Lennie from *Of Mice and Men*.

Teddy started down a thin, dark hallway. At the end of it, he pushed open a door and motioned for them to go inside. Emily heard the flip of a light switch, and the room appeared bathed in a dim yellow glow.

"Oh, I guess the other bulb's out," said Teddy.

The group fell quiet. Everything in the room, from the silver tray of perfumes to the housedresses and furs piled on the bed, telegraphed the space as an old lady's bedroom. A rocker sat in front of the only window. The room smelled like someone's attic had thrown up.

"This was Mom's room," said Teddy, his voice soft. "She died here last spring."

"Oh *hell* no," mumbled Sebastian.

"She lived here the last five years of her life. It still doesn't feel real to me, you know?" Teddy hung his head.

Ryan slapped his shoulder. "I'm sorry to hear that, Ted."

Emily looked at Ryan. He caught her looking and winked. He knew Sebastian wouldn't live in this house if it came with a new truck and a lifetime supply of bacon. He either brought Sebastian for sheer amusement or didn't know the state of things at Teddy's Funhouse. Either way, same result.

Teddy sniffed. He was crying.

"Give me a second. You all go and take a look out that window. Momma used to love sitting in that chair and looking at that view. I think you're going to love it too."

Teddy excused himself and clumped down the hall. A moment later, they heard the horn-like blow of his nose.

"Go on, Sebastian. Check out your new view," said Ryan.

"You have got to be kidding me. I'm not living in this house 180

of wax."

"The chair at the window," said Emily, motioning to the rocker in front of the view. "It's like *Psycho*."

Sebastian nodded. "I know, right? That's what I thought."

Ryan snickered. "You don't want this gem?"

Sebastian gritted his teeth. "I want to get the hell out of here."

Emily felt a bout of giggles building in her chest.

"You don't want to take a peek at the view?" she teased. "Maybe try on a wig?"

Sebastian side-eyed her. "*No*. If I walk past that bed, something will grab my ankles."

The hall bathroom door opened, and Emily bit her lip to stem the giggle-tide. She knew if she met eyes with Sebastian, she'd explode.

"Sorry about that. Whatcha think of that view?" asked Teddy.

Sebastian thrust his hands into his pockets. "Beautiful. Really nice. Too nice for me, really—"

"Isn't it? Did you see the dock?"

"Uh...Sure?"

"Let's go down the dock," said Teddy, striding down the hall.

"Let's go down the dock," echoed Ryan, pointing his index finger in the sky. He followed Teddy.

Sebastian looked at Emily. "What's that, Mother?" he whispered. "Please, Mother. It's just a girl, Mother."

Emily slapped his arm. "*Stop*. You'll make me laugh at the guy with a shotgun."

They followed Teddy and Ryan, pushing through a rickety, ripped screen door to the backyard. They couldn't avoid the view from the patio, and, to be fair, it was breathtaking. Although the night was dark, the river sparkled beneath the lights of the large houses lining its banks. It reminded Emily of the magical boat ride and glowing shrimp.

The group walked downstairs to a long ramp leading to the

pier, Emily last in line. She felt her smooth-bottomed shoes slip on the sharply angled ramp. Sliding, she flailed for the handrails, flying two feet off the ramp and directly into Sebastian, who caught her under her armpits as she sped by. They wobbled, both in danger of falling. Emily's left leg dipped off the dock and into the river before Sebastian won the battle and righted her.

"Whoa, *easy*, Flash," he said, yanking her up.

Her soggy shoe lifted from the water and she steadied herself against him, panting, adrenaline coursing through her veins.

"*Thank you*," she said, still unsure of her footing. "I'd have gone in head first if you hadn't caught me."

Teddy's mouth hooked to the right. "I should put traction on that ramp. Need a few repairs around here."

"No. This place is *perfect*," said Ryan.

Sebastian stood behind Emily and put his arms around her. "I have to lock you down, Spazz, before you go flying off the dock."

"Excellent idea," she said, nestling into his arms.

Ryan looked at them and smirked.

Teddy told a story about jumping off the dock with his brother as kids. Cozy in Sebastian's arms, Emily listened to the tale and glanced toward the house.

A dark figure darted behind the garage.

"I'm sorry—is there someone else here, Teddy?" she asked, interrupting his story.

"Hm?"

"I saw someone moving by the garage?"

Everyone looked towards the house.

Teddy scowled. "Shouldn't be. Are you sure?"

She opened her mouth and then shut it. She *thought* she'd seen someone shrink from the light into the darkness of the trees, but she didn't want Teddy running for his gun.

"I don't know. Maybe I'm seeing things."

"Probably hallucinating from your near-death experience," said Sebastian.

"Could be."

The group made their way up the ramp to Ryan's car. No one saw anyone.

"Well, I appreciate the tour," said Sebastian, shaking Teddy's enormous paw. "I'm looking at a few different places, but I'll let you know."

"No problem. Nice to see you again, Ryan," said Teddy.

Ryan said his goodbyes, and they drove back down the winding driveway. Although there was enough room to turn

182

the car around, Ryan reversed the entire way.

"You are on *crack* if you thought I'd live there," said Sebastian.

Ryan laughed. "I had no idea. I swear. I haven't seen that guy in *years*. I bumped into him, and he mentioned he was renting a room on the river, and I thought of you."

He paused before pulling onto the main road. Sitting in the back seat, Emily had the best street view. The left clear, she checked right in time to see a dark sedan peel from the side of the road and roar away.

"All clear?" asked Ryan.

"Looks good," said Emily, wondering about the car pulling away.

Had that been the person near the garage?

She couldn't shake the feeling that it had.

"Where to?" asked Ryan.

"If you could drop us back at Emily's house, that would be cool. Is that okay, Em?" asked Sebastian.

"Sure," she said, trying not to sound *too* happy.

"You don't want to go to the Rover or something?" asked Ryan. "I can take you home afterward?"

Sebastian looked at Emily and made a face like a man trapped on a rollercoaster. Emily understood. The only thing scarier than spending the night in Teddy's dead mother's room was the idea of Ryan driving them home after drinks at the Rover.

Sebastian clapped his friend on the shoulder. "Nah. I have work tomorrow, and then I have to go to my niece's birthday party."

Ryan shrugged. "Your loss."

"No doubt," said Sebastian. He turned to Emily. "Hey, you want to go to a little kid's birthday party tomorrow?"

"Me?"

Sebastian looked around the back seat. "Is there someone else back there?"

Emily shrugged. "Sure. I love cake."

184

CHAPTER TWENTY-SEVEN

Emily met Tessa for lunch the following day. She needed to tell her about Greta and the emails she'd read on Sebastian's phone.

"What do you think?" she asked after spilling the story of Greta's and Sebastian's lingering involvement and her spying techniques.

"You're reading his emails?" Tessa asked, looking uneasy.

Emily's head hung. "Uh-huh. I know. It's awful. I feel horrible about it." She looked up. "I'd do it again in a heartbeat."

Tess nodded. "My first thought is, if he goes back to Heidi, then he was never yours to begin with."

"*Greta*," corrected Emily. "Not *Heidi*."

Tessa rolled her eyes. "Whatever *Sound of Music* kid she is."

Tessa stabbed her salad. Emily watched her eat. She couldn't figure out how people ate salads for *meals*. It was like eating air. Unless you added a ton of dressing, then you might as well have had a bowl of ice cream.

She sighed. "Okay, I get what you're saying, in theory. But you don't know Sebastian like I do. He's not good at change."

"Ah, so you *know* him. After observing him in the wild for a few months."

Emily nodded.

Tessa stirred her iced tea and stared off into the distance. Emily suspected her friend had moved on to making mental grocery lists or daydreaming about bringing rival lawyers to tears in court.

"Hello?" asked Emily.

Tessa refocused on her. "Sorry. I'm mulling. You think he'll go back to—"

"*No.* I don't think he'll go back to her. But I could see him putting us on hold until he got his life straightened out, and I don't want to be on hold."

"*So* unlike you to be impatient."

"I know, right?"

"But, don't you think that might be the best thing? For him to get free and clear, and then you guys do things *right*?"

Emily frowned. "*No.* Look, I didn't ask you to lunch so you could talk *sense* into me. I asked you here to plot Greta's destruction."

"*Oh*," said Tessa leaning back in her chair, visibly relieved. "My bad. That does sound like more fun."

"I wonder if they stole her handbag," Emily mumbled before taking a bite from her turkey sandwich.

"What?"

"She was in the bar the other day yapping about her new super-expensive purse. She said Sebastian bought it for her, but he says he didn't. Anyway, she told him she was mugged, but—"

"You think she made up a thief?"

"Maybe to get his attention. But if it was real I—"

Emily stopped, mid-thought.

"Wait a second. In that email I read on Sebastian's phone, Greta said the robber hurt her knee and stole her *wallet*."

"He was after her expensive purse."

"That's just it. If you were going to slam into someone, knock them over and rob them, would you take time to take their wallet out of their expensive purse?"

"Maybe she was holding on to the handbag," said Tessa. "Maybe the wallet fell out? Maybe the handbag was stolen, but *wallet* was faster to type? Or maybe you could find a guy *without* a girlfriend making her way through drama school?"

"Maybe. Or maybe if you're going to fake a robbery, you don't want to have to throw away your brand-new purse to do it. Maybe she was buying a new wallet anyway."

"To match the purse, naturally. I always fake having my wallet stolen before buying a new one. Doesn't everyone?"

"And *purse* is shorter to type than *wallet*," added Emily. "So there."

"Touché, Sherlock."

"You know, if I didn't know better, I'd say you're not taking this seriously."

Tessa grinned sweetly.

"I wish I knew if she still had her license," said Emily under her breath. "Then I'd know if her wallet was stolen or the

186

contents just moved."

Tessa made disapproving clucking noises with her tongue.

"Frankly, I think you and Greta both have issues, and Sebastian should run screaming until he finds a *sane* girl."

"Again, I'm going to have to ask you to stop being so logical. What sucks is, no matter what I find out, anything I say to Sebastian about Greta makes me look psychotic and spiteful."

Tessa dabbed her napkin to her lips. "Unlike you reading his phone and flat-out *being* psychotic and spiteful."

"Shut up."

"Seriously, relationships are *not* supposed to be this hard."

"You have been absolutely no help, *you,* and all your *common sense.* I was hoping you could help me hatch a dastardly plan."

"Unless you want to sue her for being in love and refusing to fade away, I'm afraid I'm no help."

"She's not in *love*," Emily spat.

Several people swiveled their gazes toward their table.

She cleared her throat and began again at a less screechy pitch.

"She's not in *love*," she hissed, leaning toward Tessa. "*I'm* in love. She just doesn't want to be alone while she's moving on to the next guy."

Tessa shrugged. "Maybe. Who can say other than Greta?"

Emily sighed. "Shut *up*. I have to go. Sebastian invited me to his niece's birthday party this afternoon. That's got to be a good sign, right?"

"Maybe. Or he's a genius at getting extra gifts for his niece."

"Oh jeez, a *gift*," Emily stood. "Holy hell, what do six-year-old girls want nowadays?"

"iPhones."

"Seriously?"

"I wish I was kidding," said Tessa.

CHAPTER TWENTY-EIGHT

Emily sat in her car outside the suburban home of Sebastian's brother and his family.

What am I doing here?

She felt both excited and idiotic. Sebastian had asked her to a family gathering, which had to be a good sign, but he didn't *take* her to the family gathering. He was planning to stay at his brother's house that night, so he'd suggested separate vehicles.

Emily sat in her car, staring at Sebastian's brother's house, watching people with brightly packaged gifts arrive and disappear inside.

She felt like a stalker—funny time for that to bother her.

Emily didn't see Sebastian's truck, and he was already half an hour late. She felt inside her purse, only to find she'd forgotten her phone. *Stupid.* Sebastian might already be inside, wondering where she was.

Emily stared at her party gift, a science kit the woman at the toy store insisted a six-year-old couldn't eat and choke on. She bought the kit because she disapproved of shoving pink, sparkly things at children just because they were girls and because she wasn't sure the child *was* a girl. She was 99.9% sure Sebastian said "niece" and not "nephew," but at the last moment, she'd panicked and bought unisex. She'd agonized over what the child already owned, what she liked, and the appropriateness of every toy. That she'd arrived with anything was a miracle.

Then she realized she had no birthday wrapping paper. Already late, she'd wrapped the gift in reindeer paper, hoping no one would notice.

The reindeer looked a *little* like dogs. It could work.

Then she rushed out of the house without her phone.

She couldn't wait any longer. She grabbed the gift and sauntered toward the house, hoping to spot Sebastian's truck along the way.

No such luck.

She knocked and waited. Inside, music blared, so she tapped again—still nothing.

"You have got to be kidding me," Emily mumbled. Being a stranger arriving alone was embarrassing enough; entering with a battering ram wouldn't improve first impressions.

She raised her fist to pound.

A matronly woman with short, reddish-brown hair opened the door and eyeballed her, her face betraying no emotion. Her gaze lifted to lock on Emily's raised fist.

She lowered her hand to point at her chest.

"I'm...uh...*Emily*?"

"Are you sure?" asked the woman.

The question confused her. Concentrating on details like her name when her brain was in a blender set to liquefy was hard.

"Sebastian told me to meet him here?"

The woman's stony demeanor melted into a warm smile of recognition. Emily felt a flush of relief.

"Oh, *Emily*," said the woman. "Come in. Sebastian told us so much about you."

Emily straightened.

He has?

"I'm Sebastian's mother, Mariska," the woman said, making room to enter. Emily stepped into a large living room. She saw through to the kitchen, where people stood holding red Solo cups and chatting.

"Nice to meet you. Is Sebastian here?" she asked, shaking Mariska's hand.

"No. But I'm sure he will be. He called a little while ago to ask if you were here yet."

"Oh, good. I wondered if I'd imagined him inviting me, and I forgot my phone."

"Here, I'll take your gift."

Emily handed her the package. The woman turned it over, inspecting the paper.

Emily winced. "Christmas paper is all I had. I'm sorry. They kind of look like dogs. Horny dogs."

Emily slapped her hand to her mouth. "I mean dogs with horns," she said, scrambling. "Not *horny* dogs."

Mariska laughed. "It's *darling*. And they do look like little horned Datsun dogs."

Emily opened her mouth to correct, *Dachshunds* but caught herself in time.

"I thought so... Or, I guess, I *hoped* so."

Mariska put Emily's present on a pile of others and led her to the kitchen. Emily grew nervous again, surrounded by people she didn't know, the quasi-girlfriend of a missing man.

"Garrett, this is Emily," said Mariska, putting her arm behind Emily and pushing her toward a dark-haired man. "This is Sebastian's brother, Garrett, the birthday girl's father."

"Hi," she said, thrusting out a hand.

Garrett sized her up. She must have passed some initial review because he switched his beer to his left hand, wiped his right on his pants, and shook her hand, grinning.

"Hey, nice to meet you," he said in a booming voice. "You want something to drink?"

Oh yes for the love of everything holy please.

"Yes, please," she said aloud.

"Where did you meet Sebastian?" asked Mariska as Garrett fetched a beer from the keg on the porch.

"Uh..." She realized telling Sebastian's mother they'd met at a bar could create a poor impression, but she couldn't lie.

"Playing darts. My girlfriend took me to a dart night at a local bar downtown, and there he was."

Mariska nodded. "Really..."

"I don't usually hang out in bars, so I guess it was lucky I was there that day."

"*He's* probably there all the time," said his mother, rolling her eyes. "So what do you do?"

Emily relaxed. The "we met in a bar" exchange had gone reasonably well, and Mariska's welcoming demeanor put Emily at ease.

"I write and own a web design business."

"You make the Internet?"

Emily laughed. "Parts of it, I guess, yes."

"And it's *your* company?"

She nodded.

"Oh my. Isn't that *wonderful*," said Mariska as Garrett returned with her beer. "Garrett, Emily owns her own company making websites."

Garrett handed Emily her cup. "Very cool. Hey, do you watch

190

movies?"

Emily took a sip, resisting the urge to guzzle the thing to quiet her nerves.

"Movies?" she echoed, wiping foam from the tip of her nose. "Sure."

"I'm trying to remember the name of a movie. Maybe you can help. Sebastian said you're smart."

"Hit me." She loved trivia almost as much as she loved hearing Sebastian say she was smart.

"There's this guy in prison, I think, and he gets out and starts killing all these people. And he's got a flame thrower."

"A flame thrower?"

Garrett nodded. "Yeah, and he starts killing all these people."

Mariska, shook her head. "What kind of movie is *that*?"

Emily scowled. "He's killing people with a flamethrower? I'm not a detective or anything, but flamethrowers seem like a conspicuous way to kill people. I'd remember that. Was it sci-fi? Like *Alien*?"

"No. And I don't think he *always* uses a flamethrower."

Emily was lost. "I don't think I saw it."

Garrett shook his head. "No, it's famous. I'm sure you did."

"Any actors you can name?"

"I can't think of their names, but some of them were famous."

"Was it in Vietnam?"

"No, it was in America. The West, I think, but not the old cowboy West."

"Flamethrowing cowboys, I'd remember," Emily mumbled. "Is he a *bad* guy? Or a good guy seeking vengeance on the bad guys who killed his family or something like that?"

Garrett considered this for a moment. "I don't know. I couldn't decide if I liked him or not."

In her mind, Emily threw aside the image of burning bodies and instead zeroed in on the flamethrower itself. The shape of it did trigger an idea.

"Wait..." she said, shaking a finger in the air. "Not a *flamethrower*...you mean like a pneumatic bolt shooter thing? Are you thinking *No Country for Old Men?* The 'friendo' dude?"

"*Yes!*" yelped Garrett. He slapped his thigh and pointed at Emily. "That's it. *Thank you.*"

Emily beamed. Sebastian's whole family made her feel like a superstar.

Garrett turned and screamed out to the porch. "Hey, Nicole, it was *No Country for Old Men!*"

A thought occurred to Emily. The smile faded from her lips.

"Wait. Did you say you couldn't decide if you *liked* him?"

"Yeah," said Garrett, finishing his beer.

"He was a psychotic who killed just about everyone in the movie."

"Yeah, that guy. He was *awesome.*"

"He flipped a coin to decide whether he'd kill a convenience store clerk."

Garrett's face flooded with excitement. "Yeah, *yeah. That guy.*"

"And you couldn't decide if he was good or bad?"

Garrett blinked at her as if she spoke a language he didn't understand.

"Yeah. So, anyway, thanks," he said. "That was driving me crazy. I'll take you out to meet Nicole."

Emily looked at Mariska, but Garrett's mother was scanning the room, happily sipping on a soda. She'd stopped listening to the conversation some time ago. Garrett's adoration of psychotic murderers was passé.

Emily followed Garrett to the porch, where he introduced her to his wife, Nicole, a curvy brunette wearing a baseball jersey. Emily shook Nicole's hand and turned in time to see Sebastian walking towards her through the kitchen.

"Hey, I'm so sorry I'm late," he said, arriving at her side.

He leaned down as if he was going to kiss her and then, glancing at his brother, turned the whole movement into a supportive pat on the shoulder.

"Yeah, nice going, dude. She had to meet your crazy family all by herself," said Garrett.

Sebastian grimaced. "I am sorry. Hey, I'm going to get a drink. Do you need anything? I'm breaking into the vodka."

Emily nodded.

"I'll be right back."

"Bastian's not a beer guy," said Garrett.

"You'd never believe they were brothers," said Nicole. "Sebastian's sort of fancy, and Gar is..." Nicole met eyes with her

192

husband.

"A redneck," said Garrett, finishing her sentence. "And proud of it."

Nicole nodded. "See?"

Emily laughed and glanced toward Sebastian in the kitchen. His mother had cornered him by the counter. Mariska shot Emily a look and refocused her son.

"Looks like your mother is talking to Sebastian about me. Hope it's going well."

"Oh, I'm sure it's all nice," said Garrett.

Nicole rolled her eyes. "She didn't like Greta at *all*. You'll look good by comparison no matter what, so you've got that going for you."

Emily's gaze whipped towards Nicole. "Really?"

Nicole rolled her eyes. "Greta's *miserable*. Everything is all about *her*. She's not friendly at all."

Garrett shook his head. "Nope."

"I think she wants him back," Emily heard herself say. She couldn't help it. It felt good to talk to people who knew Sebastian.

Nicole huffed. "Oh, *whatever*. She always ignores him and then throws herself at him. That's how she rolls."

"We were glad to hear he broke up with her," said Garrett.

Emily chuckled. "Not as much as me. Though now I'm ninety percent sure she's faking a knee injury to keep him from moving out."

She looked away, mortified by her comment. Garrett and Nicole were so friendly and supportive that she felt urged to share her relationship burdens. She made herself promise to stop.

"You think Greta is faking an injury? How did she hurt her knee?" asked Nicole.

"She got 'mugged'," Emily said, making air quotes. "But strangely, her wallet was stolen and not her brand new expensive purse."

Emily grimaced.

So, the plan to keep silent is going well...

"What kind of purse?" asked Nicole.

"Marc Jacobs, I think."

"Really?" Nicole slapped Garrett in the stomach with the back of her hand.

"What the hell?" said Garrett.

"You never buy me expensive purses."

Garrett held his stomach and glared at Nicole. "*Ow.*"

Nicole turned back to Emily. "So, the thief took the wallet but not the expensive handbag. That *is* pretty suspicious. And that *totally* sounds like Greta. Sebastian doesn't know she's faking?"

"No, I don't think so," Emily looked over and saw Sebastian returning them. "And maybe she's not making it up. I don't know. I shouldn't have said anything."

Emily felt a knot tighten in her stomach. She shouldn't have said anything about Greta to Sebastian's family. She knew if he found out, he wouldn't appreciate the violation of his privacy. In addition, she wasn't supposed to *know* about the robbery. She only knew, thanks to her snooping.

Oh, what a tangled web...

Emily watched Sebastian approach with impending doom. Behind him, the front door opened.

Greta hobbled in.

The blood drained from Emily's face, her skin growing cold and prickly.

"Hole. Lee. Shit," said Garrett.

"What is *she* doing here?" asked Nicole.

Nicole looked like she was about to run across the room and attack Greta. Emily made a mental note never to piss off Nicole.

Sebastian's brows knitted with confusion as he surveyed the expressions of the people awaiting his return.

"What?" he asked.

He followed their gazes, turning to look behind him.

"What the—"

Sebastian handed Emily both drinks and strode toward Greta.

Greta closed the door behind her, struggling with her crutches. Sebastian's mother intercepted her. Greta smiled, handing Mariska the gift she'd brought for his niece. She motioned to her knee brace and sat her expensive purse on the entry table to steady herself on her crutches as she talked. She winced with what looked like pain.

Emily felt like an interloper—like a fly on the wall, watching the party as it might have been, had she not come into 194

Sebastian's life.

"She's *really* pushin' it," said Garrett. He clapped Emily on the shoulder. "Don't worry. Mom can't stand her. She won't let her stay."

Garrett's words meant nothing. Sebastian needed to tell Greta to leave. It concerned her that Garrett had put the onus on his mother. Didn't he think *Sebastian* would tell Greta to leave?

Greta spotted Sebastian. She smiled. Her gaze drifted past him and settled on Emily.

Her mood visibly darkened.

There was no question as to whether Greta knew about Emily's presence in Sebastian's life anymore.

Sebastian leaned to whisper something in Greta's ear. She recoiled as if shocked. He shook his head and gently guided her into a one-eighty-degree turn. He opened the front door and ushered the hobbling girl outside.

"She forgot her purse," said Nicole, nodding towards the table where Greta's handbag sat perched.

Garrett's eyes lit, a huge grin growing across his mug.

"Hey, Croix," Garrett barked into the yard.

A little girl with dark, curly locks bounded to the edge of the porch and stared up at him through the banister slats.

"Do you remember Miss Greta?" asked Garrett.

The girl nodded. She looked at Emily.

"Hi," she said.

Emily chuckled.

Nope. Close, but no cigar. You can tell by the boobs.

"Come up here," said Garrett.

Croix ran around the porch and up the stairs to her father. He picked her up and held her against his side with one hand.

"You see that purse over there on the table? The green one?" he asked, pointing toward the foyer.

"Orange. It's orange," said Nicole to her husband. She turned to Emily and whispered. "He's color-blind. So is Bastian."

"The orange one?" Garrett echoed to his daughter.

Croix nodded.

He crouched down with the girl. "Okay, listen to me. I want you to get that bag and take it out front, but come back this way, out back, and go *around* the house to go out front. Got it? Don't use the front door. Understand? When you get out front, show Miss Greta that you have her bag. But, no matter what you do, don't give it back to her. Okay? And don't let her catch you. If she comes after you, run away, okay? It's a game. *Keep away.*"

Croix grinned and shook her head, eager to get started.

Garrett stood. "Go get it!"

Croix ran to get the bag.

"Fetches better than a dog," he said, taking a sip of his beer.

"Garrett!" scolded Nicole, slapping his shoulder.

He grinned. "You girls go upstairs to the bedroom. I'll tell Sebastian I need him and get him inside so Greta thinks no one is watching her. Then we'll see how hurt her knee is when Croix shows up with her bag."

"Oh my god, that's brilliant," said Nicole.

"You're kind of an evil genius," said Emily.

"You have no idea," he said, winking.

Croix ran back out to the porch, bag clutched in her tiny hands. She ran past Emily and downstairs to the yard, stopping to pick up a naked Barbie doll and put it in the bag.

Nicole shrieked with giggles. "Follow me!" she said, grabbing Emily's arm.

Nicole dragged Emily through the kitchen toward the stairs, the two vodka drinks in Emily's hands sloshing with every step. She put one drink down on the kitchen counter as they passed and the second on a glass table in the foyer. The two bounded up the stairs to the second floor. Below them, Emily heard Garrett open the front door and call for Sebastian.

When Emily and Nicole pressed their faces against the bedroom window, they saw Garrett, Sebastian, and Greta on the front porch below. Sebastian waved Garrett away, but his brother grabbed his arm and tugged on him, insistent. Finally, Sebastian threw up his hands, said something stern to Greta, and followed Garrett inside.

A moment later, Croix ran into view holding the large orange bag. It was bigger than her head, but she held it high like a prized trophy. She stood at the bottom of the front porch and taunted Greta, shaking her tiny tush as she danced.

Greta's eyes popped wide as she demanded the girl return the bag.

Nicole opened the window to hear. The windowpane groaned and cracked, and Greta glanced up toward the sound.

196

Emily and Nicole dove from the window, Nicole splashing beer on her chest as she fell onto her bed. She laughed hysterically, unable to catch her breath.

Nicole covered her mouth with her hand to quiet herself, her eyes squinty with laughter. Emily crept toward the window and peered down.

Croix again shook her booty in Greta's direction, bag held high. Greta called to her, pointing at Croix and then to herself, demanding the return of the purse.

Tiring, Croix walked back and forth across the yard, dragging the bag through the grass.

Emily heard Greta's horrified screech. Nicole jumped off the bed and ran to the window.

A single phrase ran through Emily's head.

This is insane.

Croix turned the bag over and shook the contents into the grass. The Barbie fell out, followed by a set of keys and a wallet.

Greta glanced toward the front door. Seemingly furious, she set her crutches against the railing and lunged down the stairs toward Croix, who squealed with excitement and ran. Greta sprinted twenty feet before she grabbed the girl by the arm and yanked the handbag away from her. She held it high in the air as Croix jumped to retrieve it. Greta scolded the girl, shaking her finger in her face. Finally, Croix gave up and ran toward the backyard. Greta dropped to her knees and gathered the items that had fallen from the purse. She looked around and sprinted back to her crutches, bounding the porch steps two at a time.

"No way—Her knee is totally *fine!*" yelped Nicole.

Emily felt giddy. "I *knew* it."

"She ran after Croix like a track star. Ooh, *let's go tell Sebastian.*"

"No, *wait*—" said Emily grabbing for Nicole's arm, but the woman easily dodged and headed for the stairs.

Emily ran after Nicole, unsure whether telling Sebastian would cast *her* in the loveliest light. She hadn't been at Garrett and Nicole's house for more than an hour before becoming an accomplice in a sting operation.

Nicole stopped dead at the bottom of the stairs, and Emily plowed into the back of her. Nicole grabbed the handrail to support Emily's weight and keep from falling. Still standing at the bottom of the stairs beside Sebastian, Garrett looked at them. Sebastian opened the front door and stepped outside to rejoin Greta. A flash of confusion crossed his face when he noticed Nicole and Emily crash at the bottom of the stairs, but he hadn't stopped to ask questions.

"Did it work?" Garrett asked.

"She is *totally* faking. She *ran* after Croix," said Nicole.

Emily took a step back to keep from leaning her weight on Nicole's back. "I don't know if it's such a great idea to tell Sebastian about all this."

"We'll keep you out of it," said Nicole.

Emily opened her mouth to protest, but Nicole took the last few steps to join Garrett, and the two went out front. Emily moved to the landing and lingered just inside the door, which remained cracked open. She saw Greta at the bottom of the stairs, wobbling as if touching her toe to the ground was painful.

"How's your knee there, Greta?" asked Nicole.

"Hey, Nicole, how are you?" said Greta, her voice laced with sugar. "I got *mugged*. Did Sebastian tell you?"

"Like how you just mugged my daughter?"

Sebastian looked at Nicole.

"What are you talking about?"

Greta's face grew ashen. She glared at Nicole, set her jaw, and began hobbling away. "I can't stay. I wanted to drop off Croix's gift. I bought it before I was *dumped*, but there's no reason why Croix should suffer."

"She ran after Croix," said Nicole.

Sebastian scowled. "Who? What are you talking about?"

"Greta. Garrett told Croix to play keep away her bag, and she was awesome."

"Was she? I missed it. She's pretty fast—" said Garrett, his voice laced with pride.

Nicole nodded. "She was *amazing*. She danced at the bottom of the stairs, then dragged the bag across the lawn—"

"She dragged her bag?" asked Sebastian. "You can't let Croix drag that around. It was expensive, I think."

Nicole sighed. "Sebastian, you're missing the point. Greta *ran* after Croix to get the bag. We set her up to prove her leg wasn't hurt, and she fell for it."

"It was my idea," said Garrett, slapping his chest.

"Why would you think she was faking?" asked Sebastian.

Emily froze, praying Sebastian wouldn't turn his head slightly to the left and spot her lurking inside.

"If she was mugged, wouldn't they have taken her fancy purse and not just the wallet?" said Nicole. "Don't you think that's suspicious?"

"Yeah," said Garrett.

"Greta, is that true?" Sebastian asked.

Halfway down the walkway, Greta paused. She turned back to look at the three on the porch.

"It is," she said, a sob in her voice. "I did run after Croix. I had to, but now thanks to your cruel games, my knee is ten times worse, and I need to go home and get my pain meds."

"Our *cruel games*?" echoed Nicole. "Who says that?"

Greta crutched away, and Emily watched her struggle into her car.

Her black car.

Emily stepped into the doorway and opened the door wider, staring. The car that peeled away from the creepy house was dark, and the silver emblem was the same. The logo hadn't registered the night at Teddy's home, but now that she saw it again, she was sure it matched.

It looks like I'm not the only stalker in town.

Sebastian turned toward the house and met Emily's gaze. She stared back at him, unsure what to say.

"Let's go back in," suggested Garrett.

Garrett led the way, with Nicole and Sebastian following.

"Shoot, we didn't think to video it," said Nicole.

Emily tried to smile and failed. The excitement of catching Greta had faded into anxiety. She could feel Sebastian's tension and his gaze on her. Nicole and Garrett left to prepare the birthday cake for serving and left them alone in the front living room. She watched them go, feeling helpless. She wanted to run and hide behind them.

"Did you see it?" asked Sebastian.

"Hm?"

"Did you see Greta run after Croix?"

She nodded. "Yes. Nicole and I were watching from upstairs."

The muscles in Sebastian's jaw clenched.

"You guys have to let me do this my way."

She felt ashamed, but another emotion fought past her embarrassment.

Anger.

"Are you going to spend forever letting her manipulate you?"

Sebastian gaped. "What?"

"I know you feel sorry for her, but she's taking advantage of you."

Sebastian pursed his lips, staring at her for what felt like an hour. He took slow, controlled breaths.

"I'm not getting into this here," he said.

Voices in the kitchen sang 'Happy Birthday', and Sebastian walked towards them. Emily followed, lipping the words, her voice tight in her throat as she fought back the tears of frustration.

Sebastian had always planned to spend the night at his brother's house. After the cake, he excused himself to go to the bathroom, and Emily gathered her things to leave.

"Where you going?" asked Nicole.

"I'm going home."

"I'm going to go, too," said Mariska, appearing beside them. "Emily, it was *so* nice to meet you."

"Oh, it was nice to meet you, Mrs. Krzyzanowski," she said.

Too bad we'll never meet again.

Mariska gave Emily a bear hug, and she hugged her back. She'd never met such a cuddly woman. She wanted to melt into her, sobbing.

Sebastian returned.

"See ya, Ma," he said, hugging his mother.

Emily stood next to his mother, keys in hand.

"See you, Em," he said. He leaned in and kissed her on the cheek.

He glanced at his mother and stepped back, feeling decidedly standoffish.

That was it.

"I'll walk with you, Mrs. Krzyzanowski," said Emily.

"Call me Mariska," she said, grabbing her bag from the front table.

"I'll give you a call tomorrow," said Sebastian as Emily 200

opened the front door.

Emily nodded and shut the door behind her.

CHAPTER TWENTY-NINE

The last party guests left, and Sebastian sat on his brother's back patio, nursing a vodka and soda. Garrett filled the fire pit with enough wood to create a supernova.

"It's a fire pit, not the world's deadliest game of Jenga," muttered Sebastian.

Garret stuck his tongue out and attempted to balance one last stick against the kindling teepee he had created.

"You have to admit. *That* is impressive," he said, stepping away and surveying his work.

Sebastian sighed.

Garrett jogged to the back deck and snatched a yellow plastic bottle from beside the grill. Returning, he squeezed the bottle, dousing the fire pit with a relentless stream of lighter fluid.

"How have you lived this long?" Sebastian asked, standing and taking a few steps back as Garrett retrieved his lighter. "At least throw a match at it from a safe distance; don't use a lighter."

Wincing, Garrett flicked the lighter and stretched his arm toward the kindling as far as he could. With a terrifying *whoosh!* the teepee transformed into a towering inferno. Garrett jumped back and eyed his forearm.

"I singed all the hair off my arm."

Sebastian backed his chair six feet from the blaze. "Shocker. I'll have to sit in the neighbor's yard to keep from roasting now."

Garrett grabbed a bottle of beer from a cooler and sat beside him.

Sebastian looked at him. "What was up with the purse thing? That wasn't cool."

"Pfft, she deserved it. She's a liar, and we proved it."

Garrett pulled out a pack of cigarettes and offered one to Sebastian, who declined.

Sebastian threw an ice cube into the fire, where it sizzled and disappeared.

202

"I don't understand what you were trying to accomplish," he said, unable to drop the topic. "Greta shouldn't have come, but I was handling it."

"She faked an injury to rope-a-dope you. Her knee isn't even hurt. That was all a trick to get you away from Emily."

"What would even make you think that?"

"Uh..." Garrett took a long gulp from his beer.

Sebastian waited for his brother to answer.

Garrett pulled the beer from his lips and grabbed a stick beside his chair. He poked the fire.

"Gar?" said Sebastian.

"Hm?"

"I asked you a question."

"Oh. Sorry. What did you say?" Garrett poked the fire with greater enthusiasm.

"I said, *what made you think Greta was lying*?"

"Her purse," said Nicole from the porch. She walked down the stairs and dragged over a chair to join the boys.

"Good one, hon," she said, nodding at the blaze.

"What are you talking about, *her purse*?" asked Sebastian.

"She said she was mugged, and the guy stole her wallet, but he didn't take her thousand-dollar purse?"

"A thousand? It couldn't be that expensive."

"Oh, I think it is."

"How could she afford a thousand-dollar purse? That's crazy."

"I don't know. But my guess is she had an old wallet that didn't match the purse, one she didn't mind 'losing' in a mugging. Does she have a new wallet?"

Sebastian scowled. "I don't know. Apparently, I don't know anything."

"You stay at Emily's house, and suddenly Greta gets mugged, and you have to come running when she calls. You don't find that convenient? She faked the injury for sympathy."

"You don't know that for sure," grumbled Sebastian.

"She *sprinted* after Croix like a cheetah on meth."

Sebastian felt embarrassed, but he wasn't sure why. He hated hurting people. Hated everything his relationship with Greta had become and the way it threatened his connection with Emily. But, why should he be ashamed for giving Greta every benefit of the doubt?

"What if Greta did lie? She's just sad and confused."

"Oh, because you left her, and you're *so* amazing," said Garrett.

"That isn't what I meant."

"I know, but *shut up*. I know you don't like disappointing people, but you're also afraid to leave. You *hate* change."

Sebastian placed his palm over his right eye and hung his head. "No, you're right. And I know she does stuff like this. I think she was cheating on me the whole time we were dating. I mean, all the signs were there. I just couldn't even work up the urge to care."

He sighed. "What am I doing?"

Nicole gaped at him. "She was cheating on you? And you didn't say anything? How did you know?"

"I don't want to get into it. It's not like I have a video; just a strong suspicion."

"Maybe that's what makes it so hard for you to believe she'd try and trick you into staying now. Because you find it hard to care," suggested Nicole.

Sebastian shrugged. "Maybe."

She leaned toward him. "Give me *one* little hint how you knew she was cheating."

Sebastian shot her a look. "You're *such* a gossip."

"Move in with Emily. She seems awesome," said Garrett, throwing his butt into the flames.

"She is. And really, she could be, like, the *one*, but I don't want to hop right from Greta's house to hers. It's too fast. I should be alone for a while."

"Who made that rule?" asked Garrett.

Sebastian sighed. "We haven't known each other that long. What if it doesn't work out, and I'm in her house making the same mistake I made with Greta?"

"Then you *move*, dude. I mean, seriously, what else are you going to do? Live with Greta forever until she fakes her own death or something? She'll firebomb your relationship with

Emily every chance she gets."

Sebastian tilted his head back and stared into the darkening sky. In his pocket, he felt a vibration, and his phone chirped. He pulled it out and looked at the screen.

"What is it? Is it Emily?" asked Nicole.

Sebastian put the phone down in his lap and tilted his head back again.

"Who is it?" Nicole leaned over and snatched the phone from beneath Sebastian's hand. He didn't move.

Nicole read the text message on the screen.

"You have got to be *kidding* me."

"What?" asked Garrett.

"Greta says her dog might be dying."

"Duuuude," said Garret, scanning the message as Nicole held Sebastian's phone up for him to read.

He looked at Sebastian.

"You don't think she'd kill her dog to get you back, do you?"

Sebastian closed his eyes.

A few hours later, Sebastian lay in his brother's guest room, staring at the glowing clock on the nightstand. Greta had sent three more texts before calling. Binker was not dead, she reported. He'd had a seizure but recovered. Still, she pleaded for Sebastian to come home, saying the experience had been terrifying.

Sebastian refused. He remained stalwart in his decision as she begged until she called him a bastard and hung up.

He took a deep breath, closed his eyes, and drifted toward sleep.

His phone chirped to life once more. He ignored the first two alerts, grabbing it on the third. He squinted at the caller ID, expecting to see Greta's name.

It was Emily.

He answered.

"Hey," he said.

"Hey," said Emily.

There was an awkward silence.

"What's up?" he asked. He could feel his heart lighten. It was good to hear her voice.

"I—" began Emily, her voice soft, as if she, too, was lying in bed. "Today—"

"I'm *so* sorry about today," said Sebastian, cutting her short. "I really am. I mean, first for being late, that was a work thing. But more importantly, I'm sorry about the whole mess with Greta and the weird way I was acting."

Again, silence fell.

"Emily?"

"I'm here. I'm sorry, too, Sebastian. It's just... I can't do this."

Sebastian sat up in bed. "What are you talking about?"

"I don't want to be tugging at your one leg and Greta at the other. I don't want to be part of this."

"There's no tug of war. Really. Greta and I are done. I'm not sure we ever started, for that matter."

"You're still in her house. You need time to unravel whatever this is."

"There's nothing to unravel. And you're helping me find an apartment. I'll be out in no time."

There was a long silence.

"Em?"

He heard her sigh.

"Let me know when you're free and clear, your life *and* your head," she said.

"Emily—"

"I really liked your mom, by the way. And your brother and Nicole. Your whole family is super nice."

"Thank you. But Emily—"

"I'll talk to you later."

"Wait—Emily—"

The phone went dead.

Sebastian raised his thumb to call her back and then stopped. He put the phone on the table.

He thunked his head back against the wall.

What am I doing?

206

CHAPTER THIRTY

Devastation.

Emily was so sad she didn't even try to cry symmetrically. When the right eye spilled to her cheek, she didn't roll over to encourage the left. She didn't stare forlornly out her window. She didn't play melancholy music.

Heartache without art—the bleakest of all heartaches.

Things had been going so well, and then, thanks to an orange purse, she and Sebastian were over. When she made the phone call, she'd felt strongly about her decision to pull from the race until Sebastian was free from Greta. She felt less strong the next day when she didn't hear from him. Weaker still, the day after that. Now it had been four days. Sebastian had made his choice. His choice was Greta. Or starting over, but not with her.

Emily heard a knock on the door and knew it was Kady. They'd been talking on the phone about how much men sucked when Kady told her Joe was leaving for a baseball game with his friend and that he wouldn't be home until late. She suggested the two of them make homemade sausage. Emily had no idea why. All she knew was at one point, Kady said, "I have sausage casing in my car. And four pounds of meat. I'm on my way to your house."

Emily didn't want to socialize, but she knew Kady felt low herself and would do it for *her*. Kady was an awesome friend. If Emily wanted an authentic prison tattoo using food dye and a sewing needle, Kady would be the first person at her doorstep with a bottle of McCormick's Blue Number 3 and fourteen different-sized needles. She was that sort of friend.

Emily was ready if Kady thought it would make them feel better to make sausages.

Kady had meat; Emily had a Kitchen-Aid mixer. She never used it; once a year, she cleaned it and dumped a dead housefly from its shiny silver bowl. Now she could finally use it for something more than modern kitchen art.

Emily answered the door to find Kady holding two plastic bags.

"I have meat!" she announced.

"I can see that," said Emily, letting her in.

They threw the bags on the kitchen counter, poured a couple of glasses of wine, and opened all the packages. Kady chopped the meat into cubes, and Emily set up the mixer. Kady shoved the meat into the top bin, tentatively at first, but with increasing agitation.

"It's probably good Joe wasn't home tonight," Emily said, watching the zeal with which her friend shoved meat cubes through the blades.

Kady grunted.

Emily had never ground meat before, but she had a visceral reaction to watching the threads of fat and muscle squish through the metal screen of the mixer attachment.

"How have you not kicked Joe out of the house yet?" she asked.

Kady shoved another piece of meat in the top bin.

"I plan to, every day, but then I start thinking about telling him we saw him in a car behind a Mexican restaurant and the fight that comes after that. I get so *tired*, y'know?"

Emily nodded. She'd been there before.

She handed Kady the meat cubes while standing in front of the mixer attachment. Every time the mixer suffered a sputtery air bubble, flecks of meat spattered her face and chest. By the time they finished, she looked like the only girl left alive in a horror movie, the remains of her sorority sisters painted across her tee.

"What if Girl Scouts showed up selling cookies, and I answered the door covered in meat?"

Kady laughed. "Sure, I'd love some cookies, girls—let me finish killing this guy..."

"I have some money in the basement somewhere, girls—just follow me down..."

They collapsed into giggles.

"At least if Joe is cheating, I know how to dispose of the body now," said Kady.

"You think I could fit Greta in there?"

208

"Maybe one boob. Not two. I don't have enough casing."

Laughter died when the grinder clogged so badly Emily had to turn it off and dismantle the unit. She peered into the mechanism, her face an inch away from the exposed blade-disc.

Kady flipped on the switch.

Emily barely missed having her face sheared off, which spun them into more peals of nervous giggling.

Kady slapped her hand across her mouth. "I'm so sorry—I thought turning the machine back on might help dislodge it."

"Yeah, my *nose from my face*." Emily chuckled. "We probably should have waited until after the dangerous part to open the first bottle of wine."

They ground the last of the meat, and Emily read the recipe for the next step, eager to get to the part where they ate.

"Let the meat season for twenty-four hours."

Kady's jaw fell slack. "Whoops."

They skipped that part.

They stuffed the sausages into the casings Kady had purchased from a butcher earlier that day. Kady fed the meat into the sausage stuffer and eased it into the casing, twisting off links at varying lengths until they had a phallic string of assorted shapes and sizes.

"I remember him," said Kady, as Emily twisted one off. "I remember him. Ooh, I *really* remember him..."

Emily couldn't stop laughing. Making sausages *was* better than moping around.

After making the links, Emily read more of the recipe.

"Put sausages into the smoker."

She looked at Kady. "I don't suppose you brought a smoker."

Kady shook her head.

They skipped that part.

Emily took the links to her back patio and lit her charred, ancient grill. She put the sausages on the grill with old wood chips left over from two summers previous, thinking that might compensate for the missing smoker.

They sat in the metal patio chairs while the sausages cooked. Emily tried not to look at the hammock swinging empty beside her.

"I don't think I can wait any longer. I have to kick Joe out. You're right," said Kady.

"I mean, I understand you still don't know if he's been cheating. It doesn't look good, but—"

"No. You're right. We've been growing farther and farther apart for a long time. I thought we had so much in common, but..."

Kady trailed off and took a sip of wine. "What about you?"

"What about me?" Emily stared at the huge cloud of smoke billowing from the grill, wondering what would happen if one of the neighbors called the fire department.

"You and Sebastian."

She shrugged. "I guess it's over."

Kady stood. "Hey, that's a lot of smoke."

She opened the grill, enveloping the patio in a giant cloud. Kady poked a sausage with a fork and then removed them all from the grill. They took them inside to taste them.

Emily put the first forkful into her mouth.

She grimaced. "Ohmygod. That is *disgusting*."

They'd over-smoked the sausages and turned greasy, wonderful pork products into sawdust tubes.

Kady tasted a tiny piece and then spat it out, face twisted with disgust.

"I thought maybe I could eat it. It kills me to waste them, but that's *awful*."

"The only thing these are good for is hamster cage lining," agreed Emily.

"We are sausage failures."

Emily snickered. "That's what we've been talking about all night."

Emily turned on the television for background noise while they cleaned bits of meat from every surface in the kitchen. The baseball game appeared.

"Oh, that's perfect," said Kady, her voice dripping with sarcasm.

"I'll put something else on."

"No, leave it. I don't care. Maybe we'll see Joe and Max in the crowd. Whoo."

Emily groaned. "Don't even say *Max*. Sebastian said that's Greta's middle name. *And* she works at the stadium, so maybe we'll see her, too. Whoo."

210

"Greta's middle name is *Max*?"

"Short for Maxine. He said she tries to get people to call her Max, but it never works except with one little group of her hipster girlfriends."

"She has hipster girlfriends?" asked Kady, picking a piece of fat from the toaster. "She seems more preppy."

Emily shrugged. "Like poser Joe."

"Maybe *they* should get together. Joe and Greta. That could—" Emily trailed off. "Holy hell."

Kady stopped wiping sinew from the coffee maker.

"What?"

Emily pulled open a drawer and retrieved a pen and paper.

"What car symbol is this?" she said, quickly drawing what looked like a squiggly "H" in a square. "I'm terrible at car types."

Kady looked at it. "Honda? Or no; if it is wider and more stylized, Hyundai."

"This can't be," said Emily, dropping the pen to the counter.

"What? What? You're *killing me.*"

Emily locked eyes with Kady.

"Joe has a friend named Max he meets at the baseball stadium. Joe's becoming a hipster. Marc said Joe was with a girl in a black Hyundai..."

Kady's mouth gaped. "Greta calls herself Max and works at the stadium—don't tell me she has a Hyundai?"

"The car spying on us the other day was black. The car Greta got into at the party was a black sedan with this emblem." Emily held up her doodle. "I didn't think anything of it at the time, but if this emblem is what you say it is..."

"A Hyundai..."

"Sebastian said he thought Greta was having an affair. Could it *be*?"

Kady turned and looked at the baseball game playing on the television.

"Son of a *bitch*," she said.

212

CHAPTER THIRTY-ONE

"We have to go to the stadium," said Kady, grabbing Emily's hand. "We'll catch them *both*."

Emily put her right hand to her head. She was at a loss for words.

"My brain is screaming that this is a bad idea."

"How can we *not*?" Kady tugged on Emily's left hand like a child begging for candy money. "I mean, at least to see who Max is, right? Please? Please?"

Emily huffed. "Fine. But this is for *you*, not me. I don't care what Greta is up to except for how it affects *you*."

Kady clapped her hands together. "Quick costume change, and we'll take your car. I'm not sure mine will even make it."

"Quick costume...*what*—?"

Before she could finish her thought, Kady ran out the front door. She saw her from her kitchen's bay window, opening her car and slipping in. A whirlwind of motion erupted in the back seat, a swinging arm, a hand, a foot; all bobbing from behind the front seats and sinking back into the depths.

Kady looked like she was wrestling an anaconda in her back seat.

Emily jogged to her bedroom, changed her meat-splattered shirt, freshened her makeup, redid her ponytail, found her shoes, and gathered her phone and keys. As she slipped those items into her purse, Kady burst through the front door, now dressed in black jeans and a long-sleeved blouse with an oversized collar.

Emily eyeballed her friend.

"You look like a thrift store ninja."

"We're *spying*. It felt right."

"You keep clothes in your car?"

"I'm always filthy when I get off work, and I don't always have time to go home before I have to be somewhere civilized."

"Fair enough," said Emily. *"Let's do this."*

They drove to Camden Yards; home of the Baltimore Orioles. After several tragic attempts to find parking, they lucked into a spot for thirty dollars.

The girls hustled to the field and found they could still get tickets. The Orioles were having a poor season, and demand was not high.

They rushed through security and bolted into the stadium, where they stopped dead to survey the sea of people.

"There are thousands of people here," said Kady.

"It's a *stadium*. We forgot that part. I don't suppose you asked Joe where he sits at games?"

Kady frowned. "Nope. That little nugget never came up."

They fell silent, gazes sweeping the crowd.

"I kinda thought it would be like a movie..." said Kady.

"Where we arrived in time to spot Joe and Greta on a Megatron kissing?"

"Yes," said Kady, slapping her on the arm. *"Exactly.* It *always* happens that way."

"Always. I thought so, too," agreed Emily.

She knew spotting Joe would be impossible. Part of her was glad.

Not Kady. She grunted.

"I can't give up now. I need to know. Don't you quit on me. Leave no man behind."

Emily cocked an eyebrow. "We're Marines now?"

Kady huffed. "Don't you want to know if Greta is cheating on Sebastian? Hey, can I see your phone?"

Emily fished in her purse for her phone. "Why?"

Her friend ignored her, concentrating on the phone and tapping the screen several times.

"I think you have a better camera than me. Maybe I can use the zoom..." She pointed to the far wall of the stadium. "Hey, there's a bathroom over there. I'll right back."

She speed-walked to the bathroom.

Emily strolled a few feet left, twirled, and walked back again, searching the crowd for any sign of Joe. She was ready to go home. She didn't want to see Greta. She didn't want to see Joe cheating on Kady. The whole idea of coming to the stadium had 214

been a stupid idea.

Emily's thoughts drifted to the Rover. Not only was she losing a potential boyfriend, she was losing her new hobby. How could she keep playing darts with Sebastian?

She pouted. Now she *really* wanted to go home.

Emily heard a whooping noise behind her and felt a slap on her shoulder. Kady appeared at her side, grinning.

"Ow, what's up?" Emily asked. She looked toward the field, assuming she'd missed some amazing play.

Kady dug into her purse and pulled out her phone and Emily's. She handed Emily's back to her.

"Joe sent me a photo. A photo of the field from his angle. I texted him and asked him for a picture of the game."

"Brilliant! I can't believe he sent it. Did he ask why you wanted it?"

"Nope. He sent it right away, probably to prove he was at the game and not off, oh, I don't know...*cheating* or anything."

"Oh, the irony," said Emily.

Kady flipped through her phone, found the photo, and held up the screen so they could compare the image to the field. They compared. Phone. Field. Phone. Field...

"This is like those games where you spot the differences between photos. I *hate* those games," grumbled Kady.

"He's got to be over there," Emily said, pointing to right field.

Kady agreed. "I was about to say that."

Using the photo as their guide, Emily and Kady made their way to the matching section. They walked down the stairs, comparing the height of their view to that on the phone.

Halfway down, Kady grabbed Emily's arm.

"That's him!" Kady hissed, pointing a few rows away at the back of a man's head. "He wore that same shirt."

They froze and stared at the back of Joe's head. A large, iron-haired older woman sat to Joe's right, an empty seat to his left.

"Could Max be a sixty-five-year-old woman?" asked Emily.

"Somebody has to be in the empty chair. We have to wait for

them to come back."

Emily felt a bump against her shoulder. A woman swept past them and down the stairs. The collision nearly knocked Emily forward, and Kady, still holding Emily's arm, helped steady her.

People can be so rude.

The dark-haired woman who bumped her didn't stop to apologize. Piqued, Emily opened her mouth to say something. She was in no mood.

Emily shut her mouth.

The woman's hair looked familiar.

Kady gasped.

The woman heard Kady's gasp, stopped, and turned. Her eyes met Emily's.

"*Greta*," said Emily through gritted teeth.

Kady cupped her hands around her mouth to create a makeshift megaphone.

"I see you, Joe," she screamed.

Joe turned and spotted Kady, who waved at him with a stiff, angry gesture. He appeared surprised until he realized Greta was standing between his seat and his girlfriend.

His eyes grew wide with panic.

Joe scrambled from his seat and made his way up the stairs.

"I got you now, asshole," said Kady, leaning forward. It was Emily's turn to hold Kady's arm, preventing her from moving another step toward Joe.

"Kady," began Joe, climbing towards her.

"Not here," begged Emily, straining to hold Kady back.

"Don't *even*," snapped Kady. Her words spat like bullets in Joe's direction. "I have one word for you, mister: *Mexican restaurant parking lot!*"

"That's, like, *four* words," Emily muttered, shifting her hip in front of her friend to better restrain her.

"Whatever. How about five words? Sex in a Mexican restaurant parking lot!"

Joe went white as a sheet. Greta, too, seemed shocked.

"Aaaand that's seven," mumbled Emily.

"How about *one* word," Kady said, flashing Emily an irritated glance. She stretched over her shoulder to be sure Joe could see her face.

"*Cheater!*" she shrieked.

"Bingo," said Emily putting a free hand over the ear Kady

pierced with her scream.

"Cheater?" said Greta turning to look at Joe. "She means *you*?"

Joe stopped climbing, one stair away from Greta. He gaped at 216

her, speechless.

Greta turned back to Kady.

"You're his *girlfriend*?" she asked.

Kady nodded. "*Was.* Wait. You didn't *know* he had a girlfriend?"

Greta turned to Joe.

"*No,*" she said.

Kady raised her arms in the air. "We live together. Though, he's officially *homeless* as of now. Maybe he can move in with you when Sebastian moves out."

Greta's head swiveled so violently in Kady's direction Emily thought her neck would snap.

"Who's Sebastian?" asked Joe.

Kady turned back to Joe. "Seriously? You're *jealous*?"

"Oh my God," said Emily. "Joe didn't know about Sebastian, either. Is everyone cheating on *everyone*?"

Emily felt exhausted. She daydreamed about slipping into her bed, going to sleep, and letting this ordeal slip into darkness.

"Sebastian's the guy she was talking to that first night Emily went to darts," Kady said to Joe.

Emily remembered the evening well. She recalled watching Joe and Kady's heads pop around the corner to peer at Sebastian.

Such simple times.

As soon as Kady finished her sentence, her eyes grew wild.

"And then you ran out of the bar because your *mistress* was in the same bar as your girlfriend!"

"You said he was a *client*," said Joe to Greta.

"Will you sit your asses *down*?" called someone from a few rows behind the group.

"I don't have to stand here and listen to this," said Greta. She started back up the stairs, but Kady shifted to block her path.

Standing directly behind Greta, Joe snatched the orange purse from Greta's hand. She whirled on him.

"Hey!"

"Shuuuuut uuuup and sit down!" came another call from the

stands. A partially filled popcorn container dropped from the sky and landed at Greta's feet.

"I'm returning this," said Joe, holding the purse triumphantly.

"*You* bought her that?" screeched Kady. "That *super expensive purse*?"

A cup of soda hit an upper step, splashing the backs of Emily and Kady's legs with cold, sticky liquid. They flinched. Emily surveyed the crowd. Hundreds of angry glares shot back at her.

"Uh, Kady," she said, clamping on Kady's arm.

Kady continued to stare angry holes through Joe.

"Give it back!" yelled Greta, trying to tug her handbag away from Joe. "Sebastian and I broke up!"

"Not that long ago," said Kady. "You've been going to games with *Max* for six months!" Kady made exaggerated air quotes with both hands as she said *Max*.

Emily had never seen such sarcastic air quotes.

Joe tugged the purse with renewed verve.

"And Sebastian broke up with *her*, you idiot!" Kady added.

A buzz filled the air. Emily looked back at the crowd. People were standing and taking videos with their phones. The voices screaming for the four to find a seat grew louder.

"Hey Kady, we should maybe... uh..."

"Get your shit out of the house tonight!" barked Kady.

She whirled and pounded up the stairs. Emily moved with her, eager to leave. Half a hot dog flew through the air toward Kady's head. She ducked and Emily watched it fly by. The bun smacked Greta on the side of her cheek, a mustard blob splattering her nose.

Joe took his eyes off the purse long enough to watch the retreating Kady.

"Kady!" he called.

Joe pulled once more in his tug-of-war with Greta and then screamed, "*Fine!*"

He released the purse.

Unready to have the handbag give way, Greta stumbled backward on the steps. Scrambling to catch herself, she released the bag, flinging it over her head as she fell. It flew through the air, lipsticks and other paraphernalia soaring into the stands as it spun. The crowd erupted into cheers. A woman snatched a compact from the air and dropped it into her own purse.

Kady picked up her pace. Joe called to her again and pushed past Emily in pursuit.

Emily saw Greta sprawled on the cement steps, her mouth gaping in horror. She scrambled to her feet and scanned the 218

crowd. The contents of her bag lay scattered among the seats.

When her gaze met Emily's, she scowled.

Emily's neck retracted.

Uh oh. Is this turning into a catfight?

She'd dreamed about fighting someone before. A bully swung at her in her dream, and she calmly used her attacker's momentum against her. Then she said something cool like, "You don't know me," or, "I've always been lucky when it comes to killin' folk," and everyone cheered and bought her drinks.

In the dream, she never rolled down the stairs of a baseball stadium. She had a narrow vision of her fight and didn't want Greta to ruin it for her.

"Stealing one boyfriend wasn't enough?" said Greta.

"I didn't *steal* Sebastian. You two were already broken up."

"He would have come back. He always did before he met you."

Greta opened her mouth to continue, looked past Emily, and froze.

"Hey!" she screamed.

Emily followed Greta's gaze and saw the orange purse flying from person to person in the crowd, like a beach ball at a concert.

She pushed past Emily and ran up the stairs, periodically crouching to snatch makeup and other items rained from her purse.

Emily held her shoulder where Greta *and* Joe had smacked it when passing.

"This is going to bruise," she mumbled.

She walked up the stairs, passing Greta, who was on her knees prying her new, orange wallet from between the feet of a man wearing an Orioles jersey. He laughed as she slapped at his calves. Emily thought she heard a sob in Greta's frantic voice.

The orange purse landed in a woman's lap directly to Emily's right. The woman squealed and picked it up, ready to toss it back into the crowd.

"Wait," said Emily, putting her hand on the handbag. The woman looked at her.

"Come on," said Emily. "Don't be mean."

The woman's grin dissipated and she handed over the purse. A portion of the crowd booed their disapproval.

Emily took the bag and held it tightly to her chest; worried someone might grab it. Greta stood behind her, eyes red from crying, her wallet clutched in her hand.

Emily handed her the purse.

"Thanks," muttered Greta, taking it from her.

She nodded and headed to the top of the stairs. A few feet into the mezzanine, she spotted Kady talking to a tall man.

She stopped.

Sebastian?

She tilted back her head and closed her eyes.

Will this day never end?

"Emily?"

She sighed and opened her eyes to find Kady and Sebastian had walked to her.

"What are you doing here?' she asked.

"I called him when I stole your phone," said Kady. "He saw me screaming at Joe and came over. Joe left. I think he thought Sebastian would kill him when he found out about Greta."

"You *called* him? Why would you do that?" asked Emily, horrified.

"I thought he might like to know what Greta was up to, and you said yourself *you* couldn't be the one to tell him. I'm sorry. It was meddle-y. If that's a word."

Emily scowled. "It was *really* meddle-y."

Kady shrugged. It was clear she'd do it again if given a chance.

Emily looked at Sebastian. "How did you find us?"

"This is where Greta has her season ticket seats."

Kady chuckled. "Oh, jeez. I could have asked *you* for her seat."

"You came all the way here to prove she was cheating?" asked Emily.

Sebastian shook his head. "No. I don't care about that. I—"

His attention shifted somewhere behind her. Emily turned and saw Greta standing at the top of the stairs—purse clutched to her chest. Greta stared for a moment and then walked in the opposite direction.

"She's really upset. Should you go after her?" asked Emily.

Sebastian shook his head. "I came here for you."

She scowled. "Not to catch Greta cheating?"

"No. I mean, I can't believe she was with Kady's boyfriend..."

220

Emily felt a pain stab her heart.

Would he ever really leave Greta behind?

Sebastian must have seen a change in her expression. "Wait—I didn't mean it like I was *worried* about her cheating. I meant—"

Emily felt tears coming. She didn't want to cry in front of him. She tugged Kady's sleeve and started walking toward the exit.

"Emily!" she heard Sebastian call.

She kept walking.

CHAPTER THIRTY-TWO

"I'm *free*," said Kady as they drove back to Emily's house.

"Me too," said Emily, trying to sound happy but doing a terrible job. Sebastian hadn't followed them.

She told herself she was relieved.

Kady put her hand on her leg.

"I'm so sorry. This is so messed up. I'm super happy because I found out my boyfriend is cheating on me, and your man said he wants to be with you and you're miserable."

Emily chuckled.

"Can you forgive me for calling him? And can you forgive him for being confused? So it took him a while to get his head straight. So what?"

Emily sighed. "It isn't that. I think he didn't want to commit until he *knew* Greta was cheating on him. Like he was leaving a window open, you know? If you hadn't told him what happened, he'd be at her house for another month."

"How do you know? And they've *been* broken up. Even Greta said that."

Emily shook her head. "I don't want to be a consolation prize. I don't want to be the last remaining option."

She felt snot dripping in her nose and sniffed.

Kady found her a tissue. "No wonder he couldn't commit; you're repulsive."

Emily laughed, and a snot bubble popped in her nose before she could wipe it.

"You're such a jerk," she said, laughing.

Twenty minutes later, she pulled into her driveway. All she wanted to do was *sleep*.

"What's that?" asked Kady, pointing to Emily's front porch.

Illuminated only by the indirect glow of her headlights,

Emily saw dark shapes near her door.

"I don't know," she said, shutting off the car.

The two stepped out and walked to Emily's porch.

The shapes were boxes.

222

"Do a little online shopping, did we?" asked Kady.

"*No.*" She opened her door and turned on the porch light. "These boxes aren't sealed," she said, pointing to a loose flap.

She crouched down and opened one. It was full of men's clothes. She opened another to find mugs and silverware.

"What the hell?"

There was a flash of light, and Emily and Kady turned to see Sebastian's truck pull into the driveway.

The lights shut off, and he walked to the porch.

Emily head cocked. "What are you doing—"

"This time, I'm going to cut you off," he said.

She fell silent.

He took a deep inhale.

"If you hate me, I'll go. But I'll need to get my stuff."

He motioned to the boxes.

Emily scowled. "These are *yours*?"

He nodded. "I've been sleeping at my brother's since Croix's birthday party. I came to get my things at Greta's today while she was at work, and I—"

He looked at his feet.

"I know it was crazy to bring it all over here. But *this* is where I want to be, *here with you*. I didn't know if you'd be happy to see me or not. I was going to sit here until you came home and beg you to forgive me for being an idiot. Then I got the call from Kady, so I drove to Camden Yards."

Emily blinked at Sebastian. "So you moved out?"

"More importantly, he moved out *before* I told him about Joe and Greta," interjected Kady.

Sebastian nodded. "What she said. Greta cheating wasn't the last straw. I knew that before I even met you. What Greta and I had was just— I dunno. The status quo."

"That's sort of depressing," said Emily.

"Yeah."

Kady shook her head. "You can't *accept* being unhappy. You gave up."

Sebastian looked at her. "You're making it hard to create the romantic atmosphere I was hoping to achieve here."

"Sorry," said Kady, pantomiming zipping her mouth shut.

He turned back to Emily, stepping forward to take her face in his hands.

"*You* were the last straw. I was so afraid to look like a loser to you by moving from Greta's house to yours— I didn't want you to think I was using you for your house. I didn't trust my instincts, even though they were all screaming for you."

Emily felt her eyes brimming with tears.

She glanced down at the boxes.

"I guess you better bring those in before it rains," she said.

"I don't think it is supposed to rain," he said.

She looked up at him. "*Take a hint.*"

He smiled. Brushing the hair from her forehead, he leaned down to kiss her.

"Eww," said Kady.

Sebastian glared at her.

"I'm going home," she said.

"No. Please. Stay," he said, flatly.

Emily laughed and covered her face, worried she'd grow another snot bubble.

She touched her friend's arm. "No, you had a rough night. Stay with us. I could call Marc, and we could all hang out."

"Ugh," muttered Sebastian.

Kady looked at him with horror.

"Not you, *Marc*," he explained.

Kady chuckled. "You don't mind, Em? That would be so awesome. I can't bear the thought of talking to Joe tonight. I'd rather go home tomorrow while he's at work, move his stuff to the porch, and change the lock."

"Of course, you can stay," said Emily, handing Kady her phone. "Call Marc and see if he's around."

"Yay," said Sebastian, lifting a box. "Sure. We didn't have anything planned."

He winked at Emily.

She opened the door for him and grabbed a box.

Inside, Emily made three Chicken Clubs and threw a beer at Marc when he arrived, truck tires screeching.

"You gonna eat these?" asked Marc, finding a plate of sausages in the fridge.

Emily grimaced. "No. They're all yours."

"Cool." He ate one and bit into another, oblivious to how terrible they were.

The four of them went to the basement to play darts.
224

Emily and Sebastian took the first game, Marc and Kady the second.

"Hey, you're over the line," said Emily as Marc stepped up to start the third game.

"What?"

"The line is there," said Sebastian. He threw a dart into the Berber carpet, nicking the edge of the masking tape line inches from Marc's foot.

Marc glowered at him.

"Oh, I'm sorry. I thought it was more like *there*." Marc threw a dart left of Sebastian's foot.

Sebastian scowled. "Nope. Easy mistake to make, though, because it's right *there*."

A dart landed *between* Marc's feet.

"Enough of that," said Kady. She threw a dart into the carpet between the two boys.

"Yeah," said Emily. She threw her dart, but it didn't land on the carpet where she'd aimed. Instead, it sunk into the front of Sebastian's leg, left of his shinbone, *in the meat of his calf.*

A collective gasp filled the room.

Emily slapped a hand across her mouth.

"Oh my god! I am so sorry!"

Marc laughed and pointed at the dart hanging from Sebastian's leg. "Dude!"

The dart wiggled as Sebastian hobbled to sit on the arm of the sofa. It remained attached.

"I'll get it!" said Kady, dropping to her knees beside Sebastian. "My mother was a nurse."

Sebastian waved her off. "*No*—don't pull it out. It's a gusher."

"A *what*?" asked Kady.

"It might be in my vein. I could bleed out."

"It's a *gusher*," echoed Emily. She was laughing so hard she could barely form the words.

"It's a *gusher*," echoed Kady, leaning her head against the side of the sofa to steady herself, her body shaking with giggles.

"Here." Marc whipped off his shirt. "If it starts to bleed, I'll tie my shirt around it."

The other three looked at Marc, standing bare-chested before them, holding his tee.

Kady stopped giggling, her mouth hanging open.

"I told you. Any excuse..." mumbled Emily to her.

Sebastian scowled. He leaned over and, wincing, plucked the dart from his leg. A small red dot appeared at the point of impact.

"No gusher," said Emily, snickering.

"Shut it," said Sebastian, the side of his mouth twisted into a grin. "I could have died, you *psycho*."

"I'm *so* sorry. I thought I aimed better than that."

"He's been in the house two hours, and you've already tried to kill him," said Kady from the ground where she'd collapsed.

Marc put out a hand and helped her up.

"Oh my. You're strong," she said.

Marc grinned. "I work out."

Sebastian rolled his eyes.

The night continued without further bloodshed. When everyone grew too tired to play, they went to bed. Kady took the guest room next to Emily's. Marc collapsed on the sofa in the basement. Sebastian followed Emily to her room.

"Don't bother putting on makeup," said Sebastian as Emily entered her bathroom to wash her face and brush her teeth.

Emily poked out her head. "What?"

"Don't put on makeup, don't try and find sexy pajamas. I'm on to your tricks. Go to bed like you would if I wasn't here."

She arched an eyebrow. "You mean with another man?"

"Oh, that's hilarious."

They crawled into bed and spooned together.

"This is nice," said Emily, snuggling against him.

"Don't snuggle too much," he whispered, tickling her.

She giggled and thrashed until he stopped.

"I hoped we'd have some alone time tonight," he said.

"Me too."

"I guess we can make it one more day," she said, yawning. It *had* been a long day.

"Tomorrow. Tomorrow we'll have the sexiest sex."

Emily nodded. "The sexiest sex in the whole sexdom."

"The sexiest sex in the whole sexdom of Sextonia," said

Sebastian, his voice barely audible.

"Mmm."

"And then you can help me find an apartment," he added.

Emily's eyes sprang open.

226

She smirked.

"Suuuure. I'll get right on that."

THE END

Get the Next Slightly Romance on Amazon!

WANT SOME MORE? FREE PREVIEW!

If you liked this book, read on for a preview of the next book AND the Shee McQueen Mystery-Thriller Series.

THANK YOU!

Thank you for reading! If you enjoyed this book, please swing back to Amazon and leave me a review — even short reviews help authors like me find new fans!

ABOUT THE AUTHOR

USA Today and Wall Street Journal bestselling author Amy Vansant has written over 20 books, including the fun, thrilling Shee McQueen series, the rollicking, twisty Pineapple Port Mysteries, and the action-packed Kilty urban fantasies. Throw in a couple of romances and a YA fantasy for her nieces... Amy specializes in fun, exciting reads with plenty of laughs and action -- she tried to write serious books, but they always ended up full of jokes, so she gave up. Amy lives in Jupiter, Florida, with her muse/husband a goony Bordoodle named Archer.

BOOKS BY AMY VANSANT

Pineapple Port Mysteries

228

Funny, clean & full of unforgettable characters
Shee McQueen Mystery-Thrillers
Action-packed, fun romantic mystery-thrillers
Kilty Urban Fantasy/Romantic Suspense
Action-packed romantic suspense/urban fantasy
Slightly Romantic Comedies
Classic romantic romps
The Magicatory
Middle-grade fantasy

FREE PREVIEW

CHAPTER ONE

Emily sat up in bed as if she'd been jolted alive by Dr. Frankenstein.

The dog is barking.

Is that someone knocking on the front door?

She glanced to her right to find a strange, man-shaped lump in her bed. She was no Sherlock Holmes, but the lump brought her to an undeniable conclusion.

There's a man in my bed.

She smiled.

The dog continued to bark. The man-lump rolled, pushed to a sitting position, and blinked at her, bleary-eyed.

"Is this how you wake up every morning?" he asked.

Her smile broadened.

No, not exactly. For one, you're in my bed...

The man-lump known as Sebastian had moved into her house the night before. He'd brought three boxes of stuff from his old apartment and then slept in her bed, so it felt a lot like he'd moved in, anyway.

His boxes sat piled in her living room, and he lay tucked beneath her covers. She sat beside him, watching his bare chest rise and fall, his breathing agitated by the early morning commotion.

It would all seem pretty sexy if it weren't for a few things.

First, to her knowledge, they weren't officially dating. Sure, he'd confessed his adoration for her the night before—shortly before moving his stuff into her house— but nothing had happened to cement the deal. He'd lived in his last girlfriend's house up until that moment.

Greta's house.

Greta.

Grr.

Emily couldn't think the name without a growl rumbling in

her chest.

To say Greta had been a complication for her burgeoning relationship with Sebastian would be like saying icebergs were a complication for the Titanic. Emily met Sebastian during the bitter end of his relationship with Greta. Greta had been cheating on him, but he'd ended things with her long before confirming those infidelities. According to him, their whole relationship had been a mistake.

He broke up with Greta, but remained half-living at her house—close to his work—and half-living at his brother's house, a far away and inconvenient.

At first glance, their break-up sounded amicable.

During Sebastian's time in limbo, he and Emily grew closer, flirting at the dart bar where they first met. Meanwhile, without Sebastian or Emily realizing it, Greta did everything she could to win him back. Since Sebastian still occasionally slept in Greta's house, she had a home-field advantage. She even faked being robbed to gain sympathy.

After several failed attempts to find an apartment, he stopped fighting his reticence to hop from one girl's house to another and appeared on Emily's doorstep like a lost puppy. A lost puppy with three boxes of stuff and dreamy blue eyes.

The world's sexiest lost puppy.

A puppy Emily had been hoping to find on her doorstep for a very long time.

She knew Sebastian feared the move to her house made it look like he was using her for her roof, but she also knew their feelings. She didn't care what it looked like.

It felt right.

She'd always had the same philosophy about their situation: *Get in my damn house and out of Greta's.*

If their relationship was going to stand a chance, that had to be Step One. She wasn't worried he'd go back to Greta—but living with a viper, one was bound to get bitten.

Sebastian picked a bad night to appear on her doorstep. It was the night Emily's friend Kady discovered her boyfriend was cheating, something she'd long suspected.

Emily found herself with two house guests. Why not three? She called her hot friend, Marc—to take Kady's mind off the cheating boyfriend—and the four spent the evening drinking and playing darts in Emily's basement. It was all tons of fun, but it also meant Emily's first evening with Sebastian had been as un-sex-filled as their life before he left Greta's. He'd insisted on abstaining until he was out of Greta's house, and now there'd be no sexy-time with guests sleeping in the next room.

232

Bummer.

She was about ready to tear off her clothes and run screaming through the streets.

Watching him now, sitting in her bed, scratching his head, the muscles in his back flexing...

She inhaled.

He smells good.

First, Greta had been the chastity belt blocking their involvement. Now guests were.

Maybe tonight she'd spend quality romantic alone time with Sebastian, but first, she had to stop the dog barking. Usually, Duppy would have stopped by now.

There is definitely someone at the door.

She sat on the edge of the bed, and the world wobbled a little. The knocking on her door became more of a pounding. Someone battered on the door with what sounded like a small redwood tree.

I may have had a little too much to drink last night.

"It's barely six o'clock. Were you expecting someone?" asked Sebastian, grabbing his phone from the nightstand to check the time.

Emily slid out of bed and grabbed her robe from the wall hook. "I'm not expecting anyone. You don't think Greta came to collect you, do you?"

Sebastian snorted a laugh. "I wouldn't put it past her." He swung his long legs out of bed and peered through the shutters. "That looks like my brother's car."

"Why would your brother be here?"

Sebastian grabbed his shorts from the floor and pulled them over his boxer briefs.

"I have no idea. I'll get it."

He walked from the room, and Emily followed to grab her scruffy white rat of a dog.

Sebastian opened the door to reveal his brother Garrett standing on the stoop, his hand in the air, mid-pound. He looked tired.

"Hey," said Garrett.

Sebastian rubbed his eyes as the morning light poured into the entryway. "What are you doing here? How did you even find me?"

Garrett rolled his eyes. "You texted me the address last night, so I'd know you weren't at Greta's anymore."

"I did?" Sebastian scowled, his face the picture of confusion. Emily nodded.

Yep. Little too much to drink.

Garrett continued. "Look, dude. I need your help. Can I come in?"

Sebastian glanced at Emily, and she nodded, backing the dog an additional few feet.

Once Garrett stepped inside, Duppy snorfed him and then lost all interest. The mutt was fourteen years old and had little interest in anything that didn't involve food or sleep. He turned and padded off to find a soft spot to flop.

"Hey," Garrett said, nodding to Emily.

She offered him a little wave. "Hey."

"So, what's up?" asked Sebastian.

Garrett sighed. "Nicole needs help. You know that big contest she came up with for the station?"

Sebastian nodded. "Mindhead or something?"

"Minefield."

"What station?" asked Emily.

Garret turned to her. "She works for News at Six on channel eleven. She came up with the idea to run a local reality show competition with young couples from the area. Her bosses loved the idea. She hosts it too, so it's a big deal for her."

"That's great."

"Yeah, it *was*, but it starts today, and two couples had to drop out at the last second. If she can't find replacements, the whole thing is—"

Sebastian shook his head. "Oh no, you don't."

Garrett whined. "Come *on*. You guys would be perfect for it."

"*Us?*" Emily placed her hand on her chest. "You want us to be one of the couples? On television?"

Sebastian waved his hands in front of him as if the motion would make Garrett magically disappear. "No way. We'll end up looking like idiots no matter what we do."

Emily scowled. "Hey, speak for yourself."

"I didn't mean *we're* idiots. It's the way directors cut things to make everything more dramatic than it is. You know what I mean."

Garret slapped his hands together as if beginning to pray. "*Dude*. You have to. I told Nicky you were a sure thing."

"Don't call me *dude*."

"You have to."

"Wouldn't it be a conflict of interest? Her being my sister-in-law and all?"

"A little, but it doesn't matter. This is more of a test run than anything. You could still win twenty thousand dollars."

Emily gasped. "Twenty? *Each*?"

Garrett hooked his mouth to the side. "Mmm... *total*, I think. Either way, everyone gets two grand for participating."

Sebastian put his hands on his hips and turned to Emily, grimacing. "I guess it's up to you."

Her words spilled from her lips before he'd finished his question.

"I'm in."

Sebastian groaned. "We'll have to work on you picking up my silent signals."

She patted his chest, grinning. "I picked them up. I just ignored them."

Garrett bear-hugged her, and she whooped with the force of his appreciation. "Thank you."

Emily heard Sebastian sigh.

"I'll do it, too," said a new voice. Emily fell from Garrett's embrace to find Kady standing at the end of the hallway.

Garrett's eyes grew wide. "I need another couple. You have a boyfriend?"

Emily cringed.

Touchy subject. But at least they were all on the same page.

Kady gnawed her lip. "Um, funny story—"

"I could do it with her."

Emily heard footsteps on the stairs, and Marc appeared from the basement, where he'd slept on the sofa. Shirtless, he stretched, muscles rippling across his ribs, his arms flexing in places Emily didn't know arms could flex. He looked as if he'd just peeled himself from the pages of a beefcake calendar.

"This keeps getting better," Sebastian grumbled.

Emily snickered. Sebastian and Marc had known each other in high school, and while not enemies, they hadn't been the best of friends.

Garrett grinned. "You guys would be *perfect*. They wanted hotties to bring in the audiences, but I told Nicole I could only get you."

He elbowed his brother.

Sebastian shielded his ribs with his arm. "Ow. *Thanks*."

Garrett pulled his phone from his pocket. "Nicole's gonna flip when I tell her I got both couples. I was afraid I was going to have to ask Ralph and Tina. What a nightmare that would've—*oh*—" He stopped mid-dial to glance up at them. "The game's a week long, can you all get off work?"

"Not a problem. I work for my dad," said Marc.

"I work for myself," said Emily. She looked at Kady, and caught her staring at Marc's abs from the corner of her eye.

"Kady," she prompted.

Kady snapped to. "Huh?"

"Can you get this week off?"

"Oh, yeah. I was thinking about quitting anyway." She bounced on her toes, visibly excited.

"Bash?" asked Garrett.

Sebastian nodded. "Yeah, yeah. I can get off. What exactly do we have to do?"

"I'll pick you up at eleven, be ready," said Garrett, cutting him short and heading out the door.

"Eleven today? Be ready, how? What do we—"

Garrett called over his shoulder. "Pack a week of clothes. Bring bathing suits and shorts and—just bring one of everything. See ya, thanks again."

Sebastian stood stunned for a few seconds and then shut the door.

"So I guess we're going to be on TV," said Emily. Kady's infectious excitement had her growing increasingly giddy.

Sebastian grimaced.

"Whoopie."

ANOTHER FREE PREVIEW!

236

THE GIRL WHO WANTS

A Shee McQueen Mystery-Thriller by Amy Vansant

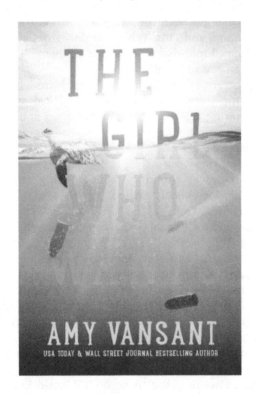

CHAPTER ONE

Three Weeks Ago, Nashua, New Hampshire.

Shee realized her mistake the moment her feet left the grass.

He's enormous.

She'd watched him drop from the side window of the house. He landed four feet from where she stood; still, her brain refused to register the warning signs. The nose, big and lumpy as breadfruit, the forehead some beach town could use as a jetty if they buried him to his neck...

His knees bent to absorb his weight and *her* brain thought, *got you.*

Her brain couldn't be bothered with simple math: *Giant, plus Shee, equals Pain.*

Instead, she jumped to tackle him, dangling airborne as his knees straightened and the *pet the rabbit* bastard stood to his full height.

Crap.

The math added up pretty quickly after that.

Hovering like Superman mid-flight, there wasn't much she could do to change her disastrous trajectory. She'd *felt* like a superhero when she left the ground. Now, she felt like a Canada goose staring into the propellers of Captain Sully's Airbus A320.

She might take down the plane, but it was going to *hurt.*

Frankenjerk turned toward her at the same moment she plowed into him. She clamped her arms around his waist like a little girl hugging a redwood. Lurch returned the embrace, twisting her to the ground. Her back hit the dirt and air burst from her lungs like a double shotgun blast.

Ow.

Wheezing, she punched upward, striking Beardless Hagrid in the throat.

That didn't go over well.

238

Grabbing her shoulder with one hand, Dickasaurus flipped her on her stomach like a sausage link, slipped his hand under her chin, and pressed his forearm against her windpipe.

The only air she'd gulped before he cut her supply stank of damp armpit. He'd tucked her cranium in his arm crotch, much like the famous noggin-less horseman once held his severed head. Fireworks exploded in the dark behind her eyes.

That's when a thought occurred to her.

I haven't been home in fifteen years.

What if she died in Gigantor's armpit? Would her father even know?

Has it been that long?

Flopping like a landed fish, she forced her assailant to adjust his hold and sucked a breath as she flipped on her back. Spittle glistened on his lips. His brow furrowed as if she'd asked him to read a paragraph of big-boy words.

His nostrils flared like the Holland Tunnel.

There's an idea.

Making a V with her fingers, Shee thrust upward, stabbing into his nose, straining to reach his tiny brain.

Goliath roared. Jerking back, he grabbed her arm to unplug her fingers from his nose socket. She whipped away her limb before he had a good grip, fearing he'd snap her bones with his Godzilla paws.

Kneeling before her, he clamped both hands over his face, cursing as blood seeped from behind his fingers.

Shee's gaze didn't linger on that mess. Her focus fell to his crotch, hovering above her feet, protected by nothing but a thin pair of oversized sweatpants.

Scrambled eggs, sir?

She kicked.

He howled.

Shee scuttled back like a crab, found her feet, and snatched her gun from her side. The weapon she should have pulled *before* trying to tackle the Empire State Building.

"Move a muscle and I'll aerate you," she said. She always liked that line.

The golem growled but remained on the ground like a good dog, cradling his family jewels.

Shee's partner in this manhunt, a local cop easier on the eyes than he was useful, rounded the corner and drew his weapon.

She smiled and holstered the gun he'd lent her. Unknowingly.

"Glad you could make it."

Her portion of the operation accomplished, she headed toward the car as more officers swarmed the scene.

"Shee, where are you going?" called the cop.

She stopped and turned.

"Home, I think."

His gaze dropped to her hip.

"Is that my gun?"

Get *The Girl Who Wants* on Amazon!

Made in the USA
Las Vegas, NV
01 October 2023

78456654R00134